13 PARK LANE

NAOMI CLIFFORD

For all misfits everywhere

Some of this story is true

London Daily News, 15 June 1872

THE PARK LANE MURDER. THE VERDICT.

At a few minutes before twelve, the jury having been absent less than half an hour, the ushers are seen to clear a path through the crowd by the door and to open the jury box. Then a gentleman of the court waves to the female warder in the dock to take away the chair on which the prisoner has sat during the trial. She must stand while the verdict is delivered. The prisoner, in her white cap and collar, with her broad shoulders draped in a black shawl, turns her anxious face to the jury and the judge. Every juryman's name is called out and the foreman reads slowly from a paper: 'The jury, having given their most careful attention to the evidence, find the prisoner guilty of wilful murder, but so far as premeditation is concerned they consider it has not been made out, and they therefore strongly recommend the prisoner to the mercy of the Crown.'

The verdict is translated to the prisoner, and two turnkeys stand between her and the warder, as if to catch her if she falls. She does not move. When asked, through the interpreter, if she has anything to say as to why sentence of death should not be passed, she mutters something, and the ashy hue her face has assumed grows deeper.

'I had no intention to kill,' is said by the interpreter, even while the folds of the judge's three-cornered flat black cap are being arranged over his wig. The prisoner stands with downcast eyes while the judge's remarks are translated sentence by sentence, and though her lips move as if she were trying to speak, no word comes forth. The ghastliness of this trial, in which the stakes are life or death, conducted in a tongue unknown to the person principally affected, comes forcibly home.

The judge announces to Diblanc that she has been found guilty of murder. The details as to her being hanged by the neck until she is dead in the prison where she is last confined, and the final prayer, 'May the Lord have mercy on your soul,' given from the bench and translated sentence by sentence, seem interminable to those looking on.

There is one more formality. The Clerk of Arraigns rises in wig and gown and from his seat below the bench directs the interpreter to ask Diblanc if she can plead that she was quick with child as a reason to stay her execution. There is a prompt and indignant 'No!' Then, to a motion from one of the turnkeys who have kept so near her, she turns obediently and disappears from sight through the door at the back.

CHAPTER ONE

Princes Street, Soho, London, January 1872
Five months before the trial of Marguerite Diblanc

'I know of a good position that's yours for the taking, Marguerite – starting today.' Madame Antoine leant across the counter. 'You could do better than this,' she said quietly, as if we were having a mundane conversation about the cheese I had wrapped for her, and put her head to one side, awaiting my reply. I kept my face blank.

'A lady from Paris – a widow and her daughter, actually – in Park Lane.' I must have looked puzzled. 'You know, Mayfair, the aristocratic quarter between Hyde Park and Green Park. You *must* know it. Not far from the royal palace. This lady's name is Madame Riel and she is looking for a cook. Madame Dumas says nice things about you, Marguerite. I've heard you can cook. You *can* cook, no? Tell me what you can do.'

'Yes, Madame Antoine, I can cook.'

I reeled off some of the dishes Madame Soulier had taught

me years before in Verdun, good solid French classics, nothing fancy, but the truth was I hadn't worked as a cook in all the years I lived in Paris, and certainly not in London.

For four months I had been behind Monsieur Dumas's comestibles counter. I felt safe, for the most part. My world was tiny. I knew little more than the shop, Berwick Street market and the French Church, which was tucked away off Leicester Square and where I attended mass every Sunday with Henriette, my only friend in London. At that time, I used to pray fervently.

Henriette and I had fled Paris together after the trouble when the Commune fell, and I was bound to her closer than I was to my own sister, whom I hadn't seen for years.

Whenever I was out of the shop, I kept a watchful eye. Amidst the clatter of carts and carriages, the bells, whistles and horns, and English people shouting in their gruff and baffling language, might be spies or secret police. That was the word amongst the French people in London and I believed it to be true.

I was not unhappy with Monsieur and Madame Dumas. They let me share a bedroom with their little girl at the top of the house. I was very fond of Jeanne, who liked to sit on my lap while I read to her or told her about my village in Belgium and how my father used to go into the forest to work at the iron forges, and how he would have to keep his eyes peeled for trolls and ogres, and how tiny fairies would dance around his lantern in the dark.

All of us, me, the Dumases, the shopmen and the sommelier, ate together every night in the kitchen at the back of the shop. Madame Dumas liked to test the quality of the products she and Monsieur Dumas brought back from the Continent by serving up tiny squares of ham, sausage or cheese on bread, a smear of pâté on toast or olives on toothpicks. *Do you prefer this one? Or this one? Is this comté better? Or that one?* Our opinions were important.

Standing in front of me at the counter, Madame Antoine looked from left to right to check no one could overhear us and bent a little further towards me. 'I think you'd be perfect for this job. Madame Riel also keeps an English maid to attend to her and to do the housework. You'd be in the kitchen. In charge. You're an intelligent girl. You could do with some responsibility at your time of life. How old *are* you?'

'Twenty-eight, Madame.'

'No admirers, I take it?'

'No, Madame.'

'So don't tell me I'm wrong. I know I'm not. I'm right, aren't I? You don't really want to be standing up in this shop all day. I pity your poor feet! And all that *Oui, Monsieur, Non, Madame.* Is that really all what you want from life?'

'Would I have Sundays free?'

Sunday was my time to see Henriette.

'Sundays? Yes, yes, of course you would. What do you say? Tell me it's yes.'

'I'm not sure,' I whispered. Normally, I make a decision in a second which, I have to confess, has not always turned out well, but Madame Antoine was rushing me. 'What about Monsieur Dumas?'

'Leave Monsieur Dumas to me,' she said. 'I'll square it with him. Don't you worry. This opportunity will disappear if you don't take it. Some other girl will gladly grab it. Oh, and you'll have a bonus of ten shillings as a gift for stepping in so quickly. You'll never get another chance like this, Marguerite. If I were in your position, I wouldn't hesitate.'

To run a kitchen again, to plan menus, to shop, to cook, to show my new Madame and her daughter what I was capable of... I looked at my hands and imagined them slicing vegetables and deboning a chicken, as I used to for Madame Soulier. This is what I needed. Proper work. Madame Antoine was right. I could at last do something I would be proud of and put the past to rest. And the ten shillings would certainly be useful – I still owed money to my friends in Paris.

While Madame Antoine spoke to Monsieur Dumas, I went upstairs to pack my possessions, including the bottle green satin gown Madame Dumas had given me a few days after I arrived. When I came back down to the shop floor, Monsieur Dumas came towards me, took both my hands in his and looked directly into my face.

'Come, come over here,' he said and guided me over towards the cash desk, away from Madame Antoine. 'It's all right, Marguerite. I'm not angry, I know you have been persuaded and I know this seems like a step up for you, but... I *am* sorry to see you go.'

He glanced over at Madame Antoine, who had picked up a jar of honey and was feigning great interest in the label.

'I'm sorry too, sir,' I said, which was true, but not the whole truth. Madame Antoine had noticed me. I had not disappeared into a well. I was not dead and forgotten. I could start afresh. Even as Monsieur Dumas was talking to me, my mind raced ahead. I saw a tall bright kitchen, its shelves stuffed with condiments and spices, window boxes full of herbs. I saw myself sitting down with a plump, friendly widow, planning the week's menus. I could be a good person again, feeding Madame Riel and her daughter and her genteel guests.

Monsieur Dumas paid me what he owed me and asked for my book of testimonials. He wrote the dates I had worked for him and some words about how honest and trustworthy I was.

'Marguerite, my dear, be a little wary at this new place,' he said.

'Of what, Monsieur Dumas?'

'Just keep your eyes peeled.'

Believe me, if I had known what he was trying to tell me, I never would have left him.

CHAPTER TWO

Once we got on to Piccadilly, it was a journey of barely fifteen minutes, even in heavy traffic. In the hansom cab Madame Antoine repeatedly told me how pleased she was that I had agreed to take the job, and that Madame Riel was a fine woman of great style, and that before she came to London she'd owned an atelier in Paris where she made and sold fashionable bonnets. Her clients were the most glamorous in the city. Madame Antoine did not say much about Madame Riel's daughter, only that she was very beautiful – it was not my place to ask about her.

'You won't regret it,' she said. 'I can guarantee it.'

I nodded politely.

Just before the big junction near the garden of the royal palace, which Madame Antoine enthusiastically pointed out to me, we turned up a narrow lane on the right and stopped in front of a run of those flat-fronted London terraced houses that you see all over the city: a short, tiled path, stone stairs and a portico with columns either side, and white stucco on the outside walls up to the first floor. There were black iron railings in front and a gate leading to steps going down to the basement.

It was much less grand than I had pictured. That was my own fault. I should have guessed that a widow and her daughter with only two female servants would live modestly, even in Mayfair.

'Here we are. No. 13,' said Madame Antoine.

I tried not to think the number was an evil omen because by then I had burnt my boats.

The house was in darkness. There was not a glimmer of light in any of the windows.

The cabman fetched down my box and I stood on the pavement in my waterproof while Madame Antoine climbed the front steps and pulled the bell. A servant opened the door. She was a good deal shorter than me and wore a plain dark-grey dress, white apron and cap. She was not young and she had that weary, washed-out look I had seen on so many Londoners, as if the soot and fog had become ingrained in their lines and wrinkles.

A short while later, a small figure emerged from behind her and when Madame Antoine moved a little to the left, I saw her more clearly. She was in her forties, petite, and clad in deep mourning with a veil over her bonnet. Tucked under her arm was a tiny white dog. After speaking to Madame Antoine, who turned her head several times to glance at me on the pavement, she came down to me and lifted her veil. The streetlamp cast a sickly green light but even so there was no mistaking it – Madame Riel was not in good health. I had seen people like that in Paris during the Siege – they were the ones who had begun to starve.

She said, 'I am so relieved that you have come to help us, Marguerite.' I caught a faint trip in her accent. It was Paris but it was also not Paris.

She looked me up and down.

'I will be out for a few minutes with little Ulysses.' She

smiled and petted the top of the dog's head. 'Have you been in London long?'

'A few months, Madame.'

I was keen to keep things as vague as possible.

'When I'm back I'll show you everything you need to know. In the meantime, do go into the house. Eliza will take care of you. She's been here only a few days herself so she's almost as new as you are.' She cocked her head towards me and out of the side of her mouth, almost as if she were attempting a stage whisper, said, 'Unfortunately, she speaks no French.' She laughed lightly. 'I'll see you a little later. Welcome to No. 13!'

I took up my box and started climbing the steps to the front door, until Madame Antoine stopped me and directed me to go through the gate to the basement. It was completely dark down there and I did not want to risk tripping over my skirts and falling, so I took the stairs backwards, shifting my box onto each step as I went. At the bottom, I tapped on the kitchen window and Eliza, carrying an oil lamp, let me in.

She led me out to the scullery, where I hung up my waterproof and bonnet. Then, wordlessly, she showed me a privy as filthy as anything I had seen in the Boulevard de la Gare, and beyond that a tiny paved yard lit only by a muzzy glow coming from the windows of the surrounding buildings.

We went back inside. In the kitchen, which stretched the depth of the house, there was the unmistakable odour of burnt and rotting food. Then she beckoned me to follow her up the stairs to the ground floor and started showing me around the house. The dining room was in front. Behind it, the door to the back parlour was ajar, and a slice of yellow gaslight glowed out from it. Because I had no English I could not ask Eliza why the rest of the house was unlit. I glanced inside the room: Madame Riel must have returned and was sitting on a snow-white sofa, wearing a pair of spectacles, with a newspaper on her lap and the dog nestled beside her. She turned to look at us, smiled, waved a hand imperiously and returned to her reading. Opposite the parlour was a door which I guessed led to a space under the stairs. Eliza whispered, 'Madame Riel,' and mimed turning a key, which I took to mean that this was the pantry.

We went through the dark up the stairs to the first floor, where she pointed out the drawing room at the front. I assumed she would next open the room behind it and took a couple of steps towards it, but she shook her head and we continued up to the second floor. This was entirely Madame Riel's domain, with a bedroom in front and an en suite dressing room at the back.

We were not yet finished. Eliza opened a narrow door revealing spiral stairs that led up to the attic. At the top, in the roof space, were two servants' rooms. Eliza opened one and indicated it was mine. I felt a wave of elation. My doubts evaporated. I had made a good decision in accepting Madame Antoine's offer. At last, for the first time in my life, I was to have my own place to sleep.

'Eliza!' we heard from downstairs.

She said something to me in English and shot back down the stairs, taking the oil lamp with her.

The room was dusty and damp, as if a roof tile had slipped and the rain had rotted the plaster. I took off my boots, and stood on the bed to peer down onto the street below. To the right, Park Lane gave way to a wide thoroughfare running by Hyde Park. To the left was the narrow lane leading to Piccadilly. When we arrived in the cab, I had not noticed that No. 13 looked onto the back end of a large building which I supposed was another of the grand palaces Madame Antoine had spoken of.

I felt my way carefully down the attic stairs and opened the door into the house. The hallways were no longer in darkness – Eliza must have been called down to light the gas.

When I was nearly at the ground floor I heard, 'New girl! Hey! Come! I'm waiting.'

Madame Riel was standing outside the locked door opposite her parlour. She bestowed a quick smile.

'Madame,' I said as I came towards her. I had a feeling I was expected to curtsy.

The first thing she did was tell me about my wages. The proper place for this would have been in her parlour or at the kitchen table or better yet before I was taken on. Distracted by Madame Antoine's promise of the ten shillings, I had completely forgotten to ask about the annual pay.

'You will have sixteen pounds a year,' said Madame Riel. 'That is one pound six shillings and eightpence a month.' She went on, 'Do not ask for more. Pay day is one month from now.'

English money with its strange pennies, and ha'pennies and farthings and guineas – I still regard it as nonsense – was hard for me to understand back then but there could be no doubt that this was a lot less than the two pounds a month I had from Monsieur Dumas. She didn't mention the bonus.

'The pantry is for *me only* to open. Not Eliza. Not you.'

All servants expect this. The pantry was her domain and provisions are expensive. What annoyed me was the way she said it, as if she expected me to be a thief.

She felt in her pocket and brought out a ring with half a dozen keys on it, unlocked the door and gestured for me to look inside.

'It's too dark to see anything, Madame.'

'Oh, silly me.' She laughed. 'Wait there for a moment.' She went back to her parlour and came back with a spill from the fire and handed it to me to light the gas. The pantry was a cramped narrow space with sparse shelves on the left-hand side.

'I keep the meat in here, as well as onions, garlic, oil, flour, spices, coffee, tea...' She reeled off a list. 'As you can see.' There were large glass jars for rice and beans. They were almost empty and I did not see any fresh food.

Screwed to the wall was a metal box, which I assumed was a safe.

She proceeded to tell me about the regime in the house. I noticed for the first time that my hands were freezing so I clamped them together.

'Every day at half past one, I will give out the provisions you need for that day and every Monday your and Eliza's own allotment of sugar, chocolate, coffee and tea' – she ticked them off on her fingers – 'which you will keep in the scullery downstairs. You will have English bread and English cheese, just as Eliza does. Half the dripping from the meat is for the two of you. The rest is for the kitchen.' She smiled and I saw that her teeth were tiny, like a child's, but rotten – small brown tombstones set at angles. 'You will dine on the leftovers of the dinners and make broth from the bones. On Sundays I pay for a jug of English beer for you and Eliza. She will fetch it from the public house on the corner. You are not to go into that place. You will work when I say so, including Sundays if required. Please ensure you use the basement entrance to the house. Only Eliza will answer the front door.' She sounded weary, as if she had given out this mantra many times before.

No good meat, no vegetables, not even good bread. I felt a band tightening around my chest. And no decent Sundays. When would I see Henriette? I had indeed made a huge mistake.

'I will issue the week's menus on Monday and you will go into Soho and order the provisions. Every day you will fetch fresh baguettes and anything else I need. Your duties include ensuring everything in the kitchen and the dining room is as I like it. The glassware must sparkle, the linen must be properly ironed and folded. And you will help Eliza.'

I did not reply, and Madame Riel said, 'That will be all.' She gave me another quick smile.

'Yes, Madame.' I turned to go.

'And Marguerite...'

'Yes, Madame?'

'You should clean the kitchen tonight.'

'Yes, Madame.'

It was then about five o'clock.

As I took the first step down to the kitchen she called out: 'You can read, can you?'

'Yes, Madame.'

'*And* write?'

I caught a note of disappointment.

'Yes, Madame.'

'You speak no English at all?'

'No, Madame.'

That seemed to make her happier.

She came towards the stairs.

'I do not tolerate gossip, Marguerite. You will do well to remember that.'

It was a strange thing to say. No servant was permitted to gossip about their employer, although we all did it.

CHAPTER THREE

The range was encrusted with fat and old food. Dirty tablecloths and linen had been piled up in a corner. The dresser was a mess of crockery and cutlery. The flagstones were gritty underfoot.

Eliza handed me a heavy canvas work apron and a striped, blue cotton dress which was already soiled with dirt and grease, and I guessed had been left by a previous cook. The fit was a little snug. I am naturally sturdily built and while I was with Monsieur Dumas I had regained some of the weight I had lost during the Paris Siege and what followed. But if I wore the blue dress, I could save the brown one I was wearing for less dirty work.

Madame Riel must have been living without servants for some time. I pictured her shopping for delicacies in Soho and wondered why I had never noticed her in Monsieur Dumas's shop, and why, if she'd had no servant in the house, she hadn't simply borrowed one from a friend or failing that put an apron over her immaculate black gown and washed her own plates in the scullery. Somehow she didn't seem the type. Although there was some indefinable rough edge to her, she was not at all down to earth like Madame Soulier, my mistress in Verdun, who had taught me to cook and was happy to stand at the kitchen table cutting onions alongside me.

I would be lying if I said I had not been a little irritated that Eliza had made no attempt to clean the kitchen – Madame Riel told me she had arrived a few days earlier – but then it dawned on me that she had been coping on her own, and goodness knows what the state of the rest of the house had been. Poor Eliza must have been running up and down the stairs carrying coal scuttles and pails of hot water and lunch trays or beating out the rugs or stripping the bed or the million other tasks that were necessary and expected in a household, as well as brushing Madame's clothes, dealing with the laundry and curling Madame's hair, so it was understandable that she hadn't had time to bother with the kitchen.

I scraped out the grate and cleaned the range. Then I lit the coals so that I could boil the dish cloths. I wiped out the seams of soot on the windowsills. The panes would have to wait for the morning. While I was on my hands and knees scrubbing the flagstones, I must have over-reached and the blue dress ripped under the arm. Eliza opened a drawer in the kitchen dresser and offered me a needle and thread and, as by then I was too exhausted to do any more cleaning, I put my brown frock back on and sat at the kitchen table mending.

I heard Madame's heels on the stone stairs and she appeared in front of us holding the little dog. She announced that she was off to spend the evening with Madame Antoine and that Eliza was to run down to the rank on Piccadilly and bring back a cab for her. I had to guess all this because, apart from a quick nod in my direction, she looked only towards Eliza and spoke in English. She said nothing about the kitchen.

After Madame left, I was ready to eat, and made signs at Eliza to say so. She set down two plates and from the scullery brought out two hunks of English bread, the kind that sticks to the roof of your mouth and tastes of chalk, and set about smearing hers with mutton fat. It was nothing worse than we had endured in the Siege, a good deal better in reality, and you'd think, wouldn't you, that as I'd been starved in the past, I'd have got used to awful food but it doesn't work like that, at least not for me.

I knew what I was allowed from the pantry so I was not expecting to dine in luxury, but this I could not tolerate. Eliza looked astonished when I put on my waterproof and indicated to her that I had to get real food. Although she didn't understand exactly what I said, she must have grasped the feeling behind it. I went up to the pavement by the basement steps and retraced the way Madame Antoine's cab had brought me. In Soho I bought myself a ham baguette and two financiers, which I ate guiltily on my way home. I was sure that if Madame Riel had caught me eating in public it would have caused a row.

When I was back at No. 13, I made a pot of camomile tea, after which Eliza opened another drawer in the dresser and fished out a sheaf of papers – dog-eared scraps bearing the addresses of Madame's favoured baker, butcher and wine supplier, a bundle of approved recipes – all, I was relieved to see, in French – as well as a detailed list of my duties annotated by the hands of Madame's previous servants.

I read them by candlelight in my room. I was to be in the kitchen at half past six. I was to clean the grate and light the range and keep myself busy by polishing the silver or re-ironing the linen, which was sent weekly to be washed and pressed at Deprez's French laundry, which also took in the Riels' bedsheets, personal linen, underwear and nightclothes. For some reason, it was my job and not Eliza's, to soak and boil their monthly rags.

I was to prepare Madame's breakfast tray – two toasts made from yesterday's baguette with a scraping of French butter and a tisane of verbena. Eliza was to take it up to Madame in her bedroom. *Madame does not want to see anyone but her maid at that hour* was underlined. After that I was to walk to Soho to buy fresh bread and anything else that was needed. The vegetables were to be bought only from the French man in Berwick Street and I was to pay him out of the red leather coin purse that Madame kept in the pantry. I was liable for anything I ruined or broke.

No gas jets were to be lit before four o'clock, no matter the time of year. She would dock our wages if she found them burning in empty rooms. No oil lamps were to be taken up to bed – Eliza and I were to have wax candles only, two a week. We were to wash our own linen and clothes using the carbolic kept in the scullery and to hang them in the yard and dry them overnight on the range or on a hanger on a pulley, along with the dish cloths.

All this time, I wondered where Madame Riel's daughter was. She appeared amongst the notes. The instructions said 'breakfast trays for Madame and Mademoiselle' and so on – but that was all.

It seemed that there would not be much cooking to do – every week a joint of beef or mutton or a ham, and sometimes a chicken, which I was to order from Madame's butcher when instructed. I was to put aside scraps for the little dog, whose legs were too short to go up and down the stairs and had to be carried to the kitchen for his meals. Madame's supper, if she was dining in, was at seven, after which I was to wash the pots, the crockery and the cutlery, serve supper for me and Eliza, and before bed lock the windows and the door to the basement area in front and the yard in the back. I was allowed up to my room at ten, unless Madame told me different.

That first night in my attic room I shivered under the blanket, occasionally briefly roused from sleep by the barking of dogs – the back of the mansion opposite was stables – and I woke at half past five to the sound of hooves on the cobblestones as the grooms brought the horses out to exercise in Hyde Park.

I was downstairs at six, rubbing my hands in the cold. A thin grey light reached through the kitchen windows. It was a relief to think that most of my time would be spent in the kitchen, which was warmed by the range. The rest of the house, except for Madame's parlour, was icy. I washed down the windows with vinegar, cleaned and reorganised the crockery and cutlery and worked on the worst of the encrusted pots and at ten, muttering under her breath, Eliza brought out the breakfast tray which I took as my cue that it was time to make Madame's toasts and to steep the verbena, but it all sat on the kitchen table, waiting for Madame's bell.

At a quarter to eleven I said to Eliza: 'Madame?' and pointed to the kitchen clock. She made a signal for me to calm down, and jerked her head as if to say, come with me. By pointing at me and with a bit of acting she let me know that my duties also included helping her do out the rooms, fill the coal scuttles and lay the fires. These jobs were not on Madame Riel's lists, but she had told me the day before that I must help Eliza. I changed into the dirty blue dress and the canvas apron.

We did out the ground floor together, she taking the parlour and me the front steps, the hall and the dining room. It was half past noon by the time we finished and went back down to the kitchen.

Madame's bell went.

I looked at the toasts, now cold and congealed.

'Marguerite,' she said, and pointed to the ceiling. 'Madame.'

I quickly changed into the brown dress, rinsed my hands and went up to the parlour.

The door was half open. Madame sat on the pale sofa attaching some black velvet trim to a bonnet.

I tapped on the door with my fingertips and she turned her head towards me.

'Well, come in then. Don't just stand out there, girl.'

In her black gown, with her dark hair and black eyes, Madame Riel reminded me of a raven landed in snow. Except for a green slipper chair, everything in the room, the walls, sofa, rug, curtains, was a shade of ivory or cream. The rest of the room was crowded with things: things on the mantelpiece, things on the floor, and in the corner a glass-fronted cabinet in which hordes of tiny little things – collectibles and trinkets – were displayed. On the walls was a rash of small paintings, of the seaside or a country lane, and either side of the fireplace ceramic figures of a woman and a man. On the floor by the escritoire I spotted a stack of French magazines and newspapers.

She got to her feet. I felt huge beside her.

'What was your name again?'

'Marguerite Diblanc, Madame.'

'Where did you say you were from?'

'I didn't, Madame. Belgium and most lately Paris.'

There was no sense lying.

'Well, we can't help the Belgium part. What does your father do?'

'He's dead, Madame.'

Her eyes went to the ceiling.

'What did he do before he was dead?'

'He worked in a forge and then in a factory.'

'Have you made breakfast?'

'Yes, Madame.'

'Where is it?'

'It went cold.'

She sighed, and paused, looking off into the corner of the room. Then she smiled and said, 'It can't be helped, Marguerite. You're new. Next time, listen for my bell or Eliza will tell you when to make breakfast. I allow one mistake. That is all. You will have the toasts for your own lunch. Right now you are to go to Soho and buy these.' She handed me a scrap of paper on which she had written a list. 'Make sure you're back here by half past one when I will open the pantry and give you your provisions. And you can make me a new breakfast when you are back.' She handed me the little red leather purse of coins. 'Make sure you bring back the change. I will be checking.'

I dashed about Soho. From the boulangerie in Lisle Street I bought two baguettes and from the Frenchman in Berwick Street market a lettuce and a bunch of watercress, and from a delicatessen in Compton Street six slices of ham. I was not yet brave enough to return to Monsieur Dumas as a customer. I feared he would guess that I was not entirely happy with what I had found at No. 13.

I rushed back down Piccadilly and up Park Lane in a steam of sweat, coming so fast down the narrow area steps that I almost tripped.

CHAPTER FOUR

'So, Marguerite, how are you finding your new place?' I was at the range with my back to Madame Antoine when she came into the kitchen. 'Something smells good.'

Madame Antoine and Madame Crosnier had come to spend the evening playing cards with Madame Riel.

'Everything all right?'

'Yes, Madame.'

'You are pleased to have made the move?'

'Yes indeed, Madame.'

'You look a little unsure... Is there something?'

'Only one thing and I don't know...'

She put herself close to me, as she had in Monsieur Dumas's shop.

'You can tell me, Marguerite. Your mistress can sometimes be a little... she can be a little hasty. She's a good soul underneath.'

'It's not that.'

There was no point complaining to Madame Antoine that there was no proper routine at No. 13, no consistency. Madame

Riel could ring her bell for breakfast at nine o'clock or at one o'clock. I was convinced that Eliza had deliberately misled me about breakfast on the first day, but I could also see that she herself was on permanent tenterhooks. And Madame was our mistress and had the right to be any way she chose to be.

'What is it?' said Madame Antoine.

'There's...' I said, trying not to sigh, 'there's not enough food in the house.'

'She pays you to cook. She pays for the shopping. No?'

'Yes, she does, and I cook exactly what she wants.'

'She doesn't eat much.'

'No, she does not, Madame.'

'So what's the problem?'

'There is not enough for *us* to eat, me and Eliza.'

'I see,' she said and turned towards the dresser at the back of the kitchen. 'Where were you before you came to London?'

'In Paris.'

'And where did you learn to cook?'

'In Verdun, Madame, before I came to Paris. Would you like to see my book of testimonials?'

She had not asked for it when she scooped me out of Monsieur Dumas's shop and Madame Riel had not asked to see it either.

'No, no, some other time.'

I was relieved. The book would show that in Paris I worked as a laundress and not much else, and it felt wrong, in that dark kitchen, to tell her about Verdun and Madame Soulier, who had saved sixteen-year-old me from the world and from the magistrate's dungeon (of course, I had no intention of mentioning this to her or to anyone).

The night I arrived at Madame Soulier's house, I was a half-drowned rat, streaked with rain and mud from my journey across the border into France. Dawn was breaking as I hauled myself up the hill to the cathedral to ask the fathers whether they knew of a place. I was lucky – the first priest I spoke to told me he knew a woman who was at the end of her tether because she had an idiot child no one could cope with.

Madame Soulier lived in a tall narrow house in the Rue du Pont-Neuf by the river. When she opened the door to me, I saw a well-built woman wearing a plain black gown and held out the note the priest had written for me.

'Thank goodness you've come!' she said, pulling me into the hall.

She did not seem to notice my bedraggled appearance and, after I had hung up my cloak, led me silently into the drawing room, where she asked me to sit on her sofa.

'I was beginning to think I would never find anyone. I'm sorry for the mess, but it's always like this.'

I looked around at the handsome black and white tessellated floors, the high ceilings, the ebony furniture, the mirrors and the oil paintings, and had to stop myself from exclaiming at how beautiful it was. The house was untidy, to be sure, things were out of place, the innards of a sewing box were strewn on the sofa, but Madame Soulier had clearly never seen real squalor.

'It's late now, Marguerite. They told you what to expect with little Iris?'

'Yes, Madame,' I said. 'I'm used to children of all kinds.'

'You have brothers and sisters?'

'I have a sister... and my mother's babies... they...'

I could not tell her about the babies without weeping. Perhaps it was the relief to have found refuge and warmth after my rain-soaked journey through the forest. Perhaps it was the memory of the babies' short lives – some had survived months, others only weeks. They were all born tiny and whey-faced and all of them now lay in the graveyard at St Hubert's. My younger sister Marie and I seemed to have been granted the life they lacked.

'You've been sent to me by God, my dear,' breezed Madame Soulier, pretending not to see my tears. 'The job is not easy, and you'll probably deserve much more than I can pay you. Come with me. I'll show you where you're sleeping. You have spare clothes? No? Not to worry. I'm sure I can find some of my old house dresses, from before I was widowed.'

She saw the look on my face and said, 'Please don't worry. I will teach you everything you need to know.'

A maid came twice a week to do out the upstairs rooms. Madame Soulier ordered the provisions and did the cooking. My duties were to answer the door, light the fires, run errands, fetch provisions from the market, clean and scour the pots, strip and make the beds, wash clothes, clean boots, and keep the kitchen and the dining room spotless. But my most important job, said Madame Soulier, as we climbed the curving staircase, was to look after Iris. She was in a room on the first floor next to her mother's and I was to sleep in a cot beside her. That first night, Madame Soulier gave me an undershift to wear and directed me to spend the night on the sofa so as not to wake the child.

'She's very delicate. You will see. Do not let her fall or she will shatter,' she said.

She woke me at ten the next morning, the promised dress draped over her shoulder. I had slept through all the clatter of the morning, even the maid dragging the rugs down to beat in the yard. Madame Soulier went to fetch Iris, who clung to her mother and hid her face. The child was all bones and no meat. Like my brothers and sisters, an early death was engraved on her body.

One evening, Madame Soulier told me how she became a widow. Her husband had been an engineer, working for

Monsieur Haussmann in Paris, but he'd died in a gas explosion. She spent all her spare time trying to get the government to give her compensation.

In those first few weeks I was clueless. Our family cottage, which had only two rooms, one upstairs and one down, was nothing like this fine home and I had only ever worked in the sugar factory unloading carts of beets and washing the mud off them before they went into the machines. I was clumsy and forgetful. I trailed wet laundry on the floor as I heaved it over the drying rack. I tracked street dirt into the kitchen. I burnt Madame's nightdress because I abandoned the iron to change Iris's napkin. I lit the fires too late in the day. Each time, I could tell that Madame Soulier was suppressing her irritation but wanted to be kind to me. She would say, 'Never mind, Marguerite. Making mistakes is a good way to learn.' I could barely keep in my tears. Why was I so stupid? How could I forget the iron? I was humiliated by my failures. But I never strayed into anger. I was never tempted to march out of the house or to lash out when she laid a hand on my arm and said, 'I have a tip that will make things go smoother next time.'

Iris did not speak but we talked in other ways. She was able to teach me that I should never give her an egg no matter how I dressed it up and that she liked to fiddle with my earlobes before she drifted to sleep. On Sundays, in church, while the fathers' voices echoed around us, she sat on my lap and we played games with our hands: gently I tapped her palm with one finger, then she did the same to me. Then two, then three, then four, then five, then four again, and three and so on. I tried to listen to the sermons, although I have to confess that not much went in, but every night I prayed to God to make me a better person and grant my wish that since I could not go home he let me stay with the Souliers for ever. Sometimes, I told myself a fable about how the Diblancs had had an ancestor who was born in Verdun, lost his fortune and was exiled to my village, until I was almost convinced that one day I would discover that Iris and I were long-lost cousins and I would be adopted into the family.

Every day at eleven, while Iris had her nap, I followed Madame Soulier around the house, where she explained some new thing to me and made me practise it. How to wash china, how to set the table correctly – things like that. Although I can't say that cleaning out the cooking range was as satisfying as my schoolteacher announcing that I had come top in a multiplication test or that my handwriting was the best in the class, when Madame Soulier praised me I felt the same kind of glow.

In our cottage, eating was mostly a way to feel warm and full. Mama and I cooked only the dishes we knew – omelettes, pâté, and pot au feu for a special occasion. Madame Soulier taught me that food could be a pleasure and that it was not sinful to like eating. She showed me how to layer dishes with flavour and texture, how to test and taste as I cooked, how to choose the right herbs from the garden. We made calves' liver, stuffed veal, marinade de volaille, cauliflower à la crème, compôtes, ice creams, mille-feuilles, madeleines. We did something new every week. She smoothed my rough edges, she encouraged and coaxed me, she made me forget what I had run from.

I did not expect the same from Madame Riel. I was there purely to perform my duties, not to be nurtured nor to be her friend. She knew nothing of me or what had happened to me before I lived in her house. For that matter, neither did Madame Soulier, who never once asked me what had brought me, muddy and soaking wet, to Verdun in the middle of the night.

At No. 13, as I was kept awake by the rumblings of hunger – Eliza and I might have shared the pickings of a poussin or a few rashers of bacon between that dreadful bread – I thought about how all servants knew the most intimate details of their employers, from the value of their jewellery, to their feelings about their relatives to the state of their underwear, even down to the dates and duration of their monthly bleeds, but they, on the other hand, knew almost nothing about us.

CHAPTER FIVE

During the morning of the Monday of the third week, in the kitchen, Eliza said, '*Madame*,' and pointed up to the ceiling, put her hand on her heart and breathed little rasping breaths as if she were pretending to be gasping for life. I had a vision of baby Edith in her final moments on the bed in Victoire's apartment at Rue Saint-Denis and wished I knew how to tell Eliza not to do such things to me.

Madame had an infection in her chest which, in my opinion, was made worse by her bird-like appetite and by inhaling the soot and grit floating around the city, which of course none of us could help doing. There was so much of it in the air you could taste it. It clung to our clothes, our skin and our hair and the inside of our noses.

Madame gave Eliza the key to the pantry and now it was she who handed me the red leather purse and a scrawled list from Madame. I could not help but feel aggrieved that Madame put Eliza over me.

In Soho, without being asked specifically to do so, I bought a chicken carcass, as I intended to make Madame a broth, and a kilo of apples for a purée. It gave me a kind of illicit thrill to know that I was making decisions for myself. When I was back at No. 13, I sent Eliza up to Madame with camomile and eucalyptus infusions.

Then Eliza caught whatever it was Madame had, not as badly but with enough of a fever to put her in bed. I was left do all my own work plus most of hers and to attend to both of them. The first time I delivered Madame her breakfast tray, she croaked out, 'Christ in heaven, you're a stupid whore, Marguerite – it's like having an elephant from the zoo in the room. Can't you be a little quieter? You're shattering my nerves.' I was so shocked I could not reply. No one had ever spoken to me like this in London, and to hear such words come out of the mouth of a lady who wore expensive silks and furs and feathers, even if she was not born to them, was so astonishing that at first I thought I had misheard her.

When Madame had spoken to me on that first day on the pavement outside No. 13, I detected a hint of a place far away from Paris, a place she was trying to veil. Who was I to judge? Like her, I had once wanted to run a winding-sheet around my origins. In Paris, in the months before the war with Prussia, I was often looked at oddly when I opened my mouth. 'You're not *German*, are you?' market traders would say. The whole country was on guard for enemies. 'No, no, not me!' I would reply. 'I'm from Belgium' – and they looked as if they wanted to say, *Have it your way, then, but I think I know a German when I see one.*

The sympathy I felt for Eliza began to grow and despite our problems in communicating I thought she was grateful for the soups I brought her and the India tea, done with milk and sugar, just the way she liked it. She ruined everything by slandering me. I can only think that when I was out in Soho running the errands, Madame must have slithered out of bed and up the attic stairs to see her because, when I was next called to her, she listed a catalogue of misdemeanours and general failings that only Eliza could have witnessed before she was ill – my not putting the crockery away at night but letting it dry on the draining board and filching two or three of the sugared almonds that Madame kept in a little silver bowl, and other such trivial matters.

Sunday came around and by then both Madame and Eliza were almost back to their routines. I went to the evening service at the French Church as usual, but Henriette was not there and I learned later that she too had caught this English cold. Sitting alone on the pews at the back of the church, I felt the loneliness of a schoolchild whose best friend has moved away. After I greeted Abbé Toursel in the lobby, I walked quickly back to No. 13. It was cold, and the fog and rain had wrapped London in a miserable shroud, which chilled me down to my bones. As I came down the stairs to the basement, I was simultaneously looking forward to the warmth of the range and dreading my next encounter with Madame.

The kitchen was unlit, so I assumed that Eliza had gone to bed early, and as Madame did not trust me with my own key to the kitchen door I had no choice but to turn around, go up to the front door and pull the bell.

It was not Madame who let me in but an old English gentleman wearing an expensive wool waistcoat and maroon cravat. He was thin, stooped and bald, with a frizz of grey whiskers, and he filled the hall with the aroma of cigars, bergamot and pomade. His shiny silk top hat and gloves lay on the hall table.

His eyes widened as he looked at me and he arched an eyebrow.

'So, you must be the cook I've heard about,' he said slowly with a heavy English accent. 'Madame will not be pleased that you've come in this way.'

It seemed to amuse him.

As I scuttled down the hall towards the kitchen, he bellowed up the stairs in French: 'It's only your cook, Madame Riel.' It was a voice made for commanding troops. 'Locked herself out, silly girl. No harm done.'

'It's all right. Madame is not too bad. I haven't seen her much because she's been ill. She tried to be friendly when I first arrived but she's not the type, really.'

'But...?' said Henriette, whispering. We were in the French Church the following Sunday, and Abbé Toursel was taking the evening service.

'But there's nothing to eat. She's starving me.'

Henriette was not yet one hundred per cent better, but she had returned to her routine – she said it was better than lying in bed trying to stay warm. In the pews at the front, I saw Monsieur Dumas and Jeanne and some of the other shop owners I recognised from Soho. Henriette and I sat at the back with the other servants and the African and Arab sailors.

'Really? There's got to be *something* to eat. There isn't a war on in London, Marguerite.'

I was stung by Henriette's scepticism. Why did she not believe me? I was exaggerating a little, I'll admit it, but it was also true.

'There's hardly any leftovers because I am not allowed to cook much. Look at me, I'm skinnier than I was in Paris. Feel my ribs.'

'Don't be silly. That was different. You're nothing like that.'

She was annoyed. Any reference to our lives in Paris set her mouth in a straight line. I couldn't start an argument about it. What could I say? That I had not asked her to do what she did on that final day before we took the boat-train to London, even if it was supposed to be 'for me'? That quite apart from the cruelty of it, her stupid act of revenge had put us both in danger?

'And the way she...' I was about to tell her about the horrible words Madame had said to me, but the thought of her in her sickbed wheezing them out – well, she was feverish and ill and that probably turned her mind. I would be surprised if she used them again. 'I have to buy loads of my own food, Henriette. I can't live on what she gives me. My savings will drain away to nothing at this rate.'

'I'm sure you'll be all right. Wait for me while I go to confession,' she said.

I had a good idea what she would be telling the priest.

On my way out of the church, Monsieur Dumas asked pleasantly how I was getting on, and I lied and said the new place was fine and that Madame Riel was most congenial. I asked Jeanne about her reading and whether she was going to school yet. When Henriette came out to join me, we walked through Leicester Square towards her place on Cranbourn Street. The rain was coming down in short bursts, creating dirty puddles on the paving. The damp got in under my waterproof and crept up the hem of my green satin Sunday dress.

A wave of misery washed through me but I didn't want to waste the time I had with Henriette whining.

She and I had arrived at Victoria Station at dawn one morning the previous August, not knowing where to go or who it was safe to speak to.

'It smells just like my village in the forest,' I said as the train pulled in.

'How so?'

'The coal.'

'It's just the train engines.'

'No, it's more than that.'

We queued at the foreign exchange kiosk to swap our francs

for English money.

When it was our turn, the clerk said in French, 'You're Catholic girls, yes? Not Communard types?'

'No!'

'You swear?'

'Yes.'

'Then you need to go to Abbé Toursel at the Church of Notre Dame de France in Leicester Square. He'll help you. Take a cab.'

He wrote down the address.

Through the window of the hansom we saw parks and grand soot-streaked buildings. Apart from the air, London seemed not so different to Paris, although more crowded. Even at that early hour the roads were jammed with carts, horses and carriages, and the pavements were filling up with people. Eventually the driver stopped in a vast noisy square, but we were so bewildered by the traffic and the people that he got down and led us to the door of the priest's house and knocked on the door for us. Before we knew it, we were in Abbé Toursel's kitchen and he was rubbing the sleep out of his eyes and nervily tightening and retightening the cord of his quilted dressing-gown.

His eyes glided past me. Whenever I was with Henriette, it was the same. I was of no interest, for which I was grateful. She was not even especially pretty, if you ask me, but she had an intriguing gap between her front teeth through which you could see her tongue flicking about, and she had a way of swaying as she walked. She made men drool, old priests included.

I stared at the Abbé's face and tried to assess whether he would be kind to us.

'Sit yourselves down, children,' he said, looking at Henriette. I was twenty-eight and Henriette twenty-five so you couldn't describe us as children, unless you were a man, I suppose. 'You're from Paris, you say? And you've just arrived? Of course, of course. I can see that. Why did you leave?'

In the warmth of his kitchen, a blanket of exhaustion and homesickness fell over me and I had a strong urge to lie on the floor and curl myself around the stove as I used to at home with Mama and Papa. Naturally, I did not.

'There's nothing for us there, Father,' said Henriette. She wriggled subtly as she leant across the kitchen table and looked directly into his eyes. 'Not work we want to do, at any rate.' She sat back. 'Marguerite and I are good girls,' she said, adding sugar to her voice.

'Oh, I'm sure you are, my dears.' He reached over and touched her arm. 'I'm sorry to have to ask you, but tell me what *did* you do in Paris during the recent troubles? Nothing against the law, I hope.'

'Indeed, we did not, Father.' She sat up straight, full of fake offence. 'I'm from the countryside and my father is a blacksmith.' None of that was true but it was easy enough for her to remember.

He tore himself away from Henriette and glanced at me.

'I am from Belgium – and I know nothing of politics or anything like that.'

I felt a fraud saying it, although it was not really a lie.

'We can work at anything: cook, laundress, shop assistant, general servant. Whatever you like,' said Henriette, keen to change the subject.

'It's not a matter of what *I* like, my dear. Either of you speak English?'

'No, Father.'

'In that case you'll have to work for French people. I'm sure I'm not the first one to tell you that places are scarce and London is already packed with French. The ones that fled here before the war with Prussia, the ones that fled because of the Commune nonsense, and the ones that went on the run afterwards. Unless you're a lady's maid, the English won't want you. Best to go back, if you can. Isn't that right, Madame?' He looked over at his housekeeper, who was polishing the cutlery.

After we finished our coffee, Abbé Toursel said Bloomsbury was chock-a-block with dangerous communists and spies. We should avoid it because we might get drawn into things we did not understand. Soho was where the respectable French establishments and businesses were. He asked his housekeeper to walk with us through the knot of streets behind the church. There were little cafés, boulangeries and restaurants, and every so often we spotted people – workers as well as richer types – wearing French clothes. Henriette got a place as a servant with Monsieur Miray, who had a business importing eggs, and a couple of hours later in Princes Street the Abbé's housekeeper and I caught Monsieur Dumas just as he was drawing down the shutters on his shop, and he agreed to take me.

Now, just a few weeks into my new place with Madame Riel, I was yearning to go back to Monsieur Dumas. I missed the smell of sawdust and cheese and I missed Madame Dumas's suppers. I missed reading stories to Jeanne.

'For lunch on Sundays, she pays for beer from the public house,' I said to Henriette.

To get out of the rain, we had stopped in the doorway of a shop and I bent down to stroke a ginger cat that was winding itself against me.

'So she's not totally awful.'

'I don't even like beer. I pour it away. As for that bread... and that cheese...'

'You didn't give your beer to the English maid?'

'Eliza? She's not my friend. She started out all right, but now I think she hates me.'

'It seems a waste to me. And she might like you better if you stopped being so resentful. Try giving her your beer and see if she warms up.'

CHAPTER SIX

No matter how much I tried to pretend life at No. 13 was bearable, each day was worse than the last. According to Madame Riel, I did nothing right. My omelettes were too wet, the champagne not cold enough. I took too long to make the breakfast tray. There was a stain on my cuff.

If I was late with the broth, Madame called me *boudin* and *bâtard*. She said those words to me all the time by then and on each occasion, I held my hands behind my back as Papa had taught me after the incident with the Widow Larue.

His voice was in my head.

She's only letting out hot air. Just let her be the way she is.

It was not just the food or the state of the table linen that Madame complained about, and it was what she said about my appearance and how I walked and talked that ate at me.

How can I describe the look on her face when I stood in front of her in the parlour waiting for my orders? An eyebrow went up a touch, the eyes widened. A corner of the mouth lifted, just a little. I was her mark. Then a darting smile from those clamped-together lips and the fake crinkle of the eyes.

'Were you *always* so large?' she said at one of these interviews. Smile, crinkle. Smile, crinkle.

'I've always been tall.'

'*Madame.*'

'Madame.'

'Have you always been so fat, was what I meant.'

Do not rise, stay quiet. Hold your wrist behind your back.

'Let me put it this way, Marguerite Diblanc. First, you seem to be growing fat at my expense. I can only conclude that you're stealing food from me. And second, I do not permit my servants to be fat.'

If Madame Riel genuinely thought I was a thief, would she not call in the English police to arrest me? I did not steal food from her because there was no food to steal.

It was not the same as when my schoolteacher caught me. Mademoiselle Lambert called me out gently and showed me a way to make amends.

As I stood in front of Madame Riel I itched to slap her.

Hold your wrist behind your back, Marguerite.

'You are accusing me of stealing, *Madame*? I pay for food from my own purse, *Madame*, because what you give us is not enough for a normal person.' I felt brazen, as if I had nothing to lose when, in reality, the opposite was true. 'Bread and cheese, a little broth from time to time – a person cannot work and live on it.'

'A fat person can't. Really, Marguerite, you must watch yourself. You thunder down the stairs. You slam the doors. I can't have such a hulking creature in my house.'

No, Marguerite. Do not.

She got off the sofa and grabbed me just above the waistband of my apron.

There was a buzz in my head, the same as during the incident with the Widow Larue.

I was sixteen. My little sister, Marie, and I were walking home through the village after the service at St Hubert's. The Widow Larue stood in the doorway of her house.

'How's your mother, Marguerite? Poor thing,' she said.

'She's fine, thank you, Widow Larue.'

I am always polite if people are polite to me.

'I'm sorry about her baby. She should...' and her hand went towards me.

Without thinking, I put my elbow up to stop her. I did not like people touching me. And her sympathy was a lie.

'No need for that.'

'Please don't touch me.'

'You Diblancs are strange. No wonder, what with your mother and her... *troubles*.'

I didn't answer. My heart grew holes. I tried to breathe but the holes grew bigger. I heard the Widow Larue speak but I don't know what she said.

At home Mama and I were enemies, circling like the caged tigers who had come through our village in a travelling show. She said I was an imbecile, a devil, a dagger in her heart, a lazy cow. For her, as for Madame Riel, I could do nothing right. In return I deliberately riled her. If she asked me to collect kindling or wash the pots or squeeze out the linen, I said I was too tired. She took the belt to me. The only thing I did well was look after her babies.

All of them were born with the same wizened bodies, the same thin white skin. We knew from the start that they would die. When Marie was born pink, fat and happy, I thought Mama would take delight in her but she did the opposite. After she nursed her she would hand her to me and sink back down in the bed, enveloped in sadness.

After the widow made her remark, Marie and I marched two paces on and then I turned around and put my face against hers, so close that I saw the dent in her forehead from her fall last spring.

'Did you say, *No wonder*?'

I was hot now.

She took a step backwards.

'I didn't mean...'

I smacked her. Hard, across the face. She had not done or said anything to merit it, I can see that now, and yet I struck her so hard my hand hurt and her head whipped back and hit the door frame.

It was a mistake. Standing in front of Madame Riel I knew I could not afford to make the same one again.

Madame Riel is like the Widow Larue – she speaks only hot air, she throws words about as if they are toys, Marguerite. Hold your wrist behind your back. Do not rise to her.

'What will people think? The quality here' – Madame Riel waved her hand towards the back of the mansion opposite – 'they don't employ people who look like you. You're quite disgusting. I have important friends, friends who are high up, friends who... are almost English royalty. You're not elegant. I can't have you serving at the table. And your dress – it's dirty.'

In those first weeks, she had not received a single visitor apart from Madame Antoine and that old English gentleman who had let me in by the front door. She had been out in the evening only to see Madame Crosnier acting at the St James's Theatre, where they put on French plays.

'I was hired to cook for you. It's not my job to be a size.'

It sounded stupid to say it out loud especially as it was not true. The world says women have to be pretty and dainty and demure, but we servants also have to be strong enough to lift wet sheets out of the copper and haul two scuttles of coal up three flights of stairs without sweating.

'I am your mistress,' she said. 'You will do as I say or before you know it you'll be out there' – she pointed towards the street – 'where you were born.'

She whispered, as if to herself, '*Salope*,' which means slut.

I was just about to say that I was born to respectable parents when it dawned on me that she was talking not about me, but about herself.

CHAPTER SEVEN

One Monday in mid-February, Madame Riel told me that her brother-in-law and his wife would be coming for lunch on the Wednesday. She had scribbled down a menu – a terrine of puréed vegetables with sauce vierge, fried whitebait, escalopes de veau à la crème and meringues with a compôte of pears.

In Verdun, when Madame Soulier invited guests – usually her father-in-law or the family lawyer and his wife – she and I decided the menus together, based on what was in season and what could be got for a good price at the market. I yearned for Verdun and Madame Soulier's bright kitchen, and for fragile little Iris, cushioned in her high chair, playing with a hunk of dough. Even though I was not sure how much Iris understood me, I liked to tell her the stories Papa told me and Marie, and which I later told Jeanne – of the forest ogre and his wife and their madness for pea soup, and of the kitchen elves who made a mince pie for every household in the land at Christmas.

During the day, as I mulled over how much I hated living at No. 13, I wondered why, if I was such a terrible person, as Madame Riel liked to say I was, Madame Soulier and Iris had loved me. But in the far corners of the night, in my little iron bed at the top of the house, I also wondered if Madame Soulier had just pretended to feel that way, for if she had truly loved me, why did she make me leave?

That Monday, when Madame Riel told me I was to make lunch for her in-laws, I was nervous and at the same time excited and hopeful. I would have to do all the shopping, she said, the meat and fish as well as the vegetables, so I felt she was beginning to trust me, at least a little. If I did well, she might be kinder to me, or the guests might say something complimentary about my cooking, which would put me in her good books.

I put on my waterproof cloak, grabbed the basket and almost ran to Berwick Street. At the fish stall I ordered the whitebait and I went into the butchers for a chicken carcass, pigs trotters, and the veal. There was no time to lose as I needed a day and a night to prepare the aspic for the terrine.

The minute I got back, I put the chicken and the pork on to simmer with bay leaves, a bouquet garni, and some carrot peelings. Eliza made a face at the smell and pretend-coughed. I ignored her.

I spent ten hours skimming off the foam and minding the pot so that it didn't boil too fast and spoil; afterwards I let the liquid cool and strained it through muslin. It was past two in the morning before I dragged myself up to bed. That night, I dreamt of pushing my way through thick forests in a panic, searching for Papa, and of standing in the sea trying to keep hold of dozens of Mama's babies, who kept falling into the freezing water.

In the morning I went to collect my orders and buy cream, fine sugar and pears. From Monsieur Dumas, who I now felt able to visit, I bought black olives, cheese, sprigs of thyme and dried basil.

On Wednesday, I woke at half past five and I lay in my bed listening to the shouts of the stable lads as they led their charges out for a run in Hyde Park. My feet were blocks of ice, so I got up, put on the blue dress, and went down to begin work. At around nine o'clock I heard a post office boy came to the front door. It was not my business, so I got on with my work.

Damp had got into the coal so it took me a good hour to light the range. Then I chopped the vegetables for the terrine and dredged the whitebait. Eliza came into the kitchen in her outdoor clothes and without a word left the house through the kitchen door.

At eleven o'clock Madame, holding Ulysses under her arm and wearing her outdoor clothes, made a rare early visit to the kitchen.

She stuck a finger in the sauce vierge and put it in her mouth.

'More lemon.'

'Yes, Madame.'

'You'd better get a move on, girl. Eliza has gone to visit her mother.' Her eyes went to the ceiling. 'Sick apparently. Dying, she said. You're on your own. I'm taking Ulysses out for a few minutes.'

She did one of her flat smiles and crinkled her eyes.

I had been counting on Eliza to do the serving.

One thing about working as a servant is that you not only have to look after the mistress or the master and their family but you also have to look after yourself, and that means finding time to wash your own underclothes, aprons and frocks and you must make sure everything is dry in time to put it back on. The blue dress happened to be clean but I could not possibly serve lunch in it – it was too worn and patched – and I had washed the brown one only the day before – it was still damp – so my only option was to wear the green satin, which I normally kept for church. Madame Dumas had given it to me, saying it was too big for her and that it had belonged to one of her customers. It was an old-fashioned style, at least fifteen years out of date, with yellowing lace at the neck and elbows, and Madame Dumas did not think it was worth remodelling it to accommodate the style for bustles. To be honest I thought the sheen too vulgar for church so I always covered it up with my waterproof. Now I had no choice but to wear it for Madame's guests. The white cotton apron would tone down the colour a tad – that was something.

I set the dining-room table at a quarter to twelve and went back down to the kitchen. At noon the doorbell went, earlier than I expected. I was still in the blue dress, so I put a good apron over it, went up to open the front door and hoped the guests would not notice.

Madame's in-laws gave me a polite smile, the type for servants, and a quick, 'Are you from Paris?' with a shade of disappointment when I said I had lived there but was originally from Belgium. They looked prosperous – pink-cheeked and wearing clothes of the highest quality. I took their coats and hats and showed them up to the drawing room. Madame gave me a look, no doubt because she had noticed the blue dress.

Back in the kitchen, I turned the terrine. It collapsed. With the sauce vierge swimming around it, it looked like the aftermath of a battle. When I brought it to the table at one o'clock Madame Riel's face told me what she thought. She ate almost nothing of it, and neither had her guests, but she thanked me pleasantly when I came to take away the plates and set down the next course. The veal was a disaster, overcooked and tough, and the cream sauce curdled. I burnt the meringues. Of the entire meal, only the whitebait and the pears were acceptable.

At three o'clock when I was laying a tray of tea to take up, I heard someone on the stairs coming down. She was *the other Madame Riel*, she informed me. Her husband, the man upstairs, was Monsieur Riel's younger brother, Théo.

'So this is the house, is it?'

There was no answer to that. She opened a drawer in the dresser.

'She won't mind if I take a quick look around. Where do you hang the laundry? Surely not out there.' She jerked her head towards the yard in the back.

'It goes to a French laundry.'

'And what's out here?' she said, pointing to the area in front of the kitchen.

'The coal cellar, Madame, under the pavement.'

'The English are strange, aren't they, with their odd little houses. How do you find your Madame? A little tricksy, eh?'

I said nothing.

'To be honest, and I probably shouldn't say this to you, we make a point of avoiding her, especially after, well, you know – or perhaps you don't – and my Monsieur Riel can't stand her, but we're moving back to Paris soon, so we've come to say goodbye, thank goodness.'

When Madame told me that she was to have family as lunch guests I wondered why I had never heard them mentioned before, especially as they lived in London. Now I knew.

The other Madame Riel set about listing all the things she hated about London and in my heart, I have to say I agreed with some of what she said.

'Horrid people, horrid houses, horrid weather, and oh my goodness – the soot! When I think of beautiful Paris and the light... and this place. We've been here for years. My husband' – she pointed a finger up to the ceiling – 'has a business importing trinkets from Paris. Inherited from his brother, *her* husband that is. Was. Their father set it up.' She waited a few seconds and then said, 'We had hoped to see the daughter, Mademoiselle Julie. Do you know why she's not here?'

'No, Madame.'

'You like it here?'

'I am pleased to work here.'

'It's an expensive area. Normally, one must have money to live in Mayfair, even at the wrong end.'

She wanted to know how much I was paid – I was evasive – and what Madame did all day. As far as I could see, it was not much but I could not say that. I said only, 'That is something you would have to ask Madame Riel yourself,' at which she looked irritated.

'After her husband, you know...' She made a hanging gesture and let out a little laugh. 'Monsieur Riel – *my* Monsieur Riel – got the business, and they got nothing. Did you know that? Before they left Paris, she was penniless, your mistress, proper paupers at one stage, she and the daughter. Did not have a sou to their name. Not a sou. My husband helped them out, out of the goodness of his heart. At the end of the day though, Marguerite, at the end of the day, she's still family, whether we like it or not, even if the daughter is not actually... But I've probably said too much. I wonder what she's doing for money these days. I heard a certain someone paid for them to come over here. Do you ever see him?'

I set out the petits-fours on a plate.

'I said, do you ever see the English earl?'

Again, I didn't answer.

'Oh, it's like that. Of course. Wouldn't want to get you into trouble. Don't mind me.'

An hour after she and Monsieur Riel had gone, I was sitting at the kitchen table with Eliza, who had returned and looked shut down and sad. I asked her about her mother and she just shook her head. We were picking at the ruins of the terrine when Madame came down the stone stairs. The next thing I knew, she was whispering loudly in my ear that it was fortunate for me that it was only that idiot Théo Riel and his imbecile wife who had been forced to eat my pigswill. The lunch was the work of a criminal, she said, and I deserved to be guillotined. In fairness, the food was so appalling I think she would have been right to sack me and certainly we would all have saved ourselves a great deal of heartache if she had.

It's strange how bad things happen so quickly but they seem to take an age to unfold, and afterwards you can remember every last little move, every action that brought you down. Madame's fingers were on the nape of my neck, pinching. For those moments, it was Lieutenant Marçeron gripping me in the same place and ordering me up the stairs of the officers' block in the prison at Chantiers. By the time I was getting up from my chair and bringing my shoulders back and forming a fist and twisting around to face Madame Riel, I was in full blood, inflamed by the fingers, and by Marçeron's words, by the Widow Larue's words too. I did not think of Papa and his instruction to let her be how she wanted to be.

It was the scrape of the chair on the flagstones and the sooty smell of the kitchen that saved Madame on that occasion. They reminded me of where I was.

'*Don't touch me,*' is all I said. That is all.

Not even very loud.

Did I frighten her? I meant to. Did I want to hurt her? Of course.

In the moment I stood up, Madame Riel and I were on a new footing. Both of us understood that we were wrestlers in the ring and one of us had to win. When she saw the look on my face, she turned her back, sprinkling insults as her little heels tapped up the stairs.

Later that evening, I pulled my box from under my bed and took out the *carte de visite* Madame Soulier had made me sit for in Verdun.

On the morning that photograph was made Madame Soulier said, 'Put your maid's cap on, Marguerite, and your best skirt. I've got a surprise for you.' I never wore my cap, unless it was Christmas or she had guests coming.

'You might want to smooth down your hair a bit.'

I felt the top of my head, searching for misbehaving strands.

The photographer's studio was on the first floor of a building in the centre of the town, reached through the back of a bookshop. Madame Soulier led the way up and I followed with Iris riding my hip and wrapped into my shawl. On the second floor we passed the open door of a storeroom and I glimpsed a neatly built barricade of props: plaster columns, wooden thrones and papier mâché balustrades.

As we waited to be called in, we walked around the showroom looking at the photographs on the walls and in the display cabinets. Dozens and dozens of brown and cream pictures pasted onto cards. The French Imperial family – 'Oh, the Empress is so beautiful,' said Madame Soulier – solemn archbishops, families with Father in a top hat and Mother on the sofa with Baby, and Dog at their feet, actors, lion tamers, explorers, notorious murderers. They looked both real and unreal, for nowhere and nobody could be that strange colour, and yet they were at the same time more like life than an oil painting or a sketch. Or were they? If a person looked happy or unhappy at the moment the camera clicked, they were frozen like that for eternity. It seemed to me that the photographs captured a person's expression that could have been on its way to another entirely different expression. What if it was the wrong expression or the wrong moment?

I told Madame that if she didn't mind, I would rather not have a *carte de visite*.

'Don't be silly. Your parents will surely want a keepsake of you, and I most certainly do. Honestly, you never know when you might need one. And they're very useful for future employers.'

The shock must have shown on my face.

'Marguerite, I'm sorry. I spoke without thinking. I didn't mean anything by it. Your place is with us. Always.'

In the studio, the photographer positioned her and Iris on a ruby-coloured velvet chaise longue and his assistant let down a painted backcloth of a well-tended wood behind them.

'Closer together, that's it, that's it – look to me – can you get the, um, little one to look at me? – perhaps, Madame Soulier, you should give her to your maid for a moment and we can take your photograph without her.'

She said that no, she and Iris would be in the photograph or neither of them would, and after several attempts the photographer was happy enough.

Then it was my turn. Madame insisted I have the same backdrop but the assistant took away the chaise longue, as the photographer said it was not suitable for a person of my station, and brought out a huge dark oak chair. He instructed me to stand next to it with my hand on the backrest, to be thinking about how best to dust bookshelves and at the same time to stare into the distance.

'Do I really look like that?' I asked Madame Soulier when we viewed the results. The photographer had taken eight pictures and in each one I looked more stupid than the last, as if I had been asked a question and had no idea what the answer was. Just as I had feared, each photograph had frozen me at precisely the wrong moment. And it was only then that I noticed that I was clenching my hand into a fist in every one of them.

'You look marvellous, Marguerite. Just choose one and we'll get it printed up. You look efficient. No nonsense. Competent. I'd give you a job!' She laughed and touched my arm. Although she had once more implied that my time with her was coming to an end, I heard only her compliments.

A few days later, she gave me a copy of the *carte* of herself and Iris and she kept one of me. I disguised my handwriting – for I did not wish the postmaster in my village to guess where I was living and inform the magistrate – and sent one to my friend Victoire, enclosing two for Mama and Papa and another for my old schoolmistress, Mademoiselle Lambert. The final two I slid behind the cover of my white leather prayer book.

CHAPTER EIGHT

It was five or six weeks after Madame Antoine came into Monsieur Dumas's shop and told me her string of lies that Eliza came down to the kitchen and beckoned me to come upstairs to the first floor. It was certainly after the débâcle of the in-laws' lunch, after my first payday at any rate – which was not actually payday because Madame was late with it and, no, I had not been given that ten-shilling bonus. Eliza unlocked the door behind the drawing room with a key only Madame could have given her.

It was, as I had known it was, Mademoiselle Riel's bedroom. The furniture was draped in dust sheets and the rug was rolled up in a brown paper sausage under the window.

Eliza led me back down to the scullery, where she pointed at the wooden box where we kept the brushes and blacking, mimed polishing the fireplace as if she thought I was simple-minded and then we both trouped back up to the bedroom, she carrying a dustpan and broom and me the box of brushes. She swept the floor and dusted the windowsill and the mantelpiece and took down the lace curtains, every so often doing her usual thing of sighing, saying 'Marguerite' and speaking in English at me and then making signals to do this, that or the other.

While I got to work on the fireplace, anger wrapped itself around me. Who was she to tell me what to do? And why was she making me do the dirtiest work? It was not as if she was a lady's maid – she was just a maid-of-all-work. She didn't even do Madame Riel's hair. Through the crack in the door, I had seen Madame in front of her mirror gluing in her own hairpieces.

I guessed that Mademoiselle Riel was expected back at the house soon, but Madame had not mentioned it to me directly. My loneliness at that moment was unlike anything I had ever known. My face burned. Waves of hot fury washed over me as Eliza wiped down the shelves and laid fresh lining paper in Mademoiselle Riel's chest of drawers and I pasted on the blacking and buffed and polished as if I were her apprentice. How dare Madame put this woman above me? It was more intense than the moments before I struck the Widow Larue, even though if you were observing me from the corner of the room you would not have noticed a thing and merely seen a red-faced woman energetically cleaning a fireplace.

After I had finished, Eliza was ready to make the bed. I was too dirty to help her so while she went up to the cupboard on the landing to fetch the bedlinen, I nipped down to the dining room, opened the dresser where the silverware was kept in a mahogany casket, lifted out a tiny silver coffee spoon, one of a set of twelve, a pointless, useless thing, and put it in the pocket of my apron. I didn't care if Madame noticed it was gone or not. If she did, I would put it back and let her think she was mistaken or mad or something, or I'd think of a way of blaming Eliza.

I never took anything at all when I was with Madame Soulier, until the end that is, and at school in my village I only acquired items of no real value. A nub of slate chalk, a bent spoon, a small French coin – things that would not be greatly missed. I did not take them to deprive another person. I took them because each time I sneaked a treasure into my palm it gave me the same feeling as when I stuffed myself with a plate of my mother's touffaye, rich with smoked sausages, bacon fat and potatoes. It made me feel replete. In the same way, the act of acquiring small objects filled a gap. I never gave much thought to what would happen if I were discovered.

One morning, after she rang the school bell, Mademoiselle Lambert drew me away into a corner of the yard.

'Marguerite, this must end. You know what I am talking about.'

I looked at the floor.

'No one wants those things. They don't need them. It's not stealing,' I said.

I knew that was a lie even before it came out of my mouth.

She made me promise to return the stolen goods, not to their owners, but to her, and I did, a few at a time. She would announce to the class that she had found something behind her desk or under a bench, hold it up and ask who had lost it. She even handed over to me a stub of my own pencil to make it look as if I were not the criminal. My friend Victoire, whose mother was a friend of my mother, guessed what was going on but kept my secret. She was my protector, telling the boys who taunted me for my square face and thick eyebrows, and who challenged me to fist fights because they said I looked like a boy, that she would speak to their fathers.

Despite my promise to Mademoiselle Lambert, I could not stop taking things and eventually she had no alternative but to inform Papa. He took me to St Hubert's to confess.

A nervous young curé spoke to me.

'Thieves go to prison, Marguerite,' he said.

'Yes, Father.'

'When they die, they go to Hell.'

'Yes, Father.'

'You know what happens there?'

'Yes, Father. I will be burned up in flames for ever.'

In my attic room at Park Lane I put Madame Riel's stolen spoon in my box. By the time Sunday came, I had forgotten all about it as by then I was almost fit for the madhouse. Madame had been accusing me of gluttony and thievery and laziness and now she had decided not to speak to me at all. I became shut off, frozen out, unable to communicate with anyone in the house. It was Eliza who received our ration of tea, coffee and chocolate at the pantry door. If Madame needed me to cook she scrawled a note in her awful French, which Eliza put down on the kitchen table with 'Marguerite' and a sigh.

At church on Sunday evening, I couldn't stop hissing to Henriette about how much I hated them both, and that I had come to the end of my tether. Mademoiselle Riel would arrive in a day or two and I had every expectation that she would be as hateful as her mother.

Abbé Toursel came slowly down the aisle of the church swinging the censer. I inhaled deeply, hoping the fumes would purify my thoughts and bring me back to sanity, but of course they did nothing of the kind.

'The English have bureaux to help servants find jobs, just like in Paris,' said Henriette as we walked towards her place. 'You could try one. I'll go with you if you like.' She also offered to walk with me through Soho to ask at the cafés and shops, as we had done on our first day in London with Abbé Toursel's housekeeper.

'I want to go home,' I said.

Going back to Paris was the one thing Henriette and I could

not do, at least not yet. Magistrate Macé had made it clear that we were not welcome in France, and then there was the matter of the business in the Rue de la Bienfaisance. For all I knew, we were being actively sought by the Paris police and that was not a subject Henriette permitted me to talk to her about. Also, we would have starved if we had returned. Even before the war and the Commune, we lived on the brink. Our basic problem was that, like most single women, we could not earn enough to eat. For us it was starvation or the streets. I had only survived by filching a little here and there, usually food, and by working extra hard – and to work hard you need fuel – more food, that is.

When we worked together in the laundry in the Rue du Faubourg Saint Honoré, Henriette told me that she was sleeping with two lonely widowers, on alternate Fridays, and that she made a few extra francs that way. I disapproved of such behaviour although I never said so, because even then I accepted that what she did was her concern and what I did was mine. Personally, I would have died before I let a man touch me. I'd decided long before that I would never marry or have children of my own. Perhaps it was living in our tiny cottage in the forest and hearing the grunting from the upstairs room, and Mama's loud objections, ignored by Papa, and the doomed babies that resulted. Besides, I had many defects as a woman, which were pointed out to me often, by stallholders in the market, by shopkeepers, by street children: my eyebrows were too thick, my jaw too heavy, my cheeks too red. I had none of the delicate gentleness that women are supposed to have. I laughed too heartily. I spoke too forcefully. I was as strong as a man – as if that was something to be ashamed of.

'If you hate it so much at No. 13 you could ask Monsieur Dumas for your old job back,' said Henriette when we reached the corner.

'He's already got someone else in. A girl from Nantes.'

'What about a laundry?'

'Never again. I'd go cross-eyed with boredom.'

'You can't afford to be picky, Marguerite.'

'Perhaps not.'

'Do you think she'll sack you?'

'If I don't leave first.'

'If she does make you leave, you should insist she pays you for the whole month or keeps you for the month while you look for a new job. Monsieur Miray's shopman told me that in England they've got to give a servant a month's notice or give us notice money. Not a week like in France. Say you'll report her to the English magistrates if she doesn't. That'll put the frighteners on her.'

'I'm not sure about that. Anyway, there's got to be something better than this.'

'Would you just up and go then? Take a chance?' said Henriette.

'I can't. Where would I go?'

'I need to leave my place too,' she said, looking at the floor.

This was a surprise. 'I thought you liked it there.'

'I did, I really did at first, but...'

I looked at her.

'Monsieur Miray's shopman, he's been... he's been bothering me. At night.'

'Henriette, are you all right?'

She knew what I meant.

'I think so. I do think so. So far, I'm all right, but if you hear of a place, anything, tell me. I need to get away from him. Marguerite, I want to go back to Paris as much as you do but I know we can't.' This was the first time she had referred to her crime, even indirectly, since the day we came to London.

'We need to wait a bit and anyway, we have no money. We have to save for the train.'

Neither of us spoke.

'Will anyone notice if we go back? We're hardly people of importance. And we seem to have got away with it...' I said, although I was not at all sure about this.

'Yes, well, I think they won't bother with us. Marguerite, what if I'm not all right? What will I do?'

'You must wait and see. And pray. Can you speak to Monsieur Miray about him, the shopman?'

'Monsieur Miray thinks the world of him. It will be me who'll have to go. I'm not sure praying does any good. I've been praying all my life and nothing's ever changed in my favour. I think God's so old he's gone deaf. He didn't exactly come to our aid in Chantiers Prison, did he?'

'We survived.'

'I want to do more than just survive, Marguerite. I expect you do too.'

It was Abbé Toursel who solved my problem, although not Henriette's. The following Sunday, after the service, as he stood in the lobby to shake hands with the congregation, Henriette dragged me over to him and announced that I was looking for a new place. Without hesitation, he said that he had heard Madame Evans, a French woman, *a Protestant*, wanted a cook for her café because her regular woman, one of the congregation, had had to go back to France for family reasons, adding that he'd heard 'not the best things' about Madame Riel. Following his directions I rushed up to Baker Street to see this Madame Evans.

She wanted first of all to know why I was looking for a new position. That proved easier than I anticipated. I started to say that I was at Madame Riel's, to which she said, 'Oh! The mother of the actress. I see!'

We agreed I would start on Thursday. She had only three weeks' work for me because her woman would be coming back, but I thought it was a risk worth taking as I would have the afternoons free to look for my next place, and I started rehearsing in my head how I would tell Madame Riel that I was leaving No. 13.

CHAPTER NINE

It was nine o'clock when I came down the stairs into the basement area in front of the kitchen and tapped on the window. Eliza let me in. There was a new expression on her doughy English face – conspiratorial.

'Mademoiselle Julie,' she said, pointing to the ceiling and then putting her finger to her lips. We both listened out.

A loud row was going on above us in the back parlour. Of course, Eliza could not understand what was being said but I heard *Paris... whore... bitch... fat... gratitude... bastard...* from Madame and almost nothing from Mademoiselle.

I was exhausted and wanted my bed, so after Eliza went up I checked that the kitchen windows and the door were locked, glanced into the scullery to see if there was anything that should be soaked or scrubbed, wiped down the kitchen table and started up the stairs to the ground floor. They were still going at it behind the parlour door. Because I was curious, I put my ear up next to the door jamb.

'Maman, Maman, please listen to me. I don't think I can...'

'*I don't think...*' whined Madame, mimicking. 'You were happy enough to *perform* for De Corneville.'

'He was not so disgusting to me... I'm being serious. We could go back to France. Saint-Germain says there are great opportunities. I could teach, Maman. We could start a school of drama, maybe not in Paris. Elsewhere. You could go back to millinery. You were the top–'

'You are more stupid than I thought.'

'Maman, please listen. Please. It's just that... he's so...'

'You're lucky he's taken you back after the games you played.'

'I wasn't playing games, Maman. I had to go. It's *my* life we're talking about.'

'*Your* life, is it? What about mine? Have you any idea, any idea at all, how much we spend? Even just to get by? You must be crazy. What you earn on stage is nothing. And to suggest I go back to millinery! I should have you locked up.'

There was a pause. I heard some rustling, as if Madame were getting to her feet.

'While you were gone, I had pennies from him. I was reduced to living in darkness. Not even able to light the gas! It's a wonder he didn't cast me out on the street. He came here once, sat and drank a lot of cognac and told me that I had a month to get you back, after which I would be out, because he couldn't wait for you for ever. He said he was impatient. You've heard what he did in Ireland, haven't you – threw those peasants off his land, to starve. Thousands of them. He's ruthless. He doesn't care. He could do that to us. Is that what you want for us? The streets? Is it?'

'You know the answer to that, Maman.'

'So why don't *you* know that your jewels, your costumes – every single thing you need for the stage and everything you need to live – none of that appears out of thin air. He paid for your diamonds and pearls. He expects a return. People like you and me, we must work for what we have.'

There was some muffled conversation, which I could not make out.

'You should know by now that you cannot exist as an actress without a gentleman. Or better yet a husband. Lord knows you should have one of those by now, even only as window dressing. And you turn your little nose up at him because he's not to your liking. *To your liking.* He's an aristocrat, for God's sake.'

The instant I heard the floorboards creak as if one of them were coming towards the door I hurried quietly up the stairs to my room. Sleep did not come. My heart beat loudly. Pictures ran through my head: Madame's wrath when I tell her I have had enough of her; Abbé Toursel when I relate to him how Madame Riel had insulted me; Henriette and me on the train back to Paris. My mind hopped from one to the other, up and down, round and round, like a carousel at a fair.

The next morning, I came down at half past six as usual and later went, as usual, to Soho for the baguette (although this time I bought two) and was back at No. 13 just as Eliza was starting up the stairs with Madame's breakfast tray, which she had laid herself. At one o'clock, after Eliza and I had had our doorstops of English bread and cheese, Madame rang the parlour bell. I ignored it, assuming it was for Eliza but she pointed at me so up I went. The door was ajar.

From behind it I heard: 'And how is that little lover of yours or whatever he is, eh?'

Mother and daughter were still at loggerheads.

'Saint-Germain is not my lover, Maman. He's my friend. Friends help each other.' Her voice was cracking as if she were struggling not to cry.

'Some friend, ruining both you and your career.'

'He didn't ruin my career, nor did he ruin me. He gave me shelter. You, on the other hand, *have* done your best to ruin me. Anyway, if my career were ruined, why would Monsieur Le

Directeur ask me to come back and why would he give me the best parts?'

'The best parts? You just play what you are. Anyway, Milord had a word with him so he had to. Don't get above yourself.'

I tapped on the door.

'Well, come in. Don't just stand there.'

It was then, when I stepped into the room, that Mademoiselle Julie came into view. She was two or three years younger than me, as tiny and elfin as her mother, but without the sharp features and the pallor. She was flushed, probably from her efforts not to cry, and decked out in a pale coral gown garnished with dove grey ruffles and her chestnut hair was piled up behind her head in a perfect weave of curls.

'Julie – this is the cook. Marguerite Something-or-Other.'

To me, Madame Riel said: 'You will address my daughter as Mademoiselle Julie. As you know, she's an accomplished actress at the French theatre. The next Madame Rachel, apparently.'

'Maman, please,' said Julie.

I had been called upstairs to be told the new arrangements. Every day except Sunday and Monday, in the afternoon, Julie would be going in a hansom cab to the St James's Theatre, and, if her friend Mademoiselle Isabelle Guy, who was also her dresser, was otherwise engaged, Madame Riel would follow her an hour or two later to help her with her costumes and make-up. On those nights, I was to prepare a cold supper on a tray and leave it for them in the dining room.

It seems strange but I felt grateful I was being told what to do to my face rather than it filtering down through Eliza. At the same time, I wasn't paying much attention to the details because I had it on the tip of my tongue to tell them both I would be gone by Thursday and they could fix their own trays for all I cared.

But I said nothing.

When I woke the next morning, I promised myself that I would give notice before the end of the day. I would have to forego what they owed me – I couldn't see them paying me for the days I had already worked that month nor the ten-shilling bonus – but it would be worth it to be rid of them.

At around one o'clock while I was in the scullery washing up the lunch things, I heard: 'Marguerite? Are you down here?'

It was almost a whisper.

Mademoiselle Julie was wearing a wrapper of lemon-yellow silk. Her russet hair was down and tied back loosely with a ribbon. She was everything I was not: soft and tiny and pretty. Next to her, in my brown dress and kitchen apron, taller, wider, bigger, I was a lumbering ogress of the forest.

'Thank you,' she said. She came forward and took my hands in hers and brought them towards her. 'Oooh, you're cold!'

We were so close I felt the sleepy warmth of her body.

'I just wanted to say thank you, Marguerite, and that I do hope you'll stay with us.' She looked like she might cry. 'All the others before you abandoned us. We really need someone like you. From what Eliza tells me, you seem to just get on with it.'

Her voice was musical and clear – she would never call me *putain* or *reine des cons*. I caught lily of the valley and lavender and the faint odour of unbrushed teeth.

'Maman can be a little hard to please, but you've done brilliantly. I know she's been rude to you but she's like that with nearly everyone, and from what she says you stand up for yourself. She doesn't like it, but I think it's good for her. You really are a breath of fresh air. I wanted to say, if at any time you can't get any sense out of her, come straight to me. There's nothing we can't sort out or put right. Do you understand?'

'Thank you, Mademoiselle Julie.' I was a doe caught in a hunter's lamp, hardly able to speak.

She asked me about my accent, and where I was from and the languages I spoke, and whether I still had family in Belgium.

I was due at Madame Evans in two days' time.

The only thing I was sure of was that I needed to speak to Henriette. On Wednesday, when I went to Soho for the baguettes, I rang the tradesman's bell at her place and told Madame Miray a lie: I had had some sad news from home and urgently needed five minutes with Henriette.

When she stood with me in the Mirays' yard, Henriette made no bones about it. I should keep my word and go to Madame Evans and forget I was ever in Madame Riel's house. I must leave No. 13 as soon as possible. She had heard things.

'But Mademoiselle Julie spoke to me so nicely. She begged me to stay. It was as if she knew what I'd been through. She will stick up for me. Henriette, she's not at all like her mother. Completely different.'

'No, Marguerite. Tell them you have found somewhere better. It's really not difficult. You need to put this behind you. You did well to get that job with Madame Evans. Don't let her down.'

'I'll never get the ten shillings Madame owes me if I leave now.' Before Julie came down to the kitchen to speak to me, I had been happy enough to let this go.

'Forget about it, Marguerite. There's no question here. They are bad women, both of them. It's a bad house.'

CHAPTER TEN

On Sunday, Madame Evans was outside the French Church waiting for me to emerge after the evening service. She grabbed my elbow and hissed in my ear, 'You will have to live with your conscience, Mademoiselle Diblanc. Very poor behaviour. I hope you understand what you've done.' She was being overdramatic, of course. It was not as if the world would stop because Madame Evans had no cook. The note I sent her gave no reason for my change of mind, but at that time I was of the opinion that when you try to justify your actions you land in even deeper water and that sometimes it's best to say as little as possible.

I gently pried her fingers off my arm, smiled and made a bland comment about the weather.

Henriette was horrified.

'That was downright rude,' she said after we had walked away from the church.

She kept on with her campaign to get me to find a new place, and when I refused, she offered me her paltry savings towards the train fare to Paris.

We parted, as usual, outside Monsieur Miray's premises. I

had only gone a few paces when Henriette ran back to me and grabbed my elbow.

'You watch out for yourself, Marguerite.'

'And you watch *yourself*!'

She had not brought up the subject of Monsieur Miray's shopman and his nocturnal demands. It was not my business to ask, of course.

I pushed her warnings to the back of my mind, distracted, I suppose, by the new mood in the house. The next day being a Monday, the theatres were closed, so Mademoiselle Julie was at home. During the week she had been appearing at the St James's in minor parts while rehearsing for what she told me was 'something really big' in a play opening in a week or so. She came down to the kitchen after lunch, not yet dressed. Her hair was down and she was wearing the yellow wrapper. I felt something when I looked at her and I didn't want to think about what it was.

Eliza's mother had taken another lurch towards death – so we had the kitchen to ourselves. It was a relief not to have to deal with Eliza's sullen intensity and instead to speak French with someone who had no reason that I knew of to resent me.

Julie seated herself at the table and read out a serialised story from a weeks-old Paris newspaper while I chopped carrots and celery for a chicken broth. I wanted very much to know why she had gone to Paris but it was not my place to ask. Then she began telling me about her life before she and her mother came to London. Her father had died when she was a child, she said. She didn't mention how – II thought of her horrible aunt on the day of the lunch disaster imitating a hanging – and afterwards her mother had opened a millinery atelier in the Rue Laffitte.

'You should have seen the customers. The most famous women in Paris. Cora Pearl – she was always nice to me and gave me bon-bons.' I had no idea who this woman was and said so. 'Oh, she was a famous courtesan. English, actually, and quite eccentric, many, many lovers, and one of the most sought-after women in Paris.' I must have looked embarrassed at the mention of lovers because she said, 'Oh, Marguerite. You're really quite naïve. Paris is full of women like that, and London too if you know where to look. It is not a thing to worry about.' It was not just mistresses who were Madame Riel's customers, though. Baroness Rothschild, and the Empress Eugénie bought her bonnets, and she kept a table of twelve girls in the workshop at the back of the studio. Her designs were in fancy magazines.

Julie looked away, towards the stairs, and said that in those days Madame Riel had been different, strict, especially with the millinery girls, but softer and kinder than she was now.

'She had one of those cabinets with lots of little drawers for all the different colours of bindings, ribbons and braids, all the notions that the millinery girls used, the needles and the special cordings and yarns. Satin rosebuds in three sizes. Darling little things. All of it miniature and exquisite. She let me unwrap the deliveries and put them away in the drawers. I thought I was in heaven, lining up all the bindings and the artificial foliage and sorting them when they became untidy, but in the end Maman said I was diverting the girls from their work and ordered me out. She spent hours designing the bonnets and kept the drawings in a locked box so that they could not be stolen. My mother was the best in Paris. It was a climbdown to lose the business and come with me to London, I suppose. She has nothing much to do here. She's bored. Perhaps that's why she has no patience with anything.'

I had a feeling that I was the first person she had spoken to in this way about her mother.

'In Paris, she was tough. Or resilient, I should say. She drove hard bargains. She fought to make us a life and at times she cut corners because she had to... It's only lately that she's become more...' She stopped. 'She wouldn't like us talking about her.'

'What did you learn at the Conservatory, Mademoiselle Julie?' I said to change the subject.

'Singing, drama, dancing. Shall I show you the first dance I learned? It's called the gavotte.'

She tied the sash of her wrapper tightly and held her arms out to the side, fingers pointed upwards, and started humming and counting out the steps, every so often lifting her skirt a little, and doing half-jumps backwards and forwards.

'It's easy. Do it with me.'

The idea of me dancing in the kitchen was ridiculous and I started laughing, and she started laughing too.

Her eyes shone and suddenly I could imagine her on the stage playing to the audience and the audience in raptures.

For a few minutes it was if we were real friends.

'Come, I'll show you how.'

'Mademoiselle, I don't think so...'

'No, you must.'

'I need to put the soup on.'

Eventually, she conceded and let me get on with my work.

'How did *you* get out of Paris and why did you come here?' she said suddenly. For a moment, I wondered if she knew about Chantiers and Lieutenant Marçeron and was trying to bait me.

'I left after all the trouble was over, after the Commune.'

'But you were there in the Siege too?'

'Yes, Mademoiselle Julie. And you?'

I already knew that the Riels had fled as the city gates were closing.

She had just made her debut when the Prussian troops surrounded the city. A friend, she said, helped her and her mother escape on the last train out. I took this to mean that he had paid a large sum for the tickets.

I wondered if their friend was the old gentleman who had let me in by the front door when I came in late, and whether that was *Milord*, who gave Julie diamonds and pearls.

'Is this his house?'

I don't know why I asked and I immediately regretted it. Servants do not speak to their employers about their financial affairs.

She bit her lip.

'Yes, it is. He has rented... lent it to us. He's very... kind.' She looked at her feet.

Did I know what she was doing? No, and also yes. I wanted to believe he was a benevolent sponsor, or that his interest was in Madame Riel, although I knew it was not.

'What was your village like, Marguerite? Why did you leave?'

I told her that my father had worked for years in an iron forge in the forest and when it closed he and I found employment at the local sugar beet factory, but that work was seasonal, and for half the year we had no money coming in.

'I don't really know what the countryside is like – I've only ever lived in Paris and London.'

I told her that we kept a pig, a goat and a few chickens, and we grew potatoes in a small field near the house.

She offered to help me cook so I tied a clean apron round her and gave her some apples to slice for a tarte tatin.

'The factory work was hard,' I said. I had an urge to tell her about coming home filthy, with cuts on my hands and grit in my clogs, about not having enough fuel for hot water to wash, about being the cleverest pupil in the school but not being able to afford a book, about Mademoiselle Lambert suggesting I should train as a teacher but not having the clothes for the interview.

'My job was to clean the beets before they went into the machines, which made a noise you wouldn't believe, humping great sacks of them over the yard, scrubbing the mud off. You should have seen me! The factory men nicknamed me Strongman. They used to do this when they saw me.' I got off my chair and knelt on one leg, an elbow on my knee, the fist to my forehead. It was indeed funny to look back on, but at the time, when the boys, half of whom I had been at school with, pranced about the yard imitating me, I wanted to punch them.

Suddenly, Julie pulled up her head and cocked it towards the stairs.

'I was easily as fast and as strong as the men,' I continued. 'But guess what, Mademoiselle Julie – they paid me less than half the men's wages.'

'Awful,' she said. 'We should...'

'I had plenty to say about it, believe me.'

'Oh, I do... but Marguerite, I...'

It was then that I heard what she had heard: Madame's boots tapping on the stairs.

'What *are* you doing, child?'

'I–'

'Julie Riel, you are wearing an apron.'

'Marguerite–'

'Marguerite made you do it?' Madame Riel looked at me and performed her smile. 'And what are *you* doing, Marguerite-the-factory-girl-from-Belgium?'

I was about to say that I was making a tarte tatin but before I could say anything she turned her head to Julie and hissed, 'Out! Out! Don't come down here. Ever. As for you.' She turned to me. Her voice was sweetly musical now. 'If I find you poisoning my daughter with your... with your... peasant nonsense, I'll drag your disgusting body out there to rot.' She pointed out to the street. 'Don't think I don't know exactly what you're up to.'

'Maman, we were not talking about you. We were just talking about Marguerite's–'

'What? What am I *up to*, Madame?' I interrupted. 'Tell me

what I'm doing wrong and I will try to correct it, Madame. I aim to please, as you know.'

She twisted back towards Julie and raised her hand, her diamond ring catching the light. 'Didn't I tell you to get upstairs? Go upstairs.'

It was as if she was talking to a ten-year-old.

'Maman, please, please stop this. There's no need. We weren't talking about you. I promise. Marguerite was telling me–'

'Look at you. Here, let me, darling,' said Madame Riel, suddenly melting. She put an arm around Julie's waist.

From her sleeve, she winkled out a handkerchief, a patch of pure white cambric against the black sheen of her gown, and dabbed at her daughter's face.

'You've made yourself red and ugly with your snivelling. Go upstairs, my dear, and fix yourself.'

———

Madame did not keep to her word. Mademoiselle Julie was not banned from the kitchen. Rather, she became my new overseer. It was now Julie at the pantry door with the orders of the day. She was efficient and polite about it. Madame Riel kept out of my way and I hers. Eliza was going every afternoon to see her mother, who was at death's door, Julie told me. When the poor woman came in at night she looked utterly bereft. I felt genuinely sorry for her.

The next Sunday after evening mass Henriette said she wanted to go to confession so, avoiding Abbé Toursel, I waited for her on the pavement. As we walked towards her place in Cranbourn Street, she said, 'I've got a couple of things to tell you, Marguerite.'

She paused.

'I was not lying when I told you Madame Riel's was a bad house. I'm just going to pass on something Monsieur Miray said. I was talking about you and your Madame and he said, "Oh, Henriette, your friend should not stay there. It's a house of scandal." Everyone knows about it, apparently.'

'What does he actually mean?' I was annoyed. 'Nothing goes on there. *Absolutely nothing*, Henriette. No gentlemen visit. They don't hold raucous parties, they don't drink, there's no unseemly behaviour. They're very quiet. I don't know why he would say that.'

I felt a kind of panic. Madame may not have been entirely what she was trying to be – I could not forget that strange lilt to her speech, with her Rs rolling too far back in her throat. Sometimes I wondered whether she herself was a Prussian or from Alsace and trying to hide it. And she was definitely on the wrong side of respectable. But if I accepted what Henriette was saying, I would have no choice but to leave, and I couldn't bear the idea of that.

'Well, Monsieur Miray must have his reasons. He doesn't say things for nothing.'

'It's probably because they are theatre people. But honestly, it's just them, and me and Eliza in the house. Barely any visitors, only Madame Antoine and Madame Crosnier, and sometimes Mademoiselle Julie's friend, Mademoiselle Guy. Anyway, Monsieur Dumas said something similar to me, Henriette, and he was wrong too. And even if there was a scandal, whatever it was, it's over. I don't deny Madame is a horror, but Mademoiselle Julie is nice and has made her mother tone herself down.'

'You don't understand. It's your Mademoiselle Julie that is the scandal.'

'Only because she is an actress.'

'No. Well, that probably comes into it, but not only that. I don't know whether the rumours are correct or not. All

Monsieur Miray said was it involves an English gentleman, a *personage*, some kind of lord. I'm only repeating what he said.'

'I'm sure it's just gossip. She goes to the theatre to act and then she comes home. Sometimes her mother goes with her.'

'Marguerite, you are perfectly aware that all the French here know everything about everybody and what they did before they came here.'

'They don't know about us.'

'We're nobodies. We're invisible. We've been over this and I don't want to talk about it. Even if they did know, they don't care. Your Madame definitely has a murky past, though, and they're interested in that. The husband killed himself because of her. Madame Miray told me. She borrowed a fortune to open her millinery shop, but she bankrupted herself sending your precious Julie to the Conservatory.'

'That's nothing I didn't know.'

We walked on towards her place. At the door, I said, 'Mademoiselle Julie is not like her mother. I'm glad I decided to stay, really I am. She has made all the difference, *and* she made sure I got paid.'

'Did you get the extra ten shillings?'

I told her I had, but that was not true.

Then Henriette said, 'Marguerite, there's something else I need to tell you.'

She looked away. I guessed what was coming.

'I'm late. Five weeks.'

CHAPTER ELEVEN

In a mauve silk day dress and with her hair down, clutching a playscript, Mademoiselle Julie had come down to the kitchen for a final run-through, and I was to be her audience.

She passed the sheaf of papers to me, posed herself, head at a little angle, her face set prettily, and said: 'Oh, I should tell you, this is the section where Agathe reads out a suicide letter her beloved has written. Don't worry – he doesn't die.'

Then she started.

'I do not feel the courage to fight any longer. Farewell, you who were my friend and who will be my only confidante.'

Her sweet clear voice filled the room and she moved effortlessly across the floor, the hem of her dress rippling and swishing. Suddenly she stopped, looking like a stricken child.

'A hopeless love was the misfortune of my life... and tonight, when you read this letter, don't pity me... I shall have ceased to suffer...

'There's a bit more along those lines,' she said, 'and then Agathe's friend says dah-dah-dah and Agathe comes back in with, *I have loved him since childhood, since the days when he called us his sisters, because then he was, for both of us, a brother, a friend, for me, even more. Even back then I admired his honesty, his uprightness, his soul which is so loving and at the same time so level-headed.'*

Was she really paid money to spout this gibberish? I supposed it didn't much matter what she said on stage. Most of the audience, the men that is, would be there not to listen but to look, at the abundant hair, the swaying hips, the trembling bosom.

'I don't say very much after that, Marguerite. Apart from one quite long bit at the beginning, which Monsieur Le Directeur has cut to almost nothing, the rest is just interjections.' She stopped and looked away, thinking. 'Agathe is decoration. She's just there to emote occasionally, nothing more. No one cares about her.'

She sat down at the table. I could think of nothing to say. Was she about to cry?

'It's always the same. I might be praised for the role, but the role hardly exists – Agathe is vapour. Pfffft! and she's gone. No one remembers her. I might as well just wear the gown and mumble the lines.' Then she sighed and said, 'Marguerite, what are we women put on earth for?'

Abbé Toursel had preached this sermon a few weeks previously.

'To look after our children, and toil in the fields, and tend to the animals... and sew clothes, and spin yarn, and nurse the sick. The Abbé says we are to be like Eve, a helpmeet for Adam.'

'Do you really believe that? That we have been created only to help the men? Well, if so, I'm sick of it and I'm sick of them. My advice: Stay away from them.' She covered her face with her hands. 'Do you wish to be married?'

'Me? No. Are you not feeling well, Mademoiselle Julie?'

'I'm fine.'

But she stayed sitting there, with her hands over her face, not shifting.

With her hair spread over her shoulders, she looked more fragile even than her mother. I wanted to put my arms around her and gently guide her back to her bed. I wanted to say that she would be all right, that the play would go well and that whatever troubled her would pass. Yet I needed to peel potatoes. I was about to say, 'Mademoiselle Julie, maybe you should take a few moments' rest,' when she said, almost barking, 'Don't speak, Marguerite. Don't pay me any attention. It's nothing. Just my monthlies probably. I had to come down and practise the lines but sometimes I can hardly find a reason to start the day. I'm sure you know how it is.'

I did know, but I did not tell her I knew, and I would never tell her or anyone else about how a curtain descended in front of me when I was working for Madame Soulier. Three months before it started, Victoire had sent on Mama's letter telling me that Papa had suffered a stroke and died a day later. Victoire included a note of condolence and an announcement of her own: she had married a man called Jacques Bouillon from a nearby village and they would be moving to Paris. To me, Papa's death was like a page on the calendar. Tear it off and carry on. I prayed for his soul in church, of course, but did not allow myself to feel anything more than a few hours of regret for an event that occurred far away.

I realise now that I was merely squashing down my grief, as if I was trying to contain an explosive. It was soon after Iris turned ten. Despite her body still being so tiny she became too heavy for me to carry about on my hip. What if she slipped from my grasp? She might break a dozen bones. So I suggested to Madame Soulier that we order a chair with wheels so we could take her around the town more easily. The day it was delivered, with its pristine wicker seat and the metal parts enamelled a shiny dark blue, a sadness spread through my body like a spill of milk on a carpet, seeping through my arms and legs, down to my fingers and toes, into every nook and cranny, turning rancid and refusing to recede. Every morning I woke thinking that the feeling had evaporated overnight, but soon enough it quickened inside me, weighing me down, strangling my heart and pinning me to the bed. I forced myself to rise, lifting my legs with my hands as if they belonged to someone else, and washed and dressed because I had to, but I did barely more than that. Iris sensed it and clung to me, and I clung to her.

I was in this state when one evening, after Iris was asleep, Madame Soulier asked me to follow her up to the drawing room. I thought she was about to suggest a remedy or tell me she'd sent for her doctor.

'I have some news, Marguerite, which is bound to come as a surprise.' We were sitting on the sofa, our knees turned towards each other. I knew she was trying to meet my gaze, but I couldn't look at her. 'It will probably make you unhappy and perhaps a little fearful.'

Disaster was coming.

'I have no choice in this – money is tight, as you know, and I'm still fighting the government for compensation for Monsieur Soulier. My father-in-law is supporting us, and I am obliged to do as he says. He has come to the decision that I must sell the house. We'll be able to live more cheaply in the countryside. I have taken the lease on a cottage in Douaumont.'

'And Iris?' My voice trembled.

'Iris will be looked after by the Sisters. I'm able only to employ a live-out woman. I'm devastated but...' she looked away, 'I know you'll understand. You should go to Paris, my dear. You will find work. Don't you have a married friend from your village who lives there? I'm sure she and her husband would look after you.'

Within a week she had bought my train ticket and paid for a carter to take me to the station at Rheims. On the morning of my departure, as he waited for me in the street, I was in the hall saying goodbye. To avoid a painful scene Madame Soulier had sent Iris out in the new chair with the daily maid.

'I can't,' I said.

'What do you mean?' said Madame Soulier.

'I feel sick. I can't go. Iris needs me.'

'You must. You have no choice. The man is waiting for you. You cannot be late. You will miss the train.'

I felt then that she had never really cared about me. From the moment she told me I must go, I was convinced that she was lying to me about moving to the countryside and that she was intending to replace me with some other servant, a better one, a prettier one, whom Iris would love more than she loved me. And anyway, a family *could* live on almost nothing, as the Diblancs were proof, so why was she not willing to do so if it meant we could all stay together?

In the canvas bag Madame Soulier had given me was my Sunday dress, a set of clean underwear, my white prayer book with the *cartes* inside and a book of testimonials she had bought for me and in which she had written nice words about me. At the bottom was *The Splendour of Paris Under Napoléon III*, which had been a gift to her from her husband and which I had stolen from her bookshelves. Its fold-out illustrations showed me a world of boulevards, bridges and grand buildings. The previous night, in my bed, as I looked at the drawings, my mind see-sawing between hating and loving Madame Soulier and tenderness and worry about how Iris would be with the Sisters, I tried to imagine the Paris I was going to. It was a fairyland – beautiful wide promenades, ladies in good dresses and bonnets and gentlemen in elegant suits and top hats, the Palais Royale from a hot air balloon, the throne room of the Hôtel de Ville.

In the hall with Madame Soulier, I could not move.

'This is not like you, Marguerite.'

I couldn't speak.

'Marguerite, you're a sensible girl. You must go now. You're letting me down.'

Tears ran down my cheeks.

'There's no need for that. On you go. I can't have this.'

Madame Soulier warned me to stay *honest* in Paris. I was not about to confess that I had never been honest with her about why I fled my village, but that was not the kind of honesty she had in mind.

As she walked me to the street and helped me into the cart, she issued me with instructions on how I was to keep my honesty: 'Do not speak to anyone at the station except your friend and her husband, especially not the women, as they will trick you into going with them to a house of evil. Do not give to beggars. The minute they see your purse they will snatch it and run off, even the ones that look like cripples, and then you will be forced to work the streets for a living.'

On the train from Rheims I cried for an hour. An old man leant forward and offered me his handkerchief, but I feared that he would want to start a conversation and that he would have the wrong idea about me and then he would take my honesty, so I smiled thinly and shook my head.

The whole way, I suffered a heart-racing anxiety that threatened to overwhelm me.

What if I was on the wrong platform?

What if I boarded the wrong train?

What if the train crashed?

What if I threw up, or worse?

What if Victoire does not come to meet me?

Eventually, after dark, we pulled into the station at Paris, a huge arched echoing cathedral of glass filled with the noise of steam, soot, metal, and boots on paving. Around me, on the platform, people trailed after porters, their children, luggage, dogs and servants in tow. We were all tired, sweaty and short-tempered. We barged into each other, swarming along the platform towards the barrier.

I went up on tiptoes, willing that man in his top hat to dip down and that lady to move a little, but even when I managed a glimpse through the crowd I could not spot Victoire waiting on the other side. Once I was through, I stood on the concourse gripping the bag, swapping it from hand to hand, afraid to put it down.

Just as I feared, Victoire had not come, so I did the only thing I could think of – I sat in the station café and ordered coffee. The bag was on the floor under my skirt between my legs – if a thief tried to move it, I would surely feel it. I prayed silently to the Virgin that Victoire was merely delayed and that she had not abandoned me but I could get no further than muttering, 'Hail, holy Queen, Mother of mercy, hail, our life, our sweetness and our hope.' In the thick warmth of the café, I closed my eyes and hovered in the space between asleep and awake.

'Marguerite?'

A tall man with a drawn-down face and wearing the blue smock of a worker stood in front of me.

'Forgive me. Jacques Bouillon. Victoire's husband.' He spoke to me in our language. 'I would have been here earlier. I've come straight from the workshop – I work as a silver burnisher. We had a big order on and I couldn't leave.'

I must have beamed out my relief.

'I'm pleased to meet you, Jacques. How did you know me?'

'Victoire described you, quite well as it happens, but I also had this...' He showed me the *carte* I had sent her. 'She's expecting and is not well. Can't leave the apartment. Constantly sick. Can't do anything, really.'

'I'll help her.'

'That would be good but you should know we've very little space.'

'I don't mean to stay long.'

I had thought we could all live together.

We set off down a wide street lit by gas lamps, past shopfronts and huge buildings where the apartments were stacked one on top of each other like the layers of a wedding cake. On we went, across the vast Place du Château d'Eau where we stopped for a moment to drink from the fountain. I was distracted by the sights – comatose beggars in doorways, brazen street women, stocky barkers outside theatres shouting out the delights within. These people were not in the pages of *The Splendour of Paris Under Napoléon III*. I lagged behind and Jacques waited for me at the junctions, impatient but trying not to show it. He did not offer to take my bag.

We crossed a bridge and passed a plain of railway lines and walked down a riverside pathway until we came to the Boulevard de la Gare, where the air was filled with screeching and scraping and whistling, metal against metal, the grinding and huffing of engines as goods trains pulled in with their cargos and out of the huge platforms on both sides of the river. It could not have been more different to Verdun or to our village, which was where I had last seen Victoire.

Jacques led me through the entrance to a building on the main road and into a dark yard beyond, in the corner of which was a small, scruffy building constructed mostly of wood. They had a room on the ground floor and shared a scullery with the family of a consumptive tailor next door. The place stank of tomcats.

'Marguerite,' said Victoire from the bed when we came in,

'so you came.' She looked awful, pale and thin. Her mousy hair hung in limp tendrils. There was a stain on the front of her nightdress. She flopped back down. 'Can't keep anything in. There's a blanket on the side there, and you can take the chair. The latrine is in the yard.'

I tried to tell myself that she couldn't help it, that she wasn't able even to rise from her bed, that one day she would be to me as she had once been, although I knew in my bones this would never be true. She was married and soon she would have a child. I was almost nothing to her.

Over the following weeks I fed her consommé and potato mash. I held her hair while she vomited into a chamber pot. She did not improve and the baby in her belly barely showed.

From time to time she would say, 'I'm dying,' and it was difficult to disagree.

The walls of the room were greasy and damp metallic grit crept into everything. At dawn, when they felt us on the move, the cockroaches scuttled to safety and all day and all night, through the thin walls, we heard the wails of the tailor's youngest child and his own hacking coughs. I longed for Iris and Madame Soulier and my life before I was told to go.

Paris was harsh. The Parisians were unfriendly. Sometimes I caught a look that said: 'How stupid is this idiot who doesn't speak French properly?' Yet we foreigners were everywhere, so they should have been used to us. As I walked past men working on building sites or laying cobblestones, I heard snippets of Belgian Dutch or the language of home. It usually turned out that we had some kind of connection, a friend of a cousin, an uncle from our village.

Eventually, I found work cleaning restaurants with the Widow Zimmermann, who had come to Paris from our village many decades earlier. She let me share her bed in a hovel in the Rue Saint-Maur in Belleville.

While I was with her, I received a note from Victoire to say that she had given birth to a baby boy who had lived for two days. He was buried in the paupers' pit at the back of Père Lachaise cemetery, near the Jews and Muslims. The following Sunday, we walked the paths of the cemetery in the drizzling rain, until we came to the place. We stood in silence.

'My breasts are still leaking,' she said.

I held her hand.

'I'll try again,' she said.

'I know you will.'

'How did your mother bear it?'

'She had no choice.'

The atmosphere in No. 13 was acrid. If there had ever been a truce between Julie and her mother, it was over. They argued all the time – you could hear it from the kitchen. Madame attacking and Mademoiselle defending and then Mademoiselle sobbing. I should have ignored it – I couldn't.

To the right of the door to the parlour there was a shallow cupboard built into the alcove where spare tablecloths and coverings were kept. I discovered that if I opened the doors and stood up close to the shelves I could hear clearly what was being said through the wall.

'He's a filthy lying bastard son of a whore, that Théo Riel. He stole your father's money from me and had the cheek to lend it back to me. There's nothing *you* can tell me about him.'

'There is, Maman.'

'What? What can you tell me?'

Silence.

'Tell me. You say there is and then you don't tell me?'

'Actually, you've always known but you'll say you don't. I was your sacrifice, your part-payment. To him. *My uncle*, Maman, *my uncle.*'

'He's not your uncle. You're not actually related.'

'That's exactly what he said.'

'It had to happen at some point. It really doesn't matter.'

There was some mumbling and then Julie said, 'How much do you still owe him? Uncle Théo, I mean.'

'How much do *I* owe him? *You* owe him too, my dear, for your education. We're a family, don't forget.'

'Much you know about family. Tell me.'

'Five thousand francs. More or less. I've paid off the rest, thanks to *your friend Milord*. He'll be at the St James's on Saturday, by the way, and will see you after your performance. Be ready for him.'

'*See* me,' said Julie. 'There's another word for it.'

There was silence.

'Don't tell me there's a problem,' said Madame Riel.

Julie let out a guttural sound of frustration.

'No. Well, yes, there is a problem, Maman,' she said loudly. 'Quite apart from the fact that he is... and the things he... it's not a good time, Maman. You didn't even ask me. My monthly...'

'Are you being difficult, my dear? Calm yourself down. There are things you can do, as if you didn't know. I gave you the equipment. It's not like I haven't taught you. God Almighty, I hope you don't show this side of your character to him.'

'What side?'

'The uncooperative side.'

'You'd know a lot about what I show him.'

'Meaning what?'

'This is all down to you. To you, I'm goods for sale. That's all I am. How much did you get for me? How much did De Corneville pay to be the first? Or Uncle Théo for that matter. Did he pay cash too?'

'Stop talking about Uncle Théo.'

Then there was a change. Madame lowered her voice and it was more difficult for me to hear what she was saying. I made out parts of it: '...ungrateful... all the help I've given you... this house...' Then she got louder. 'I hate to be candid, Julie my dear, but you'd never have achieved anything in Paris without him, or me for that matter. Pretty women like you are two a penny and believe me we need those pennies. Because he's not as generous as he likes to think he is. Everything is a squeeze. You have no idea. Anyway, you're lucky he's taken you back. Running off like a spoilt child. He was furious. You need to work on him – we need more...'

'Maman, it's just that...'

'It's only thanks to me that he took you back.'

'You're lying. It's all the other way around. He's obsessed with me... it's desperate and revolting. He's old enough to be my grandfather, Maman.'

'You're careful, I hope. We can't have an accident.'

'What? Like *you* had, you mean? Like *I* was?'

'Julie... I've warned you.'

'I'm always careful, Maman, but–'

'But? If you were clever enough you'd see that you could be his wife.'

'What do you mean? Have you finally gone crazy? He's *married* to his duchess and he's got other obligations, and other women.'

She sounded weary, as if she was going over old ground.

'The wife's not in the best of health, Julie. How do you not know this? She's almost as old as he is. Perhaps you won't need to wait long.'

'One minute you're saying he's a stingy old goat and he should cough up, now you're saying I should marry him. And anyway, what kind of life would I have? "Oh, meet my wife. Yes, she *was* my mistress, and she *was* an actress, and yes, a *French* one, and we all know what that means".'

'We'd be rich.'

'Is that all you think about?'

'Yes. And you want to know why? I know what it's like to be poor. You can have nothing one day, and everything the next, and then nothing again. I will not go back to that.'

CHAPTER TWELVE

If Papa had been with me in London he would have told me to leave No. 13. Right then. Without delay. And he would have been right. No good could come from staying, as indeed it did not.

The trouble was not only that I had nowhere to go, it was also that I was exhausted, ground to the bone. To move again, *yet again* – I could not. For years, I had been perching in one nest after another, traipsing from one place to the next, sleeping on a shelf, in a windowless cupboard, on a chair, not knowing how long I would be there, looked at sideways, never entirely welcome but, as long as I didn't misbehave, not entirely unwelcome either – on condition I worked hard and kept to the rules.

I would still be in Verdun and never have gone to Paris and never then run to London and landed in all this trouble if Madame Soulier had not pushed me out. It just goes to show that you can never trust anyone, not completely. A dog will always be a dog. If it bites you, it will have its own reasons for doing so. It just can't tell you what they are.

It was Papa who instructed me to leave our village and make for Verdun. When I appeared in front of the magistrate in the nearby town, to answer for the slap I gave the Widow Larue, I was sentenced to eight days in the town dungeon. The only reason I was not taken straight down there was that it was already full of male prisoners, and it would be unacceptable to put me in with them.

After I swore to the magistrate that I would return in a week to take my punishment, Papa and I made our way back through the forest to our cottage. It was late at night, halfway through November, a day of dirty storms and evil winds. Trees loomed around us. Somewhere in the distance two dogs barked. As we trudged, the sound of wet mulch underfoot filled the silence between us.

I glanced at the back of him – his shoulders were folded in against the cold. His short neck and square skull were exactly like mine. He was a patient man until he wasn't. We were much the same, not only in looks.

'Marguerite...' he said, turning his head a little.

I pretended that his words were lost on the wind.

'Marguerite,' he said again. 'Talk to me.' I had not told him, or the magistrate, what had actually happened. The widow's words, if you repeated them out loud, sounded like nothing.

'She was rude.'

'The widow is an old lady. For goodness' sake.'

'She insulted our family.'

I was crying now, as silently as I could manage. When I wiped the tears away the cold bit my cheeks.

'How so?'

'She said things... About Mama.'

'People will annoy you, Marguerite, and insult you, and hurt you. Most of the time it is just hot air, nothing to do with you. They have their own troubles and they take them out on other people. We are all the same like that. Your job in life, because you can be hot-tempered when you are pushed too far, is not to allow what they say to rouse you. If that happens, you have lost. You will always be in the wrong.'

We were on the main street of our village and were nearly passing the widow's house.

'You must forgive her, Marguerite. The Bible says we must forgive,' said Papa. 'She will forgive you.'

'I'm not sure about that.'

He waited before replying. 'You need to learn to ignore people who say bad things to you. You should just close your ears and...'

'I *know*, Papa.'

'...and if you feel you are about to lash out, hold your wrist behind your back and count to ten. Breathe. Wait for the moment to be over. Was your belly full or empty?'

'When?'

'Just before you came at the widow.'

'You mean was I hungry? Yes. Probably.'

'Hunger makes everything worse. You're in trouble now.'

'You don't need to tell me.'

We were almost at our cottage.

'Eight days in that lock-up is a long time for you,' said Papa.

'I'll run away.'

After a few minutes he said: 'You should go to France, child, to Verdun. It's not far – just across the border. It's about time for you to leave here, anyway. There's nothing for you. Go tomorrow, first thing. You're clever. Get an indoor job with a family. Much better than the fields or a factory. God will protect you.'

On Saturday morning, Madame Riel came down to the kitchen.

'Mademoiselle Julie will be back after midnight. It's the first night of the new play.' She looked tightly wound. 'Before you go to bed take the brandy decanter and two glasses from the dining room up to the drawing room.'

I made her wait a beat before I said, 'Yes, Madame.'

I wanted her to think me insolent, to feel that I was hardly listening to her. It was a delicious recklessness.

At noon, she and Mademoiselle Julie were in the hall, waiting to go out to their cab in the street. Julie, in a gown of frothy cream organza under a white fur cape, looked like a lamb going to slaughter.

'Well?' said Henriette as we walked to her place after evening mass the next day. 'What's up? You've got a face like thunder.'

I could have said the same about her but I didn't.

'Oh God, Henriette. Stuff *is* going on. You were right. I'm sorry that I couldn't see it. Madame came in from the theatre at eight last night and went straight up to her room.'

'And? Would she normally do that?'

'No–'

'So has something happened? What's wrong with going up to bed at eight?'

'Eliza came back from her mother's and lit a fire in Julie's bedroom and banked up the coals before she went to bed. She's never done that before.'

'This is getting interesting. Go on.'

I told her about the conversation I overheard through the linen closet, and Julie and her mother talking about the mysterious Milord; and how Madame had asked me to put brandy in the drawing room, and how from that I knew Julie would be returning from the theatre with a gentleman.

At midnight I was awake, lying in my bed, shuddering at the shame of it, not just my shame at being employed in a house where such things went on, but Julie's shame. I had been a fool, but she was not the one who had fooled me. That was me. I fooled myself.

Of course I heard them. I heard the clop-clop-clop of the hansom as it drew up in front of the house and I heard the slam of the cab door and the gruff thanks of the driver, and I heard the key turning in the lock of the front door and I heard the murmur of their voices and a thud of his cane on each step as they came up the stairs. I heard him open the door of the drawing room.

I must have dozed a little because some time later I was woken by the sound of another door clicking shut and I knew they had gone into Julie's bedroom. Then quiet. Shortly after two o'clock I tiptoed down the stairs, opened the attic door and stepped into the house. Pomade and cigars tainted the air.

Madame Riel was constantly accusing me of thundering about like an animal in the zoo but she did not know that I could also creep about like a ghost if I put my mind to it.

'Marguerite! You didn't!' said Henriette.

I massaged my brow.

'I wanted to get a newspaper from the pile in the parlour. I couldn't sleep. You know I love reading.'

I did like to read the newspapers but that was not why I sneaked downstairs.

'And then what?'

'I don't like to say.'

'Didn't you listen at her door? I would have.'

I looked at the floor.

'I thought he had gone by then. I wanted to know she was all right.'

I imagined the shopman at Monsieur Miray's with his hand on the door to Henriette's room and him telling her she must keep her mouth shut, and I thought about how anyone who discovered what he was doing, and about Henriette's situation now, would blame her, for not stopping him – the shopman would merely be following a man's inclinations. She must have encouraged him, they would say. Years before, my mother told me that it was always the woman's fault and that men are like beasts in the field and only act according to their nature, so it was down to us to fend them off.

'But what did you hear?' She sniggered.

'Nothing.'

'But it's bad enough,' said Henriette. 'To have a man in your bedroom overnight. That can only mean…'

I thought of her arrangement in Paris with her two widowers but said nothing, and of how she lived unmarried with that Communard who'd been shot in the Père Lachaise. But it was always different for poor women. They had to shift as they could. And their morals were of less importance to the world.

I did not tell Henriette that on my way back up the stairs with a newspaper in my hand I stood outside Julie's door again and listened with my ear against the crack.

'You are driving me mad, Julie.' It was a voice I had heard before. It was indeed the old English gentleman. He was loud, grunting, labouring his French. 'You are… I cannot tell you… I cannot tell you… The effect you have on me… I sometimes, sometimes, can't control myself. You have enslaved me… My friends… my friends… my friends say, they say… I am an old fool… Not finished… Don't stop… Go on… Don't stop…'

'Marguerite, I'm still not sure,' said Henriette, changing the subject. She didn't need to tell me what she was referring to.

She said she was nauseous in the mornings but it went away when she ate a cracker or a slice of bread, and anyway her bleeds had not been regular since the Siege so there was probably nothing to worry about.

As we walked on, I thought of what I had heard through the door.

After it stopped, Julie and the old gentleman were talking – about his engagements for the next day, about a speech he had given in Parliament, and then she said something I didn't hear and they were laughing. Perhaps, in reality, she did love this man.

Henriette and I stopped under a streetlamp.

'Let me look at your eyes,' I said.

She stood in front of me, like Mama used to when she suspected another baby was coming. I could always tell if that was true or not.

'I can't say for sure, Henriette, but yes, probably.'

CHAPTER THIRTEEN

A thin layer of snow crunched underfoot and I stamped on the mat as I came in through the basement door. Mademoiselle Julie, wearing a silk dress of pomegranate pink topped with a fine paisley shawl, was in the kitchen pretending to root around in the drawers of the dresser.

Anger rose up in my chest. That man was old. Rude. He had mocked me that time I had to come through the front door. His wiry grey whiskers would have grazed her cheeks. He harried her, ordered her... and his rhythmic words, commanding, ordering... *Don't stop... Not finished.*

I wanted to punish her for allowing it. For laughing with him.

'Are you looking for something in particular, Mademoiselle Julie?' I called out from the scullery as I hung up my cloak. I tried to sound unfriendly.

'I don't really know what I'm looking for, to be honest. I'm glad you're here, though. I wanted to ask if you would be interested in hearing my latest reviews.'

'Of course, Mademoiselle Julie,' I said. She didn't notice my tone.

In her hand she had a clutch of cuttings from English newspapers and she translated for me as she read:

'*Mademoiselle Riel, a charming actress whose talent we have remarked upon frequently, and with so much pleasure, has been specially selected to play those light, girlish, and pretty characters, in which she has few, if any, rivals in London.* That's the best one. Here, I've got another one: *Charming and delightful.* And this one, *Mademoiselle Riel was the piquante French girl, leaving nothing to be desired* and *She has much grace and animation.* If I continue to get notices like that Monsieur Le Directeur says he'll consider me for better parts. When I'm older, that is, more mature. Perhaps I *will* be the next Madame Rachel!'

I wondered if any of the critics had anything to say about her other than that she was young and pretty. Perhaps Madame Riel was right – that there was nothing special about her other than her looks. And then I wondered if that was the reason I liked her too.

'That's nice, Mademoiselle Julie. Madame Riel must be proud of you.'

'Oh, she says I should do better. I dare say she's right.' She looked like she was about to say something but could not bring herself to. At last, she said, whispering, 'Do you think she has changed? Maman, I mean. Lately.'

'Changed? No, I haven't noticed a change.'

'It's just that, she's been coming out with some peculiar things.'

I thought of the arguments I had overheard from the linen cupboard.

'I know she wouldn't like me to talk to you about this, but I can't think of anyone else who'd understand. Her friends don't see what I see. I've tried the priest at Farm Street' – they went occasionally to the Roman Catholic church a few streets behind Park Lane – 'but he says he doesn't know her and he just prescribed praying for help from the Virgin. Useless, if you ask me.'

I stood there, wanting to get on. It was laundry day and with Eliza at her mother's I had more than my fair share of work to do. I had beds to strip and the bundle had to be ready for collection at two o'clock, and after that I had to do the fireplaces and the coal scuttles. Cooking had been reduced to cold cuts, salads and shop-bought food, and I was thankful that neither Madame nor Julie seemed to care.

'Has Maman seemed a little more animated lately?'

'Not particularly, Mademoiselle Julie, I can't say she has. Not with me, anyway.'

Madame had barely spoken to me for weeks.

'It's just that she seems to think the world is against her, and that there are people who are out to bring her down, and she fixes on certain people.' She looked at her hands.

She is trying to tell me that she means me.

'And now she's accusing people who don't even know her.'

I said nothing for a few seconds and then: 'Do you think she's unwell?'

'I honestly don't know. When she's with Madame Antoine or Madame Crosnier... with them she seems normal, or nearly so, but when she's with me, she rails against spies and enemies. She says some quite troubling things, things that could not possibly be true. I've considered getting a doctor but...' – she looked towards the kitchen window, battling tears – 'she'll think I have betrayed her, and God only knows what will happen then.'

She slid down on a chair at the table.

'I don't know what to do.'

When I was with Monsieur Dumas, I too was worried about spies sent to get me. I felt watched and vulnerable. Now, as the events of Paris receded in time, I often forgot to be fearful, and as Henriette had pointed out, we were nobodies.

I sat down next to Julie. She was ensnaring me and I was back where I started, wanting her to bend her neck and rest her head on my shoulder, wanting to be of help to her. I yearned to tell her that this moment would pass, that better times were coming.

'Mademoiselle Julie, my own mother was sometimes ill, usually around the time her babies were born or passed away.'

Twice Mama had been found on a bridge holding the latest sick baby. I had never talked about this with anyone. Victoire knew but we had never discussed it. The Widow Larue, whose enquiry after my mother's health so angered me, knew about it.

'Your mother's feelings could be something to do with the change women go through naturally. It will pass,' I said, although I was not at all sure that this was the source of Madame's disturbance.

'What happened to your Mama?'

'She's fine.'

I didn't want to say that she had spent months at a time in the asylum.

Julie stood up.

'I'll be going away to Paris for a week. At Easter,' she said.

I was stunned that she would drop this in, without a warning. It spelled disaster. In two weeks' time I would be left with Madame Riel, and if Eliza's mother was still clinging to life, possibly without even Eliza.

Mademoiselle Julie must have decided that a roster of visits from Madame's friends was the remedy for her mother's state of mind. One afternoon shortly after Julie's casual announcement, both Mesdames Antoine and Crosnier arrived at the house at the same time. Julie asked me to bring up coffee for all four of them.

So deep were they in conversation in the drawing room that they did not hear me on the other side of the door with the tray. I stood silently and listened for a break in their conversation.

Madame Crosnier was saying, '...but can you afford to sack her, Caroline? I mean, surely you can't manage without her.'

'Manage? No. No, definitely not,' said Julie, panicked. 'That's just it. Maman, you had enough difficulty finding her in the first place, didn't you? In fact, didn't *you* find her for us, Madame Antoine? And she's *quite* a good cook. Not terrible at any rate. Now we've got her, we should try our best to keep her.'

'You should have been here for the lunch with Uncle Théo,' said her mother. 'Disgusting.'

'But it's mostly that you just don't like her?' said Madame Crosnier to Madame Riel. 'Is that it?'

'Maman thinks she's nosy,' said Julie.

'She's more than that. She lurks outside doors trying to overhear us. And she's a typical Belgian,' said Madame Riel. 'Stubborn. Stupid. And ugly.'

'She is a little strange. I don't quite know what to make of her. Tense. Intense. But I like her well enough,' said Julie.

'Stupid?' said Madame Antoine. 'I never got that impression.'

'She *is* a bit stupid,' said Julie. 'Or I should say a little rough in her manners. Direct.'

'But she can read and write. That's not always the case with female servants. Certainly not at home in France. Honestly, Caroline, I would keep her if I were you,' said Madame Crosnier.

'I can't bear her,' said Madame Riel. 'She's got to go. Untrustworthy. I hate her.'

'But Maman, Eliza is not here, at least for the next few days, weeks maybe, and anyway she can hardly prepare a decent cold tray and she certainly can't shop for French food, and we don't have anyone else.'

'We could get one of the others back. That young one, what was her name – Angèle? Or Josette.'

'No, they won't come back, and anyway, what would you do without anyone to look after you when I'm away? You can't manage on your own.'

'Are you going away, Julie?' said Madame Antoine. 'Where are you going?'

'My friend Isabelle and I will be having Easter week in Paris.'

'She's going to see that awful Saint-Germain fellow,' said Madame Riel.

'*Maman...*'

'She is. What will Milord think? Does he even know you're going? Have you told him?'

'Maman! Stop it. Stop it now. Madame Antoine and Madame Crosnier don't want to hear this. The theatre will be closed for Easter and I am going to collect some gowns from Madame Pérès and to see colleagues from the Vaudeville. And yes, Saint-Germain may be among them. He is my friend.'

I created a smile, held the tray with one hand, tapped on the door with the other and pushed it open with my back.

Eliza's mother died the next day and soon Eliza was back in the house wearing a plain black gown, which made her face look almost as papery as Madame Riel's. Once, I caught her holding on to the wall of the scullery and weeping. Of course, I had no words to express my condolences but I hoped that my general demeanour gave the right impression.

We returned to our routines. I had managed to make Eliza understand that we should share the dirty jobs more equally, and that she could not point at the blacking brushes and nod her head at me and swish off to tidy Madame's dressing table. Her manner towards me was softer than before her mother died, and there were fewer times when she sighed *Marguerite* and looked exasperated. Sometimes grief rubs the sharp edges off people.

We had a good week together. We even had the house to ourselves when Madame made an excursion to the theatre, rare for her, for one of Julie's matinées – and took that opportunity to beat all the rugs and hall runners. In the back yard, with muslin cloths tied over our mouths we took turns to swing the carpet beater as far back as we could and then quickly sheltered in the scullery while the dust settled. Afterwards, I went into the dining room and poured two glasses of Madame's red wine, which we drank at the kitchen table.

We started to use a relay system to fill the coal scuttles. As I was the stronger of us, Eliza brought down the empties and I carried them back up to the fireplaces. The first time we did this, after I put the scuttle down in Julie's room, I surveyed the mantelpiece, the dresser and cabinets, which were arranged with legions of small ornaments. Two miniature bronze soldiers in Napoleonic uniform, a tiny toy watering can that belonged in a doll's house, a porcelain leopard – I guessed they were samples from the family trinket business, perhaps chosen for Julie by her father. Over the bed, a pale oak vessel carved with flowers and fruit, she had discarded items of clothing – stockings, garters, chemises and petticoats. I had an inclination to touch them and would have done so if it had not been for the coal smuts on my hands.

On the dressing table sat a small cherrywood chest, its top drawer open. I leant over to see inside and instantly felt sick – a yellow sponge, a tangle of pink rubber tubes, pots of ointment and the barrel of a steel syringe.

CHAPTER FOURTEEN

On the morning of the next Saturday Madame again instructed me to leave the brandy and glasses in the drawing room. This time I slept through the night. I had no desire to know more about what Mademoiselle Julie was doing than I knew already, and wished I knew less.

Madame had given me permission to go to the earlier Mass at the French Church, which meant that I had Sunday afternoon to myself. I went first to Monsieur Miray's to ask Henriette if she was also free, but he told me she had left him a few days earlier and had a new place in Berwick Street with Madame Cholet. He gave me a look that told me he knew about what had gone on in his house and that he knew I knew too.

Henriette told me that on Monday she had gone to Madame Miray and said she was late and, to her surprise, the Mirays were furious with the shopman and had ordered him to provide 'expenses'. Afterwards Madame Miray handed her the address of a woman in a court behind Oxford Street and Monsieur Miray organised her a new place with Madame Cholet. The following day, soon after she arrived there, Henriette bled heavily. On Thursday, she was up and about. There was no need for her to go to Oxford Street.

'The money is going into our savings for returning home to Paris,' said Henriette. 'I think we are safe from, well, anyway... I also think we should have some fun today, and not go to church at all. We both need cheering up, Marguerite. I know I do.'

She'd seen a poster for the Colonna Troupe from Paris who were performing at a kind of pleasure garden outside London. She had an ache to see them.

We walked through Trafalgar Square and Whitehall to Westminster to catch an omnibus. Henriette knew a little bit of English, so she asked a respectable-looking woman where we should stand, and after a few minutes a green vehicle pulled by two horses stopped nearby and the conductor helped us up. The journey seemed to take for ever as the omnibus jolted through the streets, stopping every few minutes to let people on and off. At one stage, an old lady in a huge old-fashioned crinoline dress squeezed through the door and the conductor had to push down the hoops to get her in. Henriette and I avoided looking at each other as we knew we would collapse into giggles.

I had no idea where we were and found it disconcerting to travel so far away from London. We went through busy traffic junctions and past endless rows of red-brick houses. At one steep hill, the horses pulled us up agonisingly slowly and I had a sudden fear that the load would be too much and the omnibus would tumble over and we would all be killed. I felt my face redden as my secret panic set in but no one noticed, not even Henriette.

When we reached our destination nearly all the passengers, including us and the old lady, were decanted into a small street leading to Highbury Barn, where people crowded around the entrance. Lots of them were drunk and shouting, and a young woman, in a dirty white dress and with a crying two-year-old on her hip, was brawling with an equally inebriated man. The air was thick with cigarette smoke and the reek of stale English beer.

'Are you sure we should be here?' I said to Henriette, as quietly as I could so as not to attract attention for speaking French. I felt out of place amongst all the rough people and I was already dreading the journey back and imagining that the omnibus would career down the hill and that we would crash to our deaths.

'It will be amusing – you'll see.'

We went through to a courtyard filled with stalls selling raisin buns, ginger beer, souvenirs and papier mâché masks, and followed the signs to an outdoor platform. We stood towards the back of an ocean of men, trying to see through the forest of top hats. Interspersed between the men were women of the street cruising the crowd, and servants in everyday dresses, jackets and bonnets, much like ourselves. I began to feel more relaxed.

The band started playing and shouts went up from the audience. Onto the stage pranced two young women, blonde plaits roped around their crowns and wearing short floppy pink tutus, low sleeveless bodices and black heeled boots. To the thumping beat of the music, they bent forward, shook their shoulders and swayed, throwing their arms around, first pressing against each other and then easing away, swinging apart and back again, all at a tremendous pace. Two other women, in red fringed shorts and diaphanous white blousons, joined them.

'They're supposed to be the boys,' said Henriette.

The dancers' exuberance, their daring, their taunting and flaunting, their shamelessness was breathtaking. Everything was a flash of rouge, ribbons, tassels, laces, red, white, black, silver, gold, illuminated by the hissing gas jets. It was disgusting and intoxicating. My head swam, as if I were about to faint. I wanted it to stop and for it to go on for ever. I yearned to move like that, to stretch and jump and turn, to not care, to lose myself in music.

The four of them swirled and whirled and the audience roared with every swish and lift of the tutus and stamp of the boots until the music came to a peak, at which point the first two dancers, the girls, turned their backs, bent over, pulled up their skirts and one of the boys faced the audience, lifted her leg, grabbed her heel, and turned, hopping, in a full circle. And then one of the tutu girls did the same. It was as if a bolt of lightning had been thrown down. A huge noise erupted. Henriette and I looked at each other in shock. The men were howling and barking. The dancer could only have been showing her nakedness.

At the end of the number the chief dancer shouted out something to the audience.

She was not from Paris – nor anywhere in France.

CHAPTER FIFTEEN

'I'm disappointed, Julie. For your sake,' Madame said. 'London is not what I imagined. We've been cheated. The other English men reward their whores well.'

'Maman, please. Not this again.'

I was standing in the linen cupboard in my stocking feet, listening. If they had found me like that, I would have been ejected from the house there and then.

'If you remember, we were promised Mayfair, not a cottage down a lane. He's playing games.'

'It's really all right.'

'No carriage,' said her mother. 'Not even a manservant – just two idiotic skivvies who seem determined to annoy me. You must speak to him.'

'We never discuss such things. It has to end, Maman. I feel only repugnance for him. The things he...'

'Stop whingeing, will you? We all have to do things we don't like. Be patient. And think of your career. Not many actresses can say they starred on the London stage.'

'I don't have top billing or anything like it, as you well know.

But you also want me to marry him, which would be the end of my career.'

Silence.

'He won't marry me, whatever you think.'

'And why not? You'd be good for his bloodline.'

'He doesn't need an heir. I've told you before. He's got his son, a legitimate one who is forty-two with six children. And I'm not his only mistress. He has another woman, an English woman, who has I don't know how many children by him and is expecting another.'

'That is a lie.'

'It is not. It's well known. His own son told me. He wanted to warn me off, in case I, as he put it, develop ideas.'

'If I knew who this woman was I would kill her.'

'Don't be absurd, Maman.' Julie sounded weary.

'He won't marry her. Who is she anyway? Some cheap London whore, no doubt.'

'Well, Maman, I'm just a cheap French whore.'

'Don't you speak like that. He's besotted with you. I made sure of that.'

'For now, perhaps. Until he moves on to the next one. I am not besotted with him. Quite the opposite.'

'He waited for you when you chose to run away to your little friend in Paris.'

'And now he's got me.'

'You should be grateful.'

'Oh, that again.'

'Listen, Julie, you don't know this but he saw you years ago. *Years ago.* When you were a mere child. He came to me at the Rue Laffitte. Who do you think kept the business afloat all that time? Was it the Baroness and her two bonnets a year? Was it the ladies who whined and wheedled and said *"Oh I'm so sorry, Madame Riel, I've already overspent my allowance so please could I have a little tiny discount on my next order?"* Who do you think paid for your extra year at the Conservatory? Who paid off the instalments to Théo? Who do you think did that? He's already paid out. No wonder his generosity is fading.'

'You like transactions, don't you? You've loved selling me.'

'Nothing comes for free. And as for the stage, well it's the career you chose yourself.'

'*I* chose?'

'You wanted to go to the Conservatory and be an actress.'

'No, you wanted me to go to the Conservatory, be an actress *and* a whore. I was thirteen – how could I know what you had in store for me?'

Then everything went quiet.

Madame Riel said, 'Milord can have as many mistresses as he desires. That woman has children, you say? That makes her a bore. You are different. You hold the cards.'

───────────

'Marguerite! Mademoiselle Diblanc! Please forgive me. How good it is to see you. We've been a little worried.'

Monsieur Dumas came across the shop floor and took both my hands. It had been a few weeks since I'd had cause to step through his doors.

'How are you, my dear? Well, I hope, and I hope Madame and Mademoiselle Riel are, um, well.'

I replied that all was going swimmingly, although I felt he should get credit for trying to warn me before I went to No. 13, so I implied that Mademoiselle Julie tempered a difficult atmosphere, which was true enough.

When I told him that Madame had sent me to collect a bottle of Hennessy cognac he looked pained and I asked him if it was out of stock.

'It's not that, Marguerite.' He put his head close to mine. 'Between you and me, I've sent my account to Madame Riel, for the last two quarters, and I've had no reply.'

I thought of the unlit gas and the cold fireplaces, and the conversations between Madame and Julie. Despite the now frequent visits of the old gentleman, the household was almost as penny-pinched as when I first arrived. Then, as if he'd been conjured out of my thoughts–

'I couldn't help overhearing.'

The battlefield voice.

I turned around.

The whiskers, the overcoat, the top hat, the stoop, the cane.

'Madame Riel is an acquaintance of mine,' he said, looking through me at Monsieur Dumas. 'Please accept this woman's order.' Then he turned to me and said, 'Wait outside.'

I could only obey. I tried to look interested in the window display of the French pharmacist next door while fighting the knot in my stomach. After fifteen minutes, he emerged.

I couldn't look at him.

'What is your name?'

'Marguerite Diblanc, sir.'

'And you are?'

'The cook, sir, at 13 Park Lane.'

'I have seen you before, I believe.'

'Yes, sir.'

'Tell me, Diblanc, do Madame and Mademoiselle Riel receive many visitors at the house?'

'No, sir.'

'No young people? Theatre people?'

'Sometimes, sir.'

'Who?'

'Madame Crosnier.'

'Anyone else?'

'Madame Antoine.'

'Anyone else?'

'Mademoiselle Guy.'

That was Julie's friend Isabelle, who was to go to Paris with her.

'No one else?'

'No, sir.'

'That is all for now. Away you go. Do not mention our conversation to them, nor to anyone.'

'No, sir.'

I couldn't go straight back to No. 13. My heart was pounding and my fingers tingled. I needed Henriette, so I walked to Berwick Street and rang on Madame Cholet's bell. Henriette came down to answer.

'Be quick,' she said. 'I can give you two minutes. I'm supposed to be working.'

There was no need to say that.

'Henriette, if you were in a place where you thought–'

She looked irritated. 'Can this wait? Hurry up, Marguerite. Get to the point.'

'It's just that I was in Monsieur Dumas's shop and that man was there.'

'Which man?'

'Mademoiselle Julie... you know... the gentleman who...'

'And?'

She was unimpressed when I related our conversation.

'Couldn't this have waited until Sunday?'

'It's just that... Should I tell Julie about it?'

'Tell her what?'

'That he questioned me.'

'No.'

'Why not?'

'Because you live in a house of secrets. You don't really know what's going on. Anyway, what good would it do her to know he's been checking up on her? Chances are she knows he does that.'

'What shall I say about the cognac?'

'Nothing. I've got to go now. He pays all their bills. That's how it works. He pays. She... you know. You live in a bordello, Marguerite. You need to get out of there, as I have said more than once.'

'Yes, I know you're right. I should. But Mademoiselle Julie needs me.'

'For what? You're a servant. You can be replaced. We all can. When she's being nice it's because she wants something from you, that's all. You told me they'd had a stream of servants in that house. It's not just Madame Riel being an old cow, it's this Mademoiselle Julie too. They are not respectable, and if you stay there you will not be respectable either.'

Before I left, she said, 'You need to ask Monsieur Dumas who he is!'

'Who?'

'The old man, silly. Sometimes, Marguerite, I do wonder about you.'

It was nearly dark and the lamplighters were climbing their ladders. While I was dredging some beef for a casserole, Mademoiselle Julie came down to the kitchen holding Ulysses.

'Marguerite,' she said, 'I need to say something to you.'

'Are you not at the theatre today, Mademoiselle Julie?'

'No parts today. I need to speak to you. Can you stop what you're doing for a second?'

I turned around and she stepped back. She had a way of

tilting her head and gazing downward and then peeping up from under her eyebrows – her lost little girl act. She sighed.

'We... Maman... you... erm, Marguerite...'

She sighed again and took a deep breath in, dramatically, as if she were preparing to give a monologue.

'I'm sorry to have to say this, truly I am. I have no choice. Maman has asked me to tell you that you must leave.'

My heart skidded.

'Forgive me, Mademoiselle Julie. I didn't hear you properly. What did you say?'

I knew what she had said. I was punishing her by making her say it again.

She put Ulysses down and he snuffled around on the floor.

'Maman has asked me to give you your notice.'

'Are you telling me you're sacking me?' I wiped my hands on my apron.

She paused and looked over towards the kitchen window. Slowly, she drew her head round and looked at me from under her brows. The sing-song voice was gone. She pulled herself up straight. Formal.

'Yes, Marguerite. That is correct. Maman says we will pay you until the end of the week and you must go now.'

'Why?'

'No special reason.'

'Give me a reason. It's the least you can do.'

'As I said, no special reason.'

'That is not true.'

'If you insist, she says you answer back. And...'

'And what?'

'And you... well, there's no nice way to say this, she says you listen at doors and spy on her.'

'I do not.'

'Whatever the reason, she wants you to go.'

'No.'

'No, what?'

'No, Mademoiselle Julie.'

I felt a swell of hatred for them both. Julie had not fought for me; she had rolled over. She had told her mother that she needed me. I heard her say, *We should try our best to keep her*, but it dawned on me now it was only because I was of use to her. She had given no thought as to my welfare. I was nothing to her. She said I was *stupid* and *rough*.

Yet she had sought out my company and my approval. I had listened to her reviews. She had practised her lines with me. She had invited me to dance the gavotte in the kitchen. We had laughed. She had confided in me about her wretched mother's mad tirades. She told me about her father. She had relied on me to boost her, to prop her up.

Marguerite, you know how to do this. Please help me.

Be a darling and sew this button for me.

Marguerite, can I borrow you? I need to consult you for a second.

How should I attach these ribbons? Maman is too grumpy to ask right now.

She was pushing me into dangerous territory. I was now on the defensive, behind the barricade.

'You will be paid until the end of the week.'

To think I almost let this go. As I was spiralling into visions of starvation on the streets, sleeping under bridges, fending off men, Henriette's advice brought me back to the present.

'No, Mademoiselle Julie, you will pay me for the month. We live in England. English servants have a month's notice here, not a week like in France. It's the law. If you don't pay me, I'll go to the magistrates.'

I wanted to say, *And your old gentleman will not appreciate that.*

'You will pay me as you should. It's what you would have to give Eliza if you sacked her. And you will pay the ten shillings promised to me by Madame Antoine before I even came here.'

'I don't think Maman will agree to it.'

'*Maman* does not have to. I'm not leaving this house until I get it. And in any case, you can't do without me. You've told me you're going to Paris for Easter. So who will shop and cook for your mother then? *Eliza?*'

I spat out her name. Was she behind this?

'She's useless at cooking – you know that. She knows nothing about food. And you won't find anyone to take my place. All the French in London know what your household... your mother is like.'

'Marguerite, but... well, you're not wrong. About some things.'

She looked defeated and I felt a frisson of power, as if I had a baton and it was my turn to conduct. After a pause she said: 'Stay. You're right. You must stay, for now – until we find someone else, but *after that* you must be gone. I'll talk to Maman. You must leave by the twentieth of April, a month from today.'

'And if I find another place before that I'll be off. And I'll be looking.'

'Don't do that just yet, Marguerite. At least promise to stay until I get back from Paris. I'll bring you a dress, to show there are no hard feelings. I know you need one. A nice one that you can wear for work.'

'Thank you, Mademoiselle Julie.'

'Not a new one,' she said quickly.

It was the dress. Without a decent dress I had no chance of finding another place. Otherwise I would never have agreed. The blue dress was rags and despite my best efforts with bicarbonate of soda, I could not eradicate the thick yellow sweat stains under the arms of the brown dress. I was down to my last few shillings. If it had not been for the dress, I would have stamped out of the house there and then.

'Marguerite... It's not me, Marguerite. You know that. It's Maman. I don't make excuses for her. She's the way she is. You know what she's like.'

'I do know what she's like and I know what she makes you...'

I stopped. There was no point going any further. Saying it would change nothing.

CHAPTER SIXTEEN

'Marguerite, come.'

Eliza touched my elbow and pointed to the laundry sack, which she had opened up on the kitchen table. Since I had been given my marching orders, Eliza had avoided my eye. I suspected that she knew of it before I did.

She rifled through the bag and brought out items I had never seen before.

'No, no, no.' She sighed.

She looked as if she was at the end of her tether. None of the pieces that had come back belonged to the Riels.

'Mademoiselle Julie,' said Eliza feebly. 'Paris.'

Julie was due to leave the next day.

What was it to me? And anyway, Julie had a stack of spares. A new wave of hatred for her gripped my heart – she had cravenly given in to her mother and batted me away but here I was worrying about her linen. I was nothing to her, just another servant to be ill-treated and discarded.

Eliza bustled up to break the news and within seconds I heard Julie coming into the kitchen. She had not yet done her hair and she looked frayed.

'Who did this?' she said to me.

'It was an error by the laundry.'

'All our things were marked, were they?'

'Yes, Mademoiselle Julie. They always are.'

'How could it happen?'

I thought she might begin to rant like her mother.

'Laundries make these mistakes all the time.'

It had been the same when I worked at Madame Wilhelm's laundry in Paris. We did the packages early in the morning, after ironing the pieces. It was easy to misread a label in poor light when we were so tired we could barely stand. Madame Wilhelm dealt with the complaints, always admitting fault and promising to track down the missing items – which usually she did. The customers, most of them, tended to be understanding because they needed Madame Wilhelm – there was no other laundry like hers nearby.

That was where I met Henriette. Cleaning restaurants did not bring me enough money to eat so Madame Zimmermann suggested I ask Madame Wilhelm for work. She was another woman who had grown up in our village and moved to Paris.

Her premises were in the corner of a courtyard tucked away in the Rue du Faubourg Saint Honoré, an area where rich people lived, but like all rich areas, the poor eked a living in its hidey-holes. Madame Wilhelm was known for her skill with the fine muslins, lace collars and dainty underclothes that only the wealthy wear. That was all we did: the delicates. No sheets, no blankets, no labourers' smocks or maids' frocks, and it was still heavy work.

It was Henriette who showed me how to fill and empty the tubs and cut the soap, how to fold and stack the clean items, layer them in tissue and wrap them in brown paper. I learned useful things such as how to remove stains of all kinds: blood, vomit, ink, semen.

Much of it was fiddly work and involved tacking expensive lace pieces onto glass bottles so that they kept their shape and soaking them in suds, and dipping muslins in starch and pressing them out between sheets of linen. I won't say I was especially skilled at it – my fingers are too thick and square – but I was good enough.

At night, when we lay on our makeshift beds on the shelves in the storeroom, we used to laugh at the ridiculous frilliness of some of the items and make up stories about their owners and how the clothes got to be in the state they were in. The cuffs dipped in gravy. The rips in the nightgowns. Her tales were often quite filthy, but Henriette, in those days, liked to talk and talk. She yammered on about herself, and her childhood in an orphanage, and the height, handsomeness and occupations of the two widowers who were her patrons. I had to beg her to stop chatting so that we could sleep.

After a year, without warning, Madame Wilhelm said she had no choice but to let us go as she was not getting enough orders to keep the business going. People were tightening their belts. Her rich customers were disappearing. There was talk of war with the Prussians.

That was three years before I stood in the kitchen at No. 13 with Eliza and Julie, three years in which I had been flotsam, tossed here and there, swept along by the actions of others, the actions of men, mostly, and ended up here, awaiting my ejection from the house, but nevertheless trying desperately to impress Julie with my helpfulness.

I said, 'I'll go now to Deprez and ask them to look, but your clothes might have been given to someone else and it could take a few days to get them back.'

Despite his fulsome apologies the manager at Deprez could not find Julie's things.

'Can't be helped,' said Julie when I got back. 'I'll manage one way or another. Perhaps I'll buy new in Paris.' She smiled at me. Although we were wary around each other, she seemed to want a ceasefire. There was a stillness about her I had not seen before, as if she were taking deep breaths to get through the day.

My own mind was a racecourse and my heart alternated between a gallop and a stroll. I jumped at noises. I was prone to sudden exhaustion, when I would sit and not move, unable to stop staring into corners. If I let my thoughts run, every avenue led to disaster. Unless I found a new place, I would indeed be walking the streets and I'd never see Mama or my sister, Marie, or Victoire again. Before sleep, I envisaged myself in a winding-sheet, lowered into a pauper's grave, and Henriette writing to everyone to tell them how I met my end. During the day I walked around in a cauldron of anger.

The next morning, Eliza and I brought down the carpet bags and hat boxes and I watched from the dining-room window as the cabman helped Julie and Mademoiselle Guy up the step and into the cab, the morning light catching the bright orange and purple silk of their gowns below their cloaks.

Eliza and I were now on our own with Madame Riel.

That Sunday she and I had our lunch of bread and cheese, and Eliza fetched the beer from the pub on the corner. I gave her mine. In the afternoon I made a beef broth for Madame and Eliza served it to her, and at half past four I walked to Soho to call for Henriette. She told me Madame Cholet had made her an Easter gift of an extra day's wages and she had been invited to sit down to a dinner of spring lamb with her madame's brother and his family. I could not help but be envious.

Henriette was exuberant, restored almost to the person she was when we worked at the laundry, before the disaster of Père Lachaise, Chantiers and Lieutenant Marçeron.

'I can't tell you how different I feel, Marguerite, to just a few weeks ago, when I had my small problem. While that was going on... Do you remember those men who jumped off the Buttes Chaumont at the end of the Commune? I kept seeing them in front of me. I felt like doing the same.'

She caught the look on my face. She knew what I was thinking – that it wasn't just the suicides on her mind but also what she had done on the day we left Paris. She saw something else in my face too.

'Marguerite, what is it?'

I told her.

'They've sacked you but you have to work the rest of the month before they'll pay you? And all your precious Mademoiselle Julie is giving you for putting up with Madame Riel and her nonsense is an old dress? Honestly, if I had been you I would have demanded my money there and then and walked out.'

'But, Henriette, I've got nowhere to go.'

'I see that, no, you're right and it is a roof over your head, at least for now, but what *will* you do? You should at least speak to Abbé Toursel.'

'Again? I think he's probably a bit sick of me. After what I did last time.'

I was right. After the service, the Abbé expressed surprise that I was yet again looking for a recommendation and he muttered that he would ask around before turning pointedly to talk to someone else.

CHAPTER SEVENTEEN

For the first time since I had been at No. 13 I overslept – nights of patchy sleep had caught up with me. I woke to the smell of burning.

I threw the blue dress over me, shouting for Eliza as I took the stairs two at a time. Madame's bedroom door was wide open and her bed was empty. Thin grey smoke was winding its way through the house. I followed it through the kitchen and the scullery to the back yard.

'Madame Riel, what are you doing?'

Wearing a white wrapper and with her straggly hair around her shoulders, she prodded at a bonfire with a poker she must have taken from the range. Sheets of newspaper glowed in the grey morning light like red-hot mille-feuilles and as she beat them, they released fragments that floated in the air like black butterflies.

In my mind I had a picture of old Madame Zimmermann and how at the end of the Commune, with the government troops flooding in through the city gates and tearing down the barricades and shooting people in the street, we had climbed to the roof of her place in the Rue Saint-Maur and watched the skyline of Paris glow all colours of red, pink and orange.

'It must all be burned. They're full of lies,' said Madame Riel. There was a black streak across her forehead. As she bent and jabbed at the fire, the hem of her wrapper passed close to the embers.

'Please don't stand so near the fire, Madame.'

'Full of lies. They lie about me.' She turned towards me and said quietly, 'They send whores over to spy on me. People from Paris. You're one of them. You want to steal my designs. Don't think I don't know. You listen at the door. You work for them.'

'No, Madame, I do not.'

'You're lying.'

She held up the poker.

'No, Madame.'

'You're nothing but a common prostitute. You'll do anything for money.'

All my fight drained out of me. 'If you say so.'

'You admit it! You are nothing but a fat peasant, a whore from the streets.'

'Anything you say, Madame. Now go inside and sit down. I'll make you a cup of coffee.'

'No.'

So I had no choice but to stand in the yard, ready to pounce if she caught alight.

'Madame Riel!'

Eliza was in the doorway. Madame lay the poker on the ground and followed her inside, calling out to me as she went, 'Don't think I don't know about you, Marguerite the whore from Belgium. I know everything about you!'

How could she know? I was a nobody. The tribunals were over, all the criminals of the Commune were imprisoned or executed or sent into exile, and Lieutenant Marçeron, well, I didn't know what became of him... I was too far away from it – and he probably never saw Henriette as she came running up behind him in the Rue de la Bienfaisance.

———

I spent an hour boiling water and helping Eliza carry it up to Madame's dressing room for her bath, so that by the early afternoon she was dressed and primped and in her parlour ready to receive Madame Antoine. When I came into the room to collect the tray, Madame Antoine, sitting in the green slipper chair, picked up one of the magazines from the stack to avoid catching my eye.

Madame Riel showed no sign of the madness I had seen that morning. Then she said, 'This will only take a second, Virginie, so please excuse me,' and with her chin tilted up at me, said, almost under her breath, 'Don't think I don't know. I know everything that you do. I know what you're like.'

I did not reply.

'She's going soon,' I heard behind my back. 'I'm only keeping her out of kindness and because Julie says I must, but I'm watching her closely. Worst one yet. A liar and a spy, and I have it on good authority that she's a whore like you'd never believe.'

Did I care what she thought of me?

No.

Did I think she knew about Chantiers and Marçeron?

I couldn't shake the possibility.

Whore. That is what cut me. That is what stripped away the blanket of calm I had pulled over myself. *Whore*. Did she know about Lieutenant Marçeron? Could she see the feelings Mademoiselle Julie provoked in me?

I spent the rest of the day deliberately not doing much. It was Easter Monday, after all. In the afternoon I left the house and crossed over to Hyde Park, to the corner where the horses exercised in the morning. The air was tinged with the odours of manure and cut grass. I had not expected so many people. Behind the barriers, the spectators – drunks flat out under the trees, the numerous poor and their children on the benches drinking cheap concoctions bought from the stalls, couples promenading arm in arm – had all come to see the parade of the rich and notorious. Open carriages topped with awnings in yellow, cerise and purple sailed by. Mounted men in top hats and women riding side-saddle, a blaze of black, scarlet and royal blue riding habits. The aristocrats and the upstarts, the fine ladies and the courtesans – it was impossible to tell which was which. Amongst the crowd, ignored, tiny, I was walking in a daze.

At eight o'clock, Madame appeared in the kitchen and told me to run up to Soho for six religieuses. She liked to pretend she ate like a bird but she had a sweet tooth.

'No,' I said. 'I will not. I don't like to be out in the dark.'

'You must.'

'I won't. The streets at night are dangerous. Men say things to me.'

'Not without reason, I'm sure.'

I did not go.

On Tuesday, when I got back from fetching the baguette, I came up the attic stairs to change into the blue dress to do some of the heavy work and saw that my bedroom door was open. Madame Riel was sitting on my bed. My box was beside her, the lid smashed open, and all my things were strewn across the floorboards. She was reading my book of testimonials.

At first she didn't notice me in the doorway.

'Is this your family?' she said on seeing me, picking up the photograph of Madame Soulier and Iris. 'Is she an idiot, the child?'

Hold your wrist behind your back. It's just hot air.

'And what is this, Marguerite?'

She held up the stolen coffee spoon.

She hauled herself up to standing and came towards the door. I blocked her way. She moved to the left, I moved to the left, and then I stepped aside to let her pass. Neither of us spoke but I heard her wheezy breathing.

If the fire was a warning shot, the invasion of my room was a declaration of war. Like the Communards, I raised my defences knowing I was doomed. I spent most of the night alert, falling asleep as the church bells struck five. My dreams were chaotic. I was lost in London and couldn't find my way back to my village. All the trains I took went in the wrong direction and just as I got off the right one, a woman stole my bag. I looked down to see that my bottom half was entirely naked. I woke with a start at six, infused with a shuddering sense of shame.

———

We lived through Wednesday and Thursday without much incident. As I came up the lane on Friday, after my usual errand to Soho, I saw a horse and cart in the road outside No. 13. There was turpentine in the air. Three men in the blue clothes of French workers were attaching planks across the railings in front of the house. One was at a workbench on the pavement sawing the lengths while another was screwing them in place, and another painting them in a thick black gloss.

'Your Madame doesn't like passers-by looking in through the kitchen windows, apparently. She said it was urgent,' said the foreman.

At that moment, Madame Riel appeared on the front porch with Ulysses.

'Have you not finished?'

'No, Madame,' said the foreman.

'How long will you be?'

'The rest of the day, I expect. We will need to use the tap in your scullery later, if we may.'

'You may not. You must finish earlier than that. I have a guest coming.'

'But, Madame, it takes as long as it takes. We cannot go faster.'

'What are *you* standing there for? Get inside, stupid girl.'

The basement steps were blocked by the workmen.

'I'll have to use the front door,' I said. 'I'll get paint on my clothes if I go that way.'

'You'll do no such thing,' said Madame Riel. She marched off towards Green Park.

'Ignore what she says,' I told the foreman. 'Use the scullery. I'll let you in. She's a lunatic.'

By the evening, Madame had changed her plans and went off to take supper with Madame Antoine. At ten I heard Eliza, who had been watching the street from the dining-room windows, go out to help her up the stairs. Even before she reached the hall, Madame started shouting for me.

'Marguerite! Come here! I have something for you.'

I came up from the kitchen.

'A present! To show we are not enemies. Virginie says I must be nice to you.' She breathed out a blast of red wine. 'Where is it, Eliza? Ah, on the table behind you. There it is.'

She was speaking in French to Eliza, who just smiled in return.

Madame Riel turned around and snatched up the parcel,

which I could tell, from the shape and the smell, was a leg of mutton.

'Put it in the pantry, will you, Marguerite. My *friend*, Marguerite.'

'I will need the key, Madame.'

'It's in my pocket.' She made a show of shoving her cloak to one side and diving in to get it. She handed over her key ring.

'I've forgiven her,' she said to Eliza. 'Madame Antoine says we've got to get on the right side of her, or she might murder us in our beds. Isn't that right, Marguerite? You might murder us.'

That night I lay in my bed scarcely aware whether I was talking in my head or muttering out loud.

Murder. You know nothing of the price of life, Madame. You never saw the gaping wounds of the dead. The mutilated bodies of children. You did not gasp and tremble as shells fell, or watch while Paris burnt. You left the rest of us to starve and sat in your little parlour at No. 13 Park Lane, a house paid for by a rich old man who uses your daughter to satisfy his revolting desires.

I got up from my bed and walked around my attic room in tiny circles, as quietly as I could so as not to disturb Eliza next door. I lay down but it was of no use – the bells struck half past three before I finally descended into sleep.

All the next morning, Eliza scurried up and down the stairs with a relay of hot compresses and tisanes for Madame. At four in the afternoon I was summoned to Madame's bedroom door.

'You will roast the mutton for a supper with Madame Antoine, who'll be here at six,' she croaked from her bed. I was to go to Soho to get the vegetables and a bottle of burgundy for drinking and a cheaper bottle for the pot. She sounded fussy and weary. I took no pleasure in her suffering. That is the truth, but it is also the truth that my outrage had merely subsided – it did not disappear.

The leg of mutton, Madame's 'gift', was not large but, after

Madame Riel and Madame Antoine had picked at it, there would be plenty for Eliza and me to make a good dinner for once. And I would be able to make a soup from the bone to have on Sunday and Monday.

That evening, after I had served the supper and Madame Antoine had gone home, Eliza came into the kitchen. 'Marguerite,' she said, and pointed to the ceiling.

I climbed the stairs to the drawing room. Slowly. I was not a fairground monkey dancing to her tune.

'Madame Crosnier will be coming in the afternoon tomorrow and will take supper with me. You will make a broth from the mutton bones.'

'There will be plenty for Eliza and me too.'

'No. It is Sunday – you will have bread and cheese.'

'Why, Madame?'

'Why what?'

'Why should Eliza and I not have the broth?'

'Because it is for me and Madame Crosnier.'

'There will be enough for all, and we cannot work if we don't have enough to eat.'

'You are so boring. You hardly do anything anyway. And you're too fat, as I've said on numerous occasions. I am practically bankrupt because of you.'

Don't, Marguerite. Don't.

I had to get out of the house, so I put on my waterproof and left by the basement stairs. A fine drizzle was falling and the wet pavements reflected the light of the streetlamps. I walked down Piccadilly and on up to Leicester Square.

The doors to the French Church were open. There was no sign of Abbé Toursel. I thought about calling at his residence but decided against it. He was not the most sympathetic and he'd never made a favourite of me. All he would have said was

Be patient, rise to the challenge God has set you. I knelt in a pew near the front, the part where the well-off people usually sat.

I muttered my prayers.

I believe in God, the Father Almighty, creator of heaven and earth, and in Jesus Christ, His only son our lord.

It was about nine by the time I got back to No. 13 and tapped on the kitchen window for Eliza to let me in. I ignored the dirty dishes in the scullery, sat at the table for a few minutes and then went up to my room.

As I passed Madame's bedroom, she opened the door. She was in her nightgown.

'Walking the streets, Marguerite?'

I should have pushed past her.

'Can't wait to be rid of you,' she said. 'Guttersnipe.'

So we were back on that treadmill.

'You would know all about the gutter, Madame.'

'You're hideous. Look. Fatter than ever and all at my expense. With arms like that you should have been a butcher.'

'A butcher's trade might not be as lucrative as your own, Madame Riel, that is true, but it is a little more honest.'

CHAPTER EIGHTEEN

Sunday. I was up at half past six and in the kitchen by seven.

Only one more day and Julie would be back. She would have my dress. I would look for another place. Soon I would be gone from No.13.

All I needed was to get through the next few days.

The morning was cold and damp, promising nothing of spring. I swept the kitchen floor, cleaned, oiled and lit the range, and washed last night's dishes.

Eliza was in and out of the kitchen all morning. I wasn't paying much attention to her.

Guttersnipe.

Butcher.

Whore.

Last night's insults jolted around in my mind.

Murderer.

She said I would murder her in her bed.

I re-ironed the table linen and polished the good china and the silverware. I swept the yard and wiped down the shelves in the scullery.

At half past ten, I laid out the breakfast tray – the usual: toast and a tisane of verbena. Eliza took it up.

Sometime later, when I was in the scullery, I heard the heels of Madame's boots tip-tapping on the stone stairs. I dried my hands, put on my best face, and came out into the kitchen. I assumed she had come to tell me to follow her up to the pantry so that I could get the ingredients for the broth. We would pretend we were not enemies, neither of us would reignite last night's conflagration, the bonfire in the yard would not be spoken of, nor the smashing of my box, and we would live an uneasy truce until Julie came back in the morning.

Madame Riel was in her cloak and bonnet, ready to take Ulysses out to the park.

'You haven't made the broth?' she said.

Coal black bombazine, shiny black satin ruffles catching the pallid light. A raven, a crow.

I was at the range now, feeding the fire.

Twitch, twitch. Peck, peck. I couldn't get the picture out of my mind.

'No, Madame. I could not.'

'You haven't even started it.'

She crossed the kitchen to stand behind me.

'Why in God's name not? Stupid whore...'

Beak up. Squawk, squawk.

'I told you to make a broth. From the mutton. Madame Crosnier is coming this afternoon.'

Why was she making such a fuss? Unless it was an excuse to needle me? It was Sunday. In any other house, it would have been my day of rest.

'I am fully aware that Madame Crosnier is coming, Madame, but you have not yet opened the pantry for me, so how can I make the broth? The... mutton... is... in... the... pantry.' I spoke slowly as if to a small child. She had started by being antagonistic. I would give it back to her. 'So, I have nothing to cook.'

I turned my palms up, empty, for emphasis.

'Anyway, it's only eleven or so, Madame, and you have asked for supper at five. Six hours is plenty of time, I think you'll agree, Madame, to make a soup.'

'You could have asked me to open the pantry.'

'That is not my place. You insist I am called to the pantry when you decide I should be called to the pantry.'

'You're a stupid girl.'

I let her words hang in the air.

'I missed that, Madame. What did you say?'

I looked her in the face.

'I've had enough of you. We've already sacked you, so you can leave today. Right now. This minute. Nobody has a good word to say about you. Go and pack. Out of the house. I'll do the soup myself.'

She took a step towards me.

'As you wish. Pay me and I'll go, Madame. Don't forget the ten shillings you owe me. Otherwise, I'm staying. As agreed with Mademoiselle Julie.'

Silence.

'Have it your own way, imbecile, but by God I'll make you suffer. And once you're out, where will you go? You'll have nothing. No testimonial from me – nothing. No one will want you.'

'Perhaps I'll ask Julie's gentleman for help,' I said.

'Julie will be especially pleased to see the back of you, believe me.' There was a pause before she said, 'I should have turned you out of my house weeks ago.'

'*Your* house, is it? *Your* house? That's an interesting way to phrase it, Madame. I know this is not *your* house and I know what you do for it, or should I say what *she* does for it. Speaking of streets, you've been on the streets for years or, to put it another way, running a brothel.'

'Filthy whore.'

'Say that again, Madame. Louder, like the lady you are.'

'Easy. You're a whore. And what's more you're a stupid ugly whore... Don't think I don't know all about you.'

How can she know? What does she know?

Her face was right in front of me. Her satiny ruffly feathery clothes made her seem larger than she was. That corner of the kitchen was my domain. She was the enemy, assaulting my defences.

'Julie's going to be so pleased when you're gone. She says you give her the shivers.'

She launched herself, pushing me aside, and lunged for an iron skillet. I suppose it is possible she wanted to start cooking, but my instincts told me she intended to use it as a weapon.

That's when I grabbed her, for just a few seconds, or maybe it was more, but those seconds, however many there were, turned over slowly like the pages of a book. My fingers were on the skin of her throat, wrapping around her tiny neck, my nails digging in under her ears. I felt the bones of my fingers against the bones of her jaw. Her eyes grew large.

I don't know whether wringing the necks of chickens in the yard of our cottage came to my mind, or whether that was a thought that occurred to me later and could never scrub away. Perhaps in that word *whore* I saw Lieutenant Marçeron, or the sound of Julie pleading with Madame not to make her entertain Milord, or the can-can dancers at Highbury and the way they made me feel.

Did she struggle? I don't recall. Did she try to fight me off? I don't know. Or, I didn't notice at the time. What made me stop squeezing and watch her collapse slowly to the floor like a deflated balloon? It was not because I was any less angry.

Her skirts had twisted under her and as she tried to stand she trod on them, causing her to stagger like a clown pretending to be drunk. When she was almost up she came for me and I punched her. Her head went back. Did I hear a snap? No, I can't say I did, which is not to say there was not one. She fell again and gasped once, or maybe twice. That was it.

CHAPTER NINETEEN

She lay there, her back curved, her head against one arm. Not moving. A broken bird on the floor. Her tiny black boots were claws.

She will throw me out now for sure. Maybe I'll have to go with the other desperate people and tread on a mill at an English workhouse until I die. Maybe I'll end up a beggar woman outside the French Church.

She's not dead. She cannot be.

Eliza.

Eliza was two floors up in Madame's bedroom. Madame was in her outdoor clothes – she was about to take Ulysses out.

Eliza is doing out the rooms and when she finishes she will come down to the kitchen and she will see Madame on the floor.

I did not hold my wrist behind my back.

I forgot that words were but hot air.

I knelt down.

'Madame Riel,' I whispered. 'Madame Riel. Get up.'

Give me a sign. God, help me.

I lifted her hand. My thick fingers were on hers, gentle, as servants should never touch their mistresses without permission.

Squeeze my finger, Madame.

Her eyes were open. I looked away.

I felt her neck, looking for a pulse.

She had gone.

God forgive me. God forgive me.

I had seen the dead in Paris after the Commune, stacked up in the streets, grey-skinned, the women in blood-spattered calicos, the men in thick navy-blue serge, heads back, mouths dark caverns. And at Chantiers – the old women who had drowned in grief, or whose strokes and heart failures pulled them out of life. I knew the dead. They were not like this.

You can't die, just like that, by falling to the floor.

Death was never that easy. The Communards had to be shot or hanged or beaten or stabbed. Only babies died for no reason, and even then there is always a cause.

Madame could not be alive one minute and dead the next. All I had done was hold her by the neck. For a second or maybe two. I didn't even hit her that hard. Yet she was unmoving, unbreathing, unfluttering, a dead bird on the floor.

I tapped her cheek.

Nothing.

It must be because she was ill – not just in her mind but also in her body. The thin skin, the rings under her eyes. Her scrawny frame. The coughing. The wheezing. I knew she was sick the instant I saw her that day I came to No. 13. She starved herself and then gorged on pâtisserie. She had weakened her bones. And she had driven herself insane with evil thoughts. She had done this to herself.

I pushed on her neck but no more than that. I hit her – but not hard.

Eliza.

Eliza will come down here.

I had to hide Madame.

The coal cellar. Put her in the coal cellar. Tell Eliza Madame has gone out.

I grabbed the coal scuttle, took the kitchen door keys, went outside into the front basement area, put the scuttle down and unlocked the cellar door. I went back to the kitchen. The Crow had not stirred.

She is not really dead. She cannot be.

God forgive me. Blessed Virgin, please help me.

I pulled up her cloak, hooked my hands under her armpits and dragged. The backs of her boots caught on the threshold so I laid her down and lifted her feet over. I moved her bonnet to cover her face. I locked the door behind me.

Thank you, God, for sending the workmen to board up the railings. No one can see me from the street.

Was it me or some other Marguerite who shoved Madame Riel into the coal cellar while the real me stood by like the foreman at a construction site? Perhaps that woman was Madame Soulier's efficient Marguerite.

Mind the door frame – Don't worry, Marguerite, you can do it – This way a little – No, that way – Small step coming up – Dip your head as you go in – That's right, over you go – She's in, she's in the coal cellar – Close the door as soon as you can. Good work, Marguerite!

I yearned for my father but he was dead in his grave at St Hubert's. I had no one.

I whispered, 'You must recover yourself in there, Madame, and think about how you have frightened me.'

Perhaps I am as crazy as she is.

Just as I was locking the cellar door, with my back to the kitchen, I heard 'Marguerite!' from inside the kitchen. Eliza looked at me through the window.

Oui! Je suis ici, Eliza!

I made my eyes look bright and friendly, turned around and smiled.

We acted out a conversation through the window, Eliza in the kitchen, me outside, and Madame, silent, folded up inside the coal cellar.

The scene was like the opening of one of Mademoiselle Julie's farces:

Eliza: Madame. Where is Madame? (Empty hands)

Me: Aucune idée! *No idea!* (Wide eyes and high shoulders)

Eliza: But Ulysses! (Pointing upstairs, walking fingers through the air) The dog needs to go out.

Eliza had Madame's coal scuttle in her hand and lifted it up to show me that it was empty.

Me: (Shaking my head and showing her the inside of the kitchen scuttle) *Rien* (disappointed face) – *no coal left!*

Madame was so angry when Eliza let the fire in her bedroom go out I thought she would have convulsions. Eliza would not want to risk that again. If I refused to open the cellar, Eliza would demand to do it herself, even if it was just to glean coal dust.

I will be discovered. I will be hanged.

Madame Soulier's efficient Marguerite was still with me.

You look competent, Marguerite. I'd give you a job.

I went to the kitchen door and rattled the handle to show Eliza I was locked out in the basement area. Of course, I had locked myself out to keep *her* out and now I had to pretend that Madame Riel had locked me out while I was fetching coal and had inadvertently taken the key with her when she went.

Open the kitchen window, Eliza, I mimed, *I'll have to climb in.*

I was not allowed to come into the house through the front door.

She looked confused but she undid the window latch, pulled up the sash, positioned a chair under it and helped me in.

Then she went upstairs and took Ulysses out through the front door to the pavement to do his business, while I sat at the kitchen table and shook. When I stood up and paced the floor the shaking stopped.

While Eliza gave Ulysses a bowl of water, I pretended to repolish the cutlery, pinching the metal between the cloth extra hard to stop my trembling. There was a constant pounding in my kidneys, as if my heart had split and lived in two different places in my body.

She is wondering where Madame is and why she has not taken Ulysses with her. She must know. How can she not suspect? Is she more slow-witted than I thought? And what if she insists on going into the coal cellar? I have an idea – I must move Madame.

At ten to one I set out our lunch on the kitchen table – English bread and English cheese. I said, '*Bière*,' took the jug off the dresser shelf and held it out to Eliza. She pointed to the clock on the wall and held up her fingers. Ten minutes before the public house opened.

'*Bière*,' I said again.

'No, Marguerite. *Non*.' She pointed to the clock again.

At one minute to one, I carried the jug to her and placed it in her hands. After I heard the front door click shut, I unlocked the door to the basement area, opened the coal cellar, put my hands under Madame's armpits and hauled her back inside the kitchen. I had to move her to the pantry.

I got Madame up the first run of the kitchen stairs by hefting her onto my back. At the half-landing we collapsed onto the floor. I grabbed her dress by the front and pulled. She grew heavier with every second. I left her, went through the scullery into the back yard, unhooked the rope Eliza and I hung the rugs on while we beat them and passed it around her chest, under her arms and around her neck, made a knot, and with my left hand in her armpit and the right pulling the rope, sat and heaved and sat and heaved until we reached the ground floor. I stretched her out on the runner in the hall.

Her keys.

Kneeling, I rolled her until she was face down and wormed my fingers into her pocket until I fished them out.

Jingle jangle.

The front doorbell.

I didn't move. It was Eliza with the beer.

I gripped Madame's keys to silence them.

The doorbell again.

'Marguerite!'

I stood up carefully and slowly placed the pantry key in the lock, turning it little by little until it clicked, and pushed the door gently with my foot. I dragged Madame in and laid her face down.

I waited.

'Marguerite!'

The bell again.

'Marguerite!'

She thumped on the door.

'Marguerite! Open the door. I've got the beer!'

In my hands, the keys.

On the wall, the safe.

I unlocked it and saw the red leather coin purse and a pile of English banknotes. I stuffed them all into my pocket.

Time slowed.

'Marguerite!'

I looped the rope around her neck and over the top of the safe. Her feet stuck out of the doorway into the hall. Standing with one foot either side, I bent down and shuffled her up by the pelvis. Her knees came back. I smoothed down her skirts. The soles of her boots faced the ceiling, her right cheek and her palms were flat to the floor like a sleeping child.

'Marguerite!'

More banging.

I breathed deeply once, smiled, and opened the front door.

Eliza: *Angry words. Eyes to the ceiling.*

We ate our lunch and afterwards I put the plates in the scullery sink. On the way up to my room, I stopped off in the dining room and took a bottle of wine from the dresser.

The two Marguerites spoke in whispers.

Eliza will find out.

She hasn't done so far.

Eliza will guess.

No, she has no idea.

She'll go to the police.

I should leave now.

There's no one to help me.

Father Toursel will help me.

He'll tell me to confess. He'll take me to the police. The English will hang me.

Not if I get to France. I'll hide in Montmartre or Belleville.

I have no money.

I have the banknotes.

Mademoiselle Julie will hate me.

I'll never see her again.

I lay down on the bed. Every time a picture of Madame Riel in the kitchen came into my head, I sat up abruptly and drank wine from the bottle.

At four o'clock, the doorbell jangled.

It was round, funny, clever Madame Crosnier. When she visited, Madame Riel was always a touch nicer. I heard Eliza showing her into the drawing room and going down the stairs to make her a tray of tea.

Madame Crosnier speaks English. She will talk to Eliza. She will ask her about Madame. Eliza will tell her she has gone out and left Ulysses behind. Madame Crosnier will be suspicious. She will find Madame in the pantry. No, she can't open the pantry. I have the keys. I will go downstairs and do the things I would normally do. I will act as if nothing has happened.

I took the banknotes, tied them in a roll with a piece of ribbon from my box and put them back in my pocket.

I had to make the broth, for Madame Riel and Madame Crosnier's supper, as if nothing had happened.

There was scarcely anything to go in it as the mutton bone was still in the pantry with Madame, so I made a roux of what I had in the scullery: two chopped onions, a carrot, a potato and some celery, and cooked them with a bay leaf and a bouquet garni. The house was filled with its aroma.

My hands stopped shaking. I was calm.

Eliza appeared in the kitchen, frowning.

'Marguerite – Madame Crosnier,' she said, pointing to the ceiling. She wanted to see me.

Madame Crosnier was in Madame's bedroom looking through an album of programmes for Julie's plays.

'Where did Madame Riel say she was going, Marguerite? I'm a little concerned.'

'To meet a friend.'

'Did she say which one?'

'No, Madame, but she did say she might be a while.'

'So she didn't say where she was going or who she was meeting?'

'No, Madame. Shall I take it?' I reached for the tea tray and saw red scratches on the back of my hand.

Did Madame Riel do that? She couldn't have. I don't remember her fighting.

I put my hand behind my back and pulled down my sleeve.

'It's nearly five now.'

'Yes, Madame. The soup is ready.'

'It's all most peculiar. Why would she leave Ulysses behind? I'll forgo the soup today, if you don't mind, I'm sure it won't be wasted, and take myself off home. Please tell Madame Riel that I was here and that I waited for her. I'll see myself out.'

After she left, I went up to my room. I heard Eliza in hers. I slid my box out from under my bed. The broken clasp – Madame did that. She was a criminal. I found the sous I brought with me from Paris.

I changed into the green dress, put the roll of banknotes in the pocket, tied my woollen shawl around me crossways, and slipped the *carte* of Madame Soulier and Iris and my book of testimonials in by my breast.

In the scullery I hid Madame's keys and the kitchen door key behind an earthenware jug on the shelf.

I put on my bonnet and waterproof. When I emerged into the kitchen Eliza was sitting at the table looking straight at me.

She had a pair of black kid gloves in her hands.

Madame Riel must have taken them off in the hall before...

Before.

I shrugged.

'*Église*,' I said to Eliza, pointing in the direction of Leicester Square and crossing myself. I gestured at the clock and held up both hands, fingers apart, and smiled.

Back at ten!

On my way out through the front door, I took Madame's umbrella from the hall.

CHAPTER TWENTY

I could have turned left and walked down Piccadilly towards the French Church and confessed to Abbé Toursel.

I did not.

Should I have gone to America? Probably, but I didn't have the slightest idea how to get there.

Victoria Station was somewhere on the other side of the Queen's palace, but I could not remember the route, so I darted across Piccadilly and stepped onto the footplate of the first cab in line.

'Victoria,' I mumbled from under my hood, opened the door and got in.

The cab driver did not hear me and shouted something through the trap.

'Victoria.' A little louder.

The driver asked me a question. When I didn't answer, he set off anyway.

I turned away from the window and kept my head down. Within five minutes we were in the station yard. The driver came down and I held out in my palm some English coins from the red leather purse, and he picked out his fare. I gave him one of the small silver coins as a tip.

'Paris?' I said.

We had come to the wrong side of the station. Perhaps that was the question he tried to ask me. He pointed to the other train shed and I walked there quickly, almost running. At the interpreter's kiosk, keeping my head down, I asked, 'When is the Paris train?'

'Tomorrow.'

That cannot be so. The police will find me and I will be hanged.

'No other train tonight?'

The clerk paused.

'There is,' he said slowly. 'In about a quarter of an hour, but it's the first-class express. Expensive. Three pounds.'

He could tell I was a servant.

'I must be on that one but... I don't know how to ask for the ticket.'

'You have the money?'

'Yes, sir.'

He looked doubtful. 'Come with me.'

He spoke for me at the booking office. I gave him one of Madame Riel's notes and he handed me four gold coins in change, and then I followed him to the platform.

'No luggage?'

'No.'

'An emergency?'

'Yes.'

Above the echoing clatter, he shouted something over to the train guard and watched me as I boarded. I was the last one on.

At Dover, I climbed up to the deck of the steamer and sat on a bench near the stack, with Madame Riel's umbrella over my head. I stayed there all night, ignored by the crew, battered by the wind, and sprayed by salt water as the ship plunged and rose.

My feet and hands were numb by the time we docked at Calais and I was numb inside too. I felt no fear, no pain, not even relief to be out of England. Outside the customs house I queued with the other first-class passengers, hunched over, diminishing myself, until it occurred to me that doing so made me more likely to attract attention and stood up straight.

Inside the building we lined up to have our luggage inspected.

Then – a kick in the kidneys.

Not four metres away, on the other side, were Mademoiselle Julie and Mademoiselle Guy.

My scalp contracted and I began to sweat. My heart pounded. Under my clothes my armpits prickled. There was a crushing feeling in my head, as if my brain was dying.

I'm sorry, I'm sorry. I did not mean to do it. Your mother was a monster to me. I hardly touched her. I don't know how it happened. I know you will never forgive me.

At the same time I would be arriving in Paris, she would be getting out of a cab outside No. 13. She would ask Eliza for her mother and she would look all over the house, and eventually she would take her own key and open the pantry door.

In Julie's bag would be the dress she had promised me.

Julie knew what her mother was like. She knew there would be trouble. She should never have left me alone with her.

I could not stop myself looking over at her and her friend, as if some part of me wanted them to see me, wanted to be discovered and captured, and for it all to stop and for someone to say, 'There has been a mistake, Marguerite, and she was only knocked out and now she is sitting up in her bed recovering.'

It will kill my mother to see me hang. My sister will hate me for ever.

Out of the corner of my eye I saw Mademoiselle Guy talking and Julie laughing.

People are no different to animals, who know when they are being watched. I must stop looking at them. If she sees me, it will be the death of me.

I shuffled on in my line.

A small commotion. I could not help but peep.

Mademoiselle Guy lifted her arm and pointed over towards me.

The pounding in my kidneys started again. I thought I would fall to the floor.

Did I hear her say, *Over there – she looks exactly like your Marguerite*?

No.

The trouble came from an old beggarwoman being manhandled out of the shed.

It was my turn at the customs table.

'Luggage?' said the officer.

'I have none,' I muttered.

'You've come on the first class?'

'Yes, sir.'

'Why are you travelling?'

'Family emergency.'

He raised an eyebrow. 'Thank you, Mademoiselle. Next!'

I found an empty compartment on the train and took the seat next to the corridor, so that I could flee if I needed to. An English family, a couple and their two young children, tumbled in, not noticing me until they had arranged themselves on the benches. The parents exchanged looks as if to say, what is this ill-dressed wretch doing in our first-class carriage?

For the entire journey I closed my eyes. I was barely aware of the new day dawning. By ten o'clock we were at the Gare du Nord.

CHAPTER TWENTY-ONE

I had been homeless in Paris before. In 1870, just before the Prussian war, after Henriette and I were out of work when Madame Wilhem's laundry closed, I had no choice but to fling myself once more onto Victoire and Jacques' generosity. By then they had moved from that hovel in the Boulevard de la Gare to the Rue Saint-Denis, where Victoire was employed as the concierge for a shabby apartment building. The area was run down and the streets were strewn with rubbish from the markets of Les Halles, and the heavy reek of horse manure, human filth and decaying vegetables hung on the air. They were not pleased to see me, especially not Jacques, but they took me in anyway, and naturally at first everything was awkward between us. Here at least they had a bedroom, so they had some privacy. I slept in the kitchen on a daybed.

I tried to stay out of their way and to be helpful to them. Once I had finished sweeping the yard and the stairs and washing the ground-floor windows, I went out to look for work of my own. There was nothing. My accent put people on guard. Everywhere there was talk of the Emperor declaring war on Prussia, with people saying, *How dare they insult us*, and *Bismarck deserves hanging* and *We'll show them what we're made of*. And then, inevitably, war started, but far away, at the edge of France. But as the summer went on, the news grew worse and the war came nearer to Paris.

'The Prussians are at Metz,' announced Jacques one evening when he came in from work. That was only a day's march from Madame Soulier and Iris. 'They'll be in Paris before we know it.'

Even so, none of us predicted what would befall us.

At the beginning of September the French lost the battle of Sedan and the Emperor surrendered and was arrested. The Empress fled to England. France became a republic again, which made some people happy, but didn't make any difference to us. If anything, our lives got worse. When the Prussians arrived they ringed the city with camps and set up a headquarters in Versailles.

Before the Siege of Paris started in earnest, goods trains arrived carrying tons of provisions from all parts of the country. The covered markets were filled with sacks of corn in gigantic mounds, and in every corner there were piles of smoked meat, cheeses and dried vegetables. There was not a vacant patch of ground that did not have a cow or goat grazing on it.

The roads to the city gates were choked with incoming traffic. People terrified of becoming trapped with the Germans in the suburbs came in on horseback, in carriages, carts and furniture vans, or on foot pushing wheelbarrows. I watched from the pavement as chaotic processions passed by – chairs and tables, beds, hay, firewood, bird cages and children, all teetering on rickety carts.

As people filed in, people filed out. The main railway stations were crammed with those who were desperate to leave, pleading with ticket clerks and porters to find them a seat, their luggage making brown leather mountains in the station yards.

When the gates closed we were all prisoners, and the

fighting really got going. In the early days, the Parisians were adamant they would win – simply because they were French. It was impossible for the enemy to breach the walls, they said, because we had hundreds of cannon, paid for by ordinary citizens, aimed squarely at the Prussian encampments, and the French rifles were infinitely superior to anything those German bastards could come up with. The indomitable Parisian spirit would bring victory.

There was no longer a need for silver-platers so Jacques' job disappeared. All men had to fight or contribute in some way, so he joined the National Guard and was given a navy-blue serge uniform and a tiny stipend for himself and Victoire. To begin with, I worked at the public laundry in Batignolles but after a couple of weeks it was closed because the Seine, from which we were forced to draw after the use of fresh water was banned, was polluted with floating bodies. We all, or at least those of us who were not rich, grew filthier and hungrier by the day. The animals on their tiny patches of green were slaughtered as was every other beast that could be eaten, including the elephants and kangaroos in the zoo. But the steaks were sold to restaurants so only those with money ate them. The children of the poor wept as their mothers casseroled their pets.

'The poor always suffer first,' said Victoire. She did not mean us particularly but those who were even worse off, the destitute souls who scrabbled for an existence on the street. When I went out to the market or to forage in the parks for firewood, I saw their bodies, alive or dead I was not always sure, a skinny foot sticking out from under a pile of rags or a newborn left in a bundle on the steps of a church.

The price of food and fuel climbed, slowly at first, and then it soared. We were issued with ration cards. Our rents were put on hold. All we talked of was food, where we could get it, how bad it was, who had more of it than we did.

Every day of the Siege was colder than the last. The wind whipped through the apartment's rackety windows and frost clung to the glass. We were never warm.

Then baby Edith arrived. She belonged to a woman in one of the apartments in the building.

'I heard what happened to you,' she said to me at the door of the Conciergerie. She had mistaken me for Victoire, the bereaved mother. 'Will you take her? Perhaps she'll be a comfort to you. I can pay.' The child, about a year old, was curled against the woman, asleep. I saw only an ear and soft brown hair. The woman's husband had been killed in battle and she was working as a first-aider assigned to one of the stations near the ramparts. She was not obliged to volunteer but she had no patience with the child. She leant towards me and said quietly, 'It's better you have her. When she cries, I'm frightened I'll hurt her.'

'You'll have to speak to Monsieur Bouillon. It's not for me to decide,' I said, but I craved the care of this baby. I suppose I wanted to see a small bud blossom. She needed me, as much as Iris had.

The money was poor but Jacques said he thought Edith would be good for Victoire. I'm not sure it was. For the most part she ignored the child so it was me who carried her on my hip or wrapped her into my shawl and it was me who spooned soup into her. The mother never spent time with her, although every week she came to the door with money for Jacques.

When we had nothing to make soup with, I gave Edith a thin porridge with a few grains of sugar. Sometimes it was rice or bread soaked in water, but Siege bread was little more than chopped straw and mortar mixed with a bit of rye. To get milk for Edith, I had to endure the market men making disgusting offers to me. If I would just give them a bunk-up, *just the once, love, I won't be long at it*, they would give me a discount. I pretended I hadn't heard them and handed over the money. The milk turned out to be plaster dust drifting in water and Edith vomited it up.

Then Edith had a head cold that went to her chest. Within days she was coughing so much her little frame rattled like an old man's. At night she struggled for breath. When she emitted a high-pitched keening, I knew she didn't have long. On the tenth of December, as dawn broke, I put my hand to her forehead.

I went into the bedroom and gently prodded Victoire's shoulder.

'She's burning up,' I whispered. 'Come and help me.'

We cooled her with damp cloths, but her breathing was shallow and short, and at midday she died.

'My colleague will come,' said the mother when we told her. She looked defeated, as she always did. The next day a woman arrived to collect the body, which we had wound with strips torn from my petticoat.

I cannot say I was heartbroken at the time. Edith was better off in heaven than in the hell she had left.

We were the living dead. Jacques, lugubrious when he was in health, became a ghost. The circles under my eyes grew darker. My clothes hung off me. My monthly bleeds stopped. Victoire was the same but on Christmas Day, when Jacques was out at the ramparts, she told me she was pregnant.

'Nothing short of a miracle,' she said.

She was once more assailed by nausea and clung to her bed while the sea rose around her. If she ate, the waves calmed, but I had almost nothing to give her. I shredded bread and spread it around the plate to make it look more plentiful. She could not keep it down. I confess I was annoyed at the waste.

In the early days of the new year, the Prussians decided that a continuous barrage of missiles would break Paris. Thousands of shells fell on the Jardin des Plantes, thousands more on Le Jardin du Luxembourg. People were blown to bits in their kitchens, in cellars, in the streets. Little boys in a school. Patients in their hospital beds. At night, Paris was silent except for the sound of bombs reaching their target. We heard the flump of buildings far away collapsing to the ground. Houses shook, ceilings crashed. Saint-Cloud was on fire. No one went outside.

Jacques was stationed at Bastion 24 at Porte Chaumont, which was under almost constant attack, with cannon fire all around. I went there one evening to deliver him a pitiful canteen of food. The noise was like nothing else: a volcano, a cyclone, a hurricane, fireworks, all at once. Jacques told me that he had found one of his colleagues, a young lad, curled up, knees to his chin, frozen to death.

'Best off out of it in my opinion,' he said.

A month after Christmas Victoire said, 'Listen. It's stopped.'

I listened. 'Thank the dear Lord. Perhaps it's over.'

'It was all for nothing,' she said. 'Perhaps Edith would have lived if this had ended earlier. All this was for nothing. God must hate us.'

'No, Victoire. The Lord is not to blame. Men took Edith. The war took Edith. Not God. The Prussians, who have encircled Paris and starved us, they took Edith.'

I spoke clearly and put my face close to hers, as I used to with Iris, to make sure I had her attention.

'Put your clothes on,' I said. 'We must go out.'

She sat on the edge of the bed pulling on her boots, and then she stopped, hoiked up her skirt and put her hand inside her underwear. 'I can't, Marguerite. I'm bleeding. This baby is leaving me too.'

The bombardment wasn't over. It started again, and stopped again, until the French promised to give the Prussians everything they wanted – billions of francs, of course, but what they desired more than anything was the total humiliation of Paris, and that meant their soldiers must be allowed to march down the Champs Elysées. Before they arrived, young men wrapped the statues in black cloth so that the heroes of France should not witness the shame of the city. Shopkeepers shuttered their premises and stood weeping, their backs to the parade.

After that, our previous lives were gradually restored. The city gates reopened. Jacques stuffed his National Guard uniform in a cupboard and went back to work. Bakers baked. Builders built. Women did what they always did: cleaned, washed, scrubbed, smacked their children, cooked, queued, lay back for their husbands. Victoire managed to disembark from her bed and eat a little, and after a few weeks she was able to go back to her chores.

There were new hardships. Rents became due and people were suddenly hundreds, thousands of francs in debt. Half of the tenants in the upstairs rooms did a flit before Victoire could ask them to pay up. She and Jacques were all right – their rooms came with their job – but the rest of Paris... what were they meant to do? They had already burnt their furniture for firewood and pawned their valuables.

'Soon time for you to be on your way, Marguerite,' said Jacques. Now that the Siege was over, his small store of goodwill towards me had drained out. It was reasonable to ask me to go, I can see that now, but at the time, I was stung. Did they not like having me there? Was I not helpful? Although I had not been able to bring money in, I was always ready to do the housework when Victoire could not, and I had cared for Edith without expectation of reward, even though Jacques pocketed the fee. At the back of my mind was also the fact that I owed them money for my board and could not pay it back. Poor people never forget what it is like to be poor, and we never forget a favour.

I found work, quite by chance, only a few steps away. The woman who owned a shop selling gloves on the ground floor took me on as her servant and I slept in her back storeroom, so I was still able to see Victoire from time to time.

After the fighting stopped, Paris became a place of meetings: meetings to discuss the peace and meetings to discuss the new republic, meetings to discuss education, meetings to discuss the Church. Meetings for men only. Meetings for women only. Posters were pasted up everywhere. Demands. Rallies. Petitions. Ordinary people were tired of being told what to do and how to think by people who happened to be born into greater fortune than themselves, people who had, through their stupidity, led the country down the path to disaster. They were sick of having to decide between spending on food or fuel.

'Jacques says we Belgians must not draw attention to ourselves, and anyway women should keep their noses out of men's affairs,' said Victoire when I asked if she wanted to go to a women's meeting in Montmartre with me, just to find out what people were saying. We did not go.

In the middle of March my employer, the glove shop owner, came to me looking worried.

'Marguerite,' she said. 'There's news. Another revolution has started. I can't believe it. Again! I thought all that was over.'

She told me that the people in Montmartre were up in arms – they had confronted soldiers trying to take hundreds of cannon off the hill, cannon paid for by working people, that were meant to be used for the defence against the Prussians. She'd heard there had been a riot. Shots were fired. Pockets of the city were in uproar. A general was dead. The Germans were still surrounding the city walls and everyone thought they and the government were in league against the people of Paris. In the following days the streets were filled with commotion. I don't remember all that much about it – on her orders, I stayed indoors.

The gates of the city closed again. There were more flyers and more posters pasted up on walls and telegraph poles. Your Commune has been established, they told us. The cowardly aggressors had been repelled. There had been a vote and now we were to live differently. The time of incompetent aristocrats was over. All we needed to do was watch and wait for the rest of France to rise up and join us.

Paris was like an enchanted wood governed by fairies and devils: strange things occurred, over which we had no control. Our mail sailed out of the city into the sky in balloons. A huge stone column dedicated to Napoléon I lay in pieces on the ground. We found shallow barricades built of neatly piled stones across the streets. Priests were arrested and thrown in gaol. There were assassinations and executions.

Jacques pulled his National Guard uniform out of the closet and once more patrolled the bastions but this was not like the first siege. There was no huge influx of people from the countryside. And it was spring. Although food was short, we didn't starve. Everywhere there was an air of hot-headed festivity, but under that a feeling that we were once more on the edge of death, that we were all condemned prisoners who had been allowed out to roam the streets until the time of our execution.

My employer could no longer pay me – nobody was buying gloves – and to throw myself on Jacques' mercy yet again would not do anyone any good, so I put my things in my bag, asked Victoire to stash my book *The Splendour of Paris* for me and returned to the Widow Zimmermann in Belleville.

It was a shock to see her. The starvation she suffered in the first siege had destroyed her, and she could do little more than shuffle along. Together we earned a pittance cleaning cafés. I made her sit while I washed the floors and scrubbed the ranges.

We lived this way for a couple of weeks, picking up rumours about what was happening inside the city walls and outside them, believing some, ignoring others. It no longer seemed to matter what was true and what was not.

CHAPTER TWENTY-TWO

At the Gare du Nord, in the gloom of the morning, cloaked in my waterproof, I slithered off the train and into the city. The city had the hum of normality. Men and horses dragged carts of vegetables, bakeries wafted out the aroma of fresh bread and pastries, groups of small boys made their way to school. While I had been in London, some of the scars of the war and of the Commune had healed but there were still skeletal buildings held up by scaffolding and everywhere there were tidy piles of cobblestones and rubble.

I spent the day willing time to pass by crossing and re-crossing the Seine and sitting in the Jardin des Plantes, until I was so cold I thought I might die. Did I dare show up at Rue Saint-Denis? Would Jacques and Victoire take me in or turn me away? Would they see through my lies? Should I turn myself in to the police? Should I end it now and jump in the river? Would anyone care whether I died in Paris or at the end of a rope in London?

Should I have gone to Belgium and hidden in the forests near my village? For how long could I survive there? No, best to lurk in the city. My hope was that after a while the English police would lose interest in me. Perhaps then I could return home.

At seven o'clock I walked to the Rue Saint-Denis.

'Yes? Who's there?'

The voice from behind the street door was gravelly, as if its owner had been roused from a nap. I was almost sure it was Jacques.

'Good evening, I've come to see Madame Bouillon, the concierge.'

'And you are?'

By now I knew it was Jacques.

'It's Marguerite. Your friend Marguerite Diblanc,' I said in the language of our village.

As he unlocked the door, he said, 'Why have you turned up again, Marguerite, with no warning? You told me Magistrate Macé ordered you to stay out of France.'

'I'm not a wanted person, Jacques, so I can come back to Paris any time if I wish to. I've committed no crime.'

'Last time I saw you, you and your friend were in a great hurry to leave.'

'Because we had heard that there was work to be had in London,' I said brightly.

As he led me to the apartment, he called out, 'Victoire, you'll never guess who's pitched up. Will we never get rid of her?' He turned to me. 'And was there? Work?'

I ignored him.

In the apartment, by the light of an oil lamp, Victoire looked haunted. The place was a mess.

'Don't stare at me like that, Marguerite.'

She was pregnant again.

'I'm just thinking about how I can help you,' I replied.

The yarn I span was that I had come to Paris with my master and mistress. They were called Monsieur and Madame Michel, well-off merchants who lived in a grand house in Mayfair, and they were taking a holiday in a hotel on the Boulevard Malesherbes while I was free to use my time in Paris as I wished.

'They're good to you, your employers?' asked Victoire, wearily.

'No... to be honest, not always.'

'But they give you a holiday in Paris?'

'When I said they were not always good, I meant only that they can sometimes be a little... unreliable. They can be very generous at times.'

I asked if I could stay until Thursday. Jacques glowered so I pulled out the red leather purse.

'To pay you back for your kindness to me, during the Siege, and for the train fare to London for me and Henriette, of course. I haven't forgotten. Take it,' I said. 'It's my wages. At least I'm paid well!'

I didn't know what the gold coins were worth in France.

As I passed them to him, Victoire saw the scratches on my hand.

'She has a cat, my mistress. A kitten. Very pretty but not very friendly.' I laughed and almost couldn't stop.

'English money?' said Jacques. 'Not much use to us.'

'No, take it,' I said. 'A bank will change it for you. I'll pay you the rest as soon as I can.'

A young man who lived in a room on the second floor and worked with Jacques joined them for supper and the three of us played a card game for matchsticks while Victoire rested. I drank too much wine and laughed too loudly at the young man's jokes and told them about the omnibus that took Henriette and me to Highbury Barn to see the can-can dancers who had pretended to be from Paris. At nine Victoire led me up to an unoccupied room in the attic of the building, where there was an old bed and a grubby mattress.

'I'll need a dress for tomorrow,' I said. 'This one is no good for every day.'

She fetched an old grey cotton frock of her own and a clean camisole. She did not ask me why my employers had let me come to Paris in unsuitable clothes.

'Thank you, Victoire. I love you,' I said.

'What kind of talk is that?'

'You are my friend is all I meant.'

'And you are mine.'

'Remember when those bullyboy brothers beat me up at school. You saw them off.'

'Yes, Marguerite.'

'You protected me.'

'You should sleep now. I'll help you with your dress.'

'I'm in trouble, Henriette.'

'I'm not Henriette.'

'Victoire.'

'Don't say any more. Go to sleep.'

She draped both dresses and my waterproof over me. I slept for fourteen hours. Just before I woke, I dreamt I was lost in a storm and my mother was calling to me.

I did all of Victoire's chores, just as I had when I stayed there during the Siege, and worked my way up the stairs carrying buckets of cold water, scrubbing down the walls and the skirting boards, sponging the windows. I tied a rag over my hair and another across my nose and mouth and rinsed out the privy and scrubbed it with carbolic. I broke only at lunchtime to make soup. My hands were red from the cleaning, the scratches barely noticeable, I hoped. That night, I went to bed early, but every time I began to descend into sleep, I had a feeling that I would die and jerked awake. When at last sleep came, I dreamt that Madame Riel was in the crowd watching as I climbed the ladder to the gallows and as the noose went around my neck she shouted out, *But I'm alive! There's been a mistake! It was a joke, Marguerite, you stupid whore!*

I heard the church bells strike eight, but I could not rise from the mattress and stared at the ceiling until Victoire knocked and told me that Jacques wanted me downstairs.

His face was thunder.

'The game is up, Marguerite,' he said. 'Explain this, if you can.'

He slammed a rolled-up copy of *La Liberté* on the table.

'She has lied about everything,' he said, turning towards Victoire. 'She'll put us in prison. I always said she was a bitch.'

He took up the newspaper and unfurled it.

'"London, 9th April",' he read loudly while I stared at the floor. '"The mother of Mademoiselle Riel, a French actress, has been found strangled." But you know this, don't you, Marguerite, because as it says here, "The perpetrator is thought to be a cook called Diblanc who, it is said, was involved in the recent uprising in Paris".'

I looked at Victoire, who had closed her eyes. Her hand went to her belly.

'Who could that be? A cook called Diblanc. Could that be you, Marguerite?'

'She...' I started.

'Marguerite, please...' said Victoire.

'I'm going,' I said. 'I'm going now. Right now. No need to worry about me.'

'We're not worried about you,' said Jacques. 'We're worried about us. We have a baby coming and you do this to us.'

'The police will be looking for you,' said Victoire.

'Don't worry – no one knows about you or where you live. No one will know I was here.'

'What about Henriette?'

'She knows nothing about this, I haven't told her, or anyone, and she won't say anything about you, I can guarantee that. We've always stuck together, and she owes me...' I felt a bubble of laughter coming. 'I'll go to Madame Zimmermann.'

'Don't tell us! We don't want to know.'

I ignored her. 'She won't know anything about London – and she can barely read. And then I'll get to America, somehow. Don't concern yourselves. No one will know I was here.'

Jacques would not allow me to go upstairs to collect my things.

'Out, damn you. Out.' He turned away. 'I can't even look at you.'

Victoire came with me to the street door. She said, 'Is it true? Tell me it's not true.'

'You should burn my things,' I said.

'Go to my cousin Françoise,' she said. 'You know her. She runs a hostel, the women's section, in the Avenue d'Italie. Jacques and I stayed there when we first came to Paris. Sleep in your clothes as near to the door as possible. It opens at six.'

She gave me three francs.

I headed south to the river, over the bridge to the Île, creeping like a tiny insect next to the huge buildings. On my right was the city prison, on my left the law courts, and further on the police headquarters, whose walls had been scorched by the fires of the Commune – men on scaffolding were replacing missing stones. I pulled my shoulders back. I'm like any other woman in Paris, I told myself, no one knows me or anything about me, they don't even know I am here. I am a nobody.

―――

In the Jardin des Plantes, I moved from bench to bench. The damp clung to my shawl, chilled my bones and frizzed my hair. I flipped from cold to hot. Every so often I got up and paced the paths.

You look efficient, Marguerite. No nonsense. Competent. I'd give you a job.

That Marguerite was gone.

People thought I was a madwoman. I can't say they were wrong.

At five I walked down to the Avenue d'Italie to find the hostel. It was easy. Outside a windowless building, two lines – men to the left and women to the right – waited for six o'clock to toll. It reminded me of the queues for the soup kitchens during the Siege. These were the same people: the starving, the demented, the homeless, the deluded, the sick. I held my wrist to my nose, trying not to betray my disgust at the smell of stale alcohol, filthy underclothes and rotting teeth.

The street door opened and the women were admitted first, one at a time, filing into a stone passageway leading to a reception desk. Victoire's cousin, Françoise, sat behind it. She wasn't expecting me so I doubted she would know me after all these years.

'State your name.'

'Alice Duchamps.'

'Age?'

'Twenty-eight.'

'Third floor.'

'Can I have a bed near the door?'

I instantly regretted saying it. She glanced up at me wearily and I thought she would recognise me then, but she didn't. I paid with Victoire's francs and remembered that the English banknotes were still in the pocket of my waterproof which I had left in the room at the Rue Saint-Denis. The cousin gave me a chit with a bed number.

A young girl directed me up a rickety staircase to a large

windowless room with thirty narrow beds in it. Some women were lying down in their coats and boots, others sat staring into space or chatting. The air was suffocating and cloyed in my throat. There was a sweet reek of monthly blood and ammonia from unwashed chamber pots that reminded me of the dormitory at Chantiers. Someone was coughing, thick, foul and wet. I found my bed and stretched out on it. It was as hard as a board. The rough brown sheets stank of sweat.

The matron briefly lit her oil lamp and I saw that the coughing woman was old, with the sunken green hue of the dying. At seven the door was locked from the outside. I realised that I had not eaten since the evening before.

All night, in the pitch dark, despite the noise and the stink of the room it was pictures of London that kept me awake, rolling past me like a lantern show.

In the scullery washing the pots, outside Mademoiselle Julie's room listening, Eliza, the bonfire in the yard, Madame Crosnier, the Crow with her little bird feet lying on the floor of the kitchen, me arrested, me in court, me on the scaffold...

At four, I slept. At five, I woke and lay waiting to hear someone else stir. The coughing woman was quiet. At seven the door was unlocked and I put my boots on, tied the shawl around me and left. I could not stay at the hostel another night – I would rather wait for justice to claim me.

'You're up bright and early.'

A man with the face of a boy was leaning against the wall of the hostel, smoking a cigarette. His clothes were threadbare but not ragged. There was something impish about him that reminded me of Little Ranvier and the savvy street boys who had lived in Chantiers with us.

'Where are you off to, young lady?'

He was what Madame Soulier had warned me against.

Do not speak to the men. Stay honest.

'Nowhere,' I said, which was true enough. 'Leave me be.'

'Come to the Gingerbread Fair with me.'

'Why should I do that?'

'Because you look as if you could do with cheering up, and because you look like you were once respectable... a day or so ago... and because I'm lonely and could use a companion.'

I must have looked doubtful. Was I to be a decoy?

'Don't worry – I'm not a thief, not today. And I'm not a pimp. Do you have any money? Silly question – we've both just come out of there.' He jerked his head towards the hostel.

'I have enough.'

'It's just that I can't pay for you, that's all.'

So I went with him. What did I have to lose?

His name was Pierre.

He led the way to the Place de la Nation, which was packed with gaudy tents. I heard the sweet, sad opening bars of Le Temps des Cerises, the anthem of the Commune, which we used to sing in Chantiers to annoy the guards. The air was full of chat, of the screams of children, of the wheeze of Gypsy accordions and the shouts of the barkers:

Throw hoops for prizes!

Win at cards!

Visit the anatomical waxworks – see real diseases!

Pierre bought me a mug of ginger tea and I paid for a slice of gingerbread, which we shared. Its sweet, spicy aroma was so delicious I didn't know whether to eat it quickly or prolong the pleasure and pick at it slowly.

We took a turn on the merry-go-round, which span us around and around, up and down, the machinery grinding beneath us, sending my body one way and my head another. Before Sunday, before London, I would have clutched at Pierre's sleeve, laughed and screamed but I was strangely calm, as if I was floating.

After we disembarked he took my hand and we queued for the circus. Esmerelda the goat balanced barrels on her nose and a little pack of dogs did tricks dressed in tiny clown costumes.

When Pierre spoke to me, I heard him but didn't answer. I was submerged, as if I was perpetually pushing my way through from a thick afternoon sleep.

A chill blew through the leafless trees. I pulled my shawl closer around me.

We came away from the fair, and he stood in front of me and performed a little bow.

'Thank you for an enjoyable afternoon, Mademoiselle Whoever-You-Are. See you around,' he said.

'I doubt that.'

He walked away.

He was the first person I had met in years who hadn't required something of me.

CHAPTER TWENTY-THREE

On my way to Belleville, I bought a copy of *La Petite Presse* from a kiosk. I didn't dare open it in the street and instead took it to a bench in a corner of Père Lachaise cemetery. Even though Jacques had shown me the paragraph in yesterday's *La Liberté* I was half expecting to find nothing about a crime committed so far away. I hoped that Paris was not bothered about Madame Riel, but it was not so. There was a long article and it was not Madame who was at the centre of it but Mademoiselle Julie.

Madame had been reduced to *the mother of a charming young woman who made her début at the Vaudeville three years before.*

And they were fascinated by me, the monster. There were paragraphs about how I was the one and only suspect, about how Madame and I had clashed frequently and how, after I killed her, I had fooled Eliza. Poor Eliza. Despite sitting at the kitchen table with Madame's gloves in her hands and despite finding Ulysses upstairs ready to go out for a walk, it had not dawned on Eliza that I was lying. Grief for her mother must have addled her brain.

Even though I had imagined the scene many times, my heart pounded and my fingers tingled as I read that it was Julie herself who opened the pantry door and was greeted with... well, there is no need to say.

That's when I cried.

They said Madame Riel had been strangled with a rope and that I had deliberately positioned her body to make it look like suicide.

I will be hanged for sure.

There was nowhere left to go except to Madame Zimmermann in Belleville. I couldn't be sure she would be at her old lodgings, but she was. She was a wraith, and she took a moment to recognise me. A cancer was eating her throat. She could barely speak. Her room was empty but for a cot and a chair, and the fire was unlit. I made her lie down and knelt by her side.

'I'll get you soft bread and fruit,' I said. 'I'll make you broth.'

She shook her head and showed me the rosary in her hands.

'I'll take you to the Sisters,' I said, but she didn't want that either.

'Go to Thomas Gérard tomorrow,' she whispered. 'He'll take care of you.' She told me where he lived.

How did she know that I needed taking care of?

Perhaps she did not and was merely suggesting that he might give me a bed for a night or two, or perhaps she saw that I was on the brink of an abyss.

I slept in the chair and before Madame Zimmermann woke, went out into the street, setting off north towards the city gates, taking my time, sitting wherever I could find a bench, dawdling past enormous sheds where freight trains laden with coal and coke from Belgium clanked their way in. I wanted to arrive at dusk.

Monsieur Gérard was a coal seller who had left our village as a boy. I had met him once when he had come back to visit his parents.

His premises were easy to find as his name was blazoned roughly across an ancient broken-down building thrown up on the main road, with joists at precarious angles and chunks of plaster missing. When I went up the front step I saw him in the back, taking an order from some working men. After they left, he came towards me.

'Good morning, Madame, can I help you?'

'You don't remember me, Monsieur Gérard?'

I spoke in our language.

'Oh...' he said, giving himself time. 'Of course I know you... Diblanc. Marguerite Diblanc. You look so much like your father. What brings you to me?'

I told him I needed a place to stay for a night or two and he said, 'You are most welcome.'

His wife had a cold and was in bed, he said, otherwise she would come down and greet me. I sat in the corner of the shop while he served the customers, and as darkness fell, he put two chairs on the pavement, went upstairs and returned with bread, ham and wine. While we ate, I told him I had a job in the Faubourg Saint-Honoré and I was looking for a new situation, somewhere near this place.

'You are much better off where you are,' he said. 'Look around you. There's nothing for a person like you here. No aristos, not like in Saint-Honoré. Why would you want to leave such a position anyway?'

I could carry it no longer. I had to confess, even if I didn't tell him everything.

'I had a quarrel. With my mistress.'

'I could see that something was on your mind. But arguing with your mistress from time to time – it's not a reason to leave, Marguerite. If it were, all the servants of France would do the same and the place would fall apart.'

A customer came in and Monsieur Gérard got up to serve

him. When he came back, he said: 'Marguerite, really, you can't just leave a place because of an argument.'

'It was more of a fight,' I said.

'But if she, your Madame, was in the wrong, she's bound to take you back. She'll need you.'

'I don't think so. I gave her such a good hiding... that she might be seriously hurt. She might have died.'

'Marguerite, Marguerite...' he passed a hand across his brow, 'I can't believe that. Just apologise. I'm sure it can be cleared up. Do you want me to speak up for you?'

'No. Thank you, Monsieur Gérard, but no. She wanted to send me out without paying me, with nothing. She insulted me. She did not treat me like I was a person.'

'But I insist. She'll say sorry, for sure. I'll go with you now to Saint-Honoré and talk to her, it's the only way.' He stood up.

Then I told him that my place was not in Paris but in London and he sat back down.

'That makes it a little complicated.'

I started to cry.

'I will go to Hell. They will kill me.'

'Oh come, Marguerite. Things can't be that bad.'

'You don't know.'

'Tell me then.'

I spoke without stopping. I told him everything that had happened at No. 13 on Sunday, and how I had come on the boat-train, and how I had seen Mademoiselle Julie and her friend in the customs house at Calais, and that Julie had searched the house and found her mother's body in the pantry.

'The English police will catch me,' I said. 'I'm in the newspapers.'

He passed a hand over his brow. 'Marguerite... But why...?'

There was so much to explain, and I could not bring myself to tell him everything so I merely said, 'She cannot speak to me in that way. I didn't think she would die – I wasn't thinking at all – but she wouldn't stop. Her words...'

He took me up to see his wife, and together they tried to persuade me that I must be mistaken. Then I took *La Petite Presse* from my pocket and gave it to Madame Gérard. They read it together.

I told them I needed to get out of Paris but I expected to be caught any minute, and that if I was sent back to London, the English would put me on trial and hang me. Monsieur Gérard asked for some time alone with his wife, so I went outside and sat on the threshold and looked up at the cold dark night sky and wept. After about twenty minutes a tall man in a dark coat appeared in front of me. He did not look like the type of person to order coal but he asked for Monsieur Gérard and I told him he was upstairs and to shout for him.

Five minutes later, the gentleman was back.

'You are Marguerite Diblanc?'

There was no point lying.

He introduced himself as Monsieur Raviart. He did not say he was police but I knew he was.

Madame Gérard, in her nightgown and shawl, came down to the street.

'Marguerite, in case you need these,' she said, holding out a brown paper package to me. Monsieur Raviart took it and opened it: a prayer book, a handkerchief and a chemise.

'She cannot have these,' he said. 'She's my prisoner now.'

He gave them back.

While we were in Monsieur Raviart's cab, he asked me if I had lived in London. I said, 'Yes, of course. You know that. I know why you've come for me. How did you find me?'

'Your friends. And the English police provided your photograph.'

He showed me the *carte* made in Verdun. There was the old

long-departed Marguerite – in clean clothes, fresh-faced, in the days when I made good suppers with Madame Soulier and held Iris on my hip, when I was as happy as I could expect to be, before the Siege, before the Commune, before Chantiers, before Lieutenant Marçeron, before Madame Riel and her daughter, before I became a murderess.

'What happened in London?'

I told him that I had put my hands around Madame Riel's throat and she had fallen to the floor but she had not died from that.

'I didn't mean that she should die.'

'But you strangled her with the rope.'

'No, no, no! I did not! I would never do that. I used the rope to drag her upstairs afterwards... I wanted to hide her. I didn't strangle her.'

Later he said: 'I've been asking around about your Madame Riel. She certainly had a reputation and there was the unfortunate business with her husband.'

'Will I be sent back to London?'

'Most probably. Marguerite, if you had done this in Paris, you would not be in such a predicament. It would have got you a few years of prison. But you never know. Perhaps the English will be sympathetic.'

CHAPTER TWENTY-FOUR

'Go on, go forward, Marguerite,' said Monsieur Raviart. He gave the lightest of pushes on my back. He had taken me up to the detectives' room at the police headquarters, which I had crawled past like an ant on the first day I was in Paris. I wondered how justice could be done in such a chaotic place. There was a series of bays separated by dark wood panels with frosted glass windows, each packed with small tables and stacked chairs. Yellowing files, papers and directories lay in haphazard piles.

At the back of one of them, a man stood up and beckoned to me, pointing to the chair in front of his small desk. He was smartly dressed in a dark suit, with a pristine starched collar and shirt, tall and healthy-looking, smooth complexioned with neatly trimmed whiskers, and I could smell his cologne before I got near. He was not much older than me, too young for a detective, I thought.

I expected him to be French but he introduced himself to me in English as Chief Inspector Druscovich from Scotland Yard. And then in French he told me he would be taking me back to London, when the time came, but first he would like to ask me some questions, if I didn't mind.

He had no powers in France, he said, but the British and French police were working together on my case. He was the one who had helped Monsieur Raviart track me across Paris and given him my *carte de visite*.

'Am I allowed to ask you a question, Monsieur?'

'Go ahead, Mademoiselle Diblanc.'

'Mademoiselle Riel...' I stopped, fearful that I would break down before I even began.

'Yes... Mademoiselle Diblanc, and what is your question?'

'I would like to write to her.'

'No, Mademoiselle, you will not be allowed to do that.'

'Would you give her a message, from me?'

'That I cannot promise. But tell me what your message is.'

'Please tell her I didn't intend to kill her mother and I am sincerely sorry for it.'

As we spoke he wrote notes on a lined pad in front of him, in a script so clear I was able to read it upside-down.

'While you're held here you may only speak to me, the French detectives and the magistrate, Monsieur Macé,' he said. 'And the Sisters who will look after you, but they are generally not given to chat.'

'Monsieur Macé?'

'That is correct.'

'He's the magistrate?'

'He is.'

If he remembers me from Chantiers he will tell everyone I was arrested after the Commune and I am a criminal who abused his mercy.

'May I ask another question?'

'Yes, indeed. Go ahead.'

'How did you find me?'

'I believe the French detectives were directed to Madame

Zimmermann by your friend Madame Bouillon, and to Monsieur Gérard by Madame Zimmermann.'

I had already guessed that Victoire and Jacques had given me up. I could not blame Madame Zimmermann.

'Madame Bouillon and her husband have been arrested.'

'But they've done nothing wrong.'

'They had stolen money in their possession. Money you stole from Madame Riel, I believe. There was a great deal of it.'

I thought of the roll of banknotes in the pocket of my waterproof.

'But they didn't know it was stolen. I didn't tell them.'

Victoire will never forgive me.

'And before that, Chief Inspector Druscovich. In London... who?'

'Your friend, Mademoiselle Pompille. She told us about Victoire Bouillon and gave us her address. We guessed you'd gone to Paris and the clerk at Victoria Station remembered you.'

Henriette. Henriette betrayed me. I knew it was her before I asked the question. I kept her secret and yet she gave up mine.

He saw my face.

'Don't forget that Mademoiselle Pompille is a foreigner in a foreign land, Mademoiselle Diblanc, just as you have been. Try not to blame her. We told her the consequences of not helping us. She's in a precarious position.'

When I started to weep he passed me a handkerchief.

'I must ask you about the crime now, Marguerite. Is there anything you would like to tell me before we begin?'

Should I describe how Madame Antoine lied to me in Monsieur Dumas's shop? Should I tell him what I knew about Madame Riel and what she made Julie do...? Made Julie what exactly? Did she force her? No. Julie is a grown woman. How could I explain it to this policeman? Should I tell him about the meals of bread and cheese? The accusations? The words? Whore. Stupid. Filthy. Fat. *Pinching the back of my neck? Telling me that everything about me is lacking, wrong or defective?*

The Inspector reached across the desk. 'Give me your hands, Mademoiselle Diblanc.'

He turned them over. His skin was soft, his touch gentle. My hands were rough. He ran his thumb over the scratches, which had faded but were not healed, and asked me how they came to be there.

'I don't remember. It must have been during... during what happened. I didn't notice at the time. She fell to the floor, sir. And then she came back up, to hit me, so I hit her first. That is all. I did do that, I admit it, but I didn't mean to kill her.'

'Are you saying you were trying to defend yourself? That's a little difficult to believe. I have seen her. She was tiny.'

'I didn't murder her, and you must not say I did. I didn't strangle her either.'

He looked at me, waiting for me to continue.

'She should not have died. Something was wrong with her.'

'Explain that to me.'

'She was ill. She looked like a ghost. And she wheezed. All that coal dust and soot in the air. It was bad for her health. And she had wickedness in her soul. She should not have died, from what I did. I didn't do much. Perhaps God wanted to punish her and struck her down.'

'Marguerite, it is all very well you talking about her to me in this way, but for your own sake you should be careful. Things will not go well for you if you blame Madame Riel for her own death. If you had not fought with her, she would still be alive. No matter what she did, she did not deserve to die. Please tell me now about the money. Did you take the banknotes?'

'Yes, sir. I had to have money for the train. I had none of my own, because I had spent it all on food and she never paid me on time. I didn't know how much they were worth. I just took them. I had no choice.'

'A jury might see that differently. You could have called for help or gone for a doctor. There was one living next door, after all.'

I did not know this. But the Riels did not speak to their neighbours. Or perhaps the neighbours did not speak to them.

'Did you take anything else?'

'I took the coin purse. But I would never steal. I am an honest person. I need to tell you about her. What she did. About Mademoiselle Julie... There was an English gentleman. In the house.'

'We know about the gentleman.'

'I don't know his name.'

'Marguerite, we know of this gentleman. His name is Lord Lucan. He is powerful, in his own way, and he's trying very hard to wash his hands of the Riels. That is all I will say about him.'

'Will I be taken to London?'

'Most likely, but certain legal procedures must be gone through in Paris before that.'

I started to cry again.

'Why the tears? You're not in a good situation, it's true, but you should be hopeful. Listen now to what I tell you. Listen carefully.'

He looked at me kindly. I thought I saw pity in his face.

'Perhaps certain events in the house could be said to have disrupted the balance of your mind. In London we've just had a case where a schoolmaster pleaded insanity after battering his wife in a fit of fury. It didn't work with the jury, but afterwards the public pleaded for mercy and he ended up with a life sentence. Talk to your lawyer about this, Marguerite, when you have one.'

CHAPTER TWENTY-FIVE

I spent the night in the cells in the basement and the next morning a police officer and a Sister of Mercy escorted me up a series of wide stone staircases into an oak-lined courtroom filled with a mass of people – police, lawyers and journalists. I saw Druscovich in the well of the court sitting next to Inspector Raviart.

High at one end was the magistrates' bench and sitting behind it was Monsieur Macé, wearing black robes and the same gold-rimmed glasses he had on when he came to Chantiers. He showed no sign that he remembered me and I prayed he knew nothing of what happened to Lieutenant Marçeron.

He barked question after question at me in such quick succession that I barely had time to answer.

'So, you were soon to leave the household, yes? Why did you not go when you were sacked? What makes you think that Madame Riel would have hit you with the skillet? Had she ever done such a thing before? Tell the court in your own words about the way Madame Riel treated you. So now a mistress cannot chide her servant for not carrying out her wishes?'

'She was always rude to me. She called me a...'

'You wish everyone to be polite in speaking to you?'

'Certainly, for I make a point of being so myself.'

There was laughter. I had not meant to be amusing.

'And what if the police officer, Monsieur Raviart, had handled you roughly when he arrested you? Are you saying you would have resisted?'

'No, sir, but he behaved very properly to me and I have no reason to complain.'

Again there was laughter, as if it was absurd that a servant should demand good manners.

'What did Madame Riel say to you that caused you to attack her?'

'She slandered me in ways I can't repeat in front of you.'

'So when she did this you decided to put your hands around her neck? You strangled her to stop her saying these slanders again? How could you believe that she would say them if you were strangling her? She wouldn't have been able to speak.'

What was he talking about? I did not decide anything.

I told him my nails dug into her neck because I thought she would hit me with the pan, but not so deep as to stop her breathing.

'But your nails are quite short, Diblanc, so it would have been difficult for you to dig them into her throat. I don't believe you.'

He ordered me to demonstrate what had happened, so I was made to act out the final seconds in the life of Madame Riel, dodging as she reached for the pan on the range, narrating her words and mine and stretching my arms towards her neck. The courtroom was silent, and I found myself cold with sweat.

'Then she was a heap on the floor – but she tried to get up.'

'And that is when you strangled her again?'

'No, sir. I did not strangle her. That was when I hit her.'

'You must have strangled her. There was a rope around her when she was found. You think we are stupid?'

'No, sir.'

'There is no other explanation.'

'If you'll just let me–'

'We've heard enough from you.'

Even after Detective Druscovich read out a translation of the report of the inquest, in which it stated I dragged Madame Riel to the pantry with the rope, Monsieur Macé insisted that I had strangled her, first with my hands and then again with the rope.

Then they called in the witnesses.

Monsieur Gérard was first. Monsieur Macé apologised to him for the behaviour of the crowd outside, which had heckled him.

'They think I'm Prussian,' said Monsieur Gérard. 'I don't know why. I suppose because of the way I speak. It was the same in the war. I've had people outside my coal yard non-stop since Mademoiselle Diblanc was arrested.'

He told the court about me coming to him the day before and how, after lying about why I was there, I had suddenly confessed and told him everything.

The clerk called Victoire and Jacques. Monsieur Macé announced that they were currently confined in the Saint-Lazare Prison. Victoire was pale and her face was bloated as if she had been crying, and her little baby belly stuck out. Jacques requested a chair for her, and she sat with her elbows on her knees and her hands at her temples. I thought of the day we had walked together to the back of Père Lachaise cemetery remembering her lost baby boy, and how she and Jacques had lent me and Henriette money for the train to London. And when I thought about Henriette and how she had given me up, the room started to shift. I felt unsteady, as if I were about to faint.

Someone must have noticed because Monsieur Macé asked an official to bring me a glass of water and we took a short break.

When we restarted, Jacques told the court about me staying with them when I came to Paris and later during the Siege and the Commune. Victoire agreed that when I turned up at their conciergerie, she and Jacques had allowed me to stay and she had given me a dress. Monsieur Macé said she knew from the beginning what I had done in London and that she had helped me hide from justice. She insisted she did not know the half-guineas and banknotes were stolen.

After she got down from the bar, Monsieur Macé asked me whether I had ever registered as a prostitute or had cohabited with a man or been in the lock hospital. I had to tell myself that he asked all women before the court these questions.

'What did you do during the war?'

'I lived with Monsieur and Madame Bouillon, sir, in the Rue Saint-Denis.'

'Did you work?'

'I looked after a child, sir. A neighbour's child.'

'And the Commune, what did you do then?'

'I was still living with them, sir, although the child had died by then.'

'Tell the court why you went to London.'

'I could not find work in Paris, sir, to support myself.'

It was the reason Henriette and I gave Abbé Toursel. It was not a lie exactly, but of course it was not the whole truth.

CHAPTER TWENTY-SIX

The words in the prayer book danced in front of my eyes and made me feel sick. They were all about death and nothing about living. I begged the Sister for something else, a newspaper, a picture book, anything to distract me.

'That is not permitted,' she said. 'Read your prayers, Diblanc. God will aid you. I'll call a priest to you if you need one.'

I turned my thoughts to ways to end my life. The city prison was not like Chantiers, where Henriette's friendship, the companionship of all of the women and the haphazard affections of the children created a life, however unpleasant. At Chantiers, I was an innocent person unjustly locked up. In this dungeon, I was guilty and all I had to contemplate was my humiliation, my family's shame, and my journey to the gallows. I considered it would be preferable to surrender to my fate now, but a Sister was with me at all times so I had no choice but to continue to live.

One morning – I can't remember how many days had passed – a prison officer collected me from my cell.

'Where are we going?'

'I cannot tell you.'

'Am I to go to London now?'

'It is not that.'

With the Sister walking behind us, he led me back into the police headquarters and up to a door with Magistrate Macé's name on it.

'You were in Chantiers,' said the magistrate as I stood behind a chalk line drawn on the floor in front of his desk, the officer and the Sister behind me. 'I recognised your name and checked the records.'

'Yes, sir.'

'We did not charge you with a crime and there's little point bringing all that up now. I am a fair man, I think you will agree.'

I looked at the floor and wondered if he was hinting that he required payment in kind for his sense of justice.

'I will now examine you.'

I was confused. Had not the hearing been an examination?

'Distinctive physiognomy,' he muttered.

He came around the desk and stood very close to me, holding a small notebook.

'You're an interesting specimen, Diblanc,' he said, taking my jaw in his other hand, turning it one way and then the other. 'A woman killing another woman – very unusual.'

He wrote in his notebook.

'From the look of you, I'd have you down as a born assassin. Certain physical characteristics carry predestination within them. The killing was bound to happen. You women always make the worst criminals, more bestial even than the men. Not content with throttling the poor woman, you had to hang her with the rope, and defile her body.'

'That isn't what happened–'

'Did I ask you to speak?' He went back to examining me. 'Thick eyebrows meeting, almost, above the nose.' He placed his pencil across my forehead. 'The set of the facial bones, the position of the ears, the covering of down on the face. I would have predicted you to be an infanticide, though, rather than a murderess.'

He returned to his chair and made more notes.

'Was the child yours?' he said, without looking up.

'Which child, sir?'

'The child you said you cared for, during the Siege.'

'No, sir. A neighbour's, as I said.'

'You have had no children?'

'No.'

'I cannot say I am surprised. You are not an attractive specimen. Mostly likely barren, and in any case I doubt many would want to mate with you. For which we are grateful.'

Did he expect me to reply?

'The English want to try you for your life and your own people, the Belgians, have agreed to this. France did not feel your loss last time you left these shores and will not now. Your extradition is expected to be signed any day.'

That night, I scarcely slept, once more afflicted with a fear of falling asleep and dying. A doctor visited me and prescribed a sleeping draught which gave me twelve dreamless hours, until the Sister shook me awake and told me it was time to prepare for my removal to London. She had brought me a clean undershift, a linen cap and a woollen cloak but I was still wearing Victoire's grey dress, which now stank of perspiration.

At seven o'clock, Magistrate Macé and an officer collected me from the cell. The Sister pressed a prayer book on me and said, 'May God guide you,' as she pulled my cap straight on my head and tucked an errant lock behind my ear. 'You must contemplate your crime, Diblanc, and understand how straying from God brought you to this.'

In the yard of the police headquarters I was given into the

custody of Inspector Raviart. Inspector Druscovich was there too, with Monsieur Gérard.

'Is Monsieur Gérard coming to London with us?' I whispered to Inspector Raviart as he handed me into the cab.

'Yes, because he will give evidence.'

'Will I be tried right away?'

'Not right away. The arraignment comes first and, I expect, a trial shortly after that.'

'But what about Monsieur and Madame Bouillon?'

'Well, yes, ideally they should be coming with us, but they're in custody, and your friend is not far off her time. The lawyers say they will manage without them.'

At the Gare du Nord, Detective Druscovich suggested we sit in the café while we wait for the train to be ready. He ordered me a glass of kirsch, for courage he said, and when it was time to go, he took me by the elbow and we boarded a second-class carriage that he had reserved for us.

'Marguerite, you must expect a scene when we reach the boat,' he said. 'The French feel strongly about foreigners murdering their citizens. And a number will just want to catch a glimpse of you. You are a woman and that is... not common. The newspapers have rather ramped it up because of that.'

At Calais, hundreds of people had gathered on the pier to jeer at me as I crossed the platform and walked up the gangway to the steamboat. It was not worse than our terrible trek out of Paris to Chantiers, when we were insulted and bombarded by crowds of people, but then I was one among hundreds and this time I was totally alone.

CHAPTER TWENTY-SEVEN

The matron directed me to sit at the table in the middle of the room where prisoners talked to their attorneys. After a few minutes my solicitor, Mr Godfrey, entered and sat facing me. By then I had lived in a remand cell at Newgate Prison for five weeks.

'Mademoiselle Diblanc, we must talk about the trial, which is due to commence tomorrow.'

His French was cumbersome and full of errors.

In previous meetings, I had done as Inspector Druscovich suggested and told Mr Godfrey about the presence of Lord Lucan in the house and how it had disturbed my mind, and how I had been worn down by Madame Riel's constant criticism, so much so that I had no control over myself.

Mr Godfrey was not interested.

'I need to tell the advocate what happened, Mr Godfrey. He must say she starved me. She was ready to cast me out with nothing, not even what she owed me. He must tell them about Lord Lucan–'

'Slow down, Miss Diblanc, please.' Mr Godfrey put his hands up, as if I were attacking him. 'If you speak more slowly,

I'll be able to help you better. In this country there is normally no need to consult your advocate in person before the trial. His name is Mr Powell, by the way. You will see him in court.'

'Then how can Mr Powell speak for me if I have not told him what happened?'

'It is very simple.' He addressed me as if I were a child. 'Because I have told him about you and about your case and because he has all the relevant papers. He knows all about it. You have nothing to fear. In court, Monsieur Albert will translate for you, just as he did at your arraignment at Bow Street. You remember? It is all as it should be.'

The arraignment was an ordeal, a torture that I thought would kill me. A few days after Inspector Druscovich brought me back from Paris, he collected me from Newgate and took me, along with a prison matron, in a cab to the courtroom at Bow Street. Two police constables, one in front of me, one behind, with Druscovich at one side, the prison matron the other, pushed through the roiling ocean of enemies waiting to hurt me. They screamed at me, bared their teeth, and spat. They shoved at me and at each other in their eagerness to get at me. I did not understand how I had made them so angry.

'Fix your sights on the main door,' said Detective Druscovich in my ear, in French. 'Think yourself in a tunnel heading for the light at the end.'

Then he shouted over to the prison matron, because the rule was that everything said to me in French had to be repeated to her in English.

'Why are they here? It's not even my trial,' I said once we were inside the building.

'Some of them hate foreigners, so they're going to hate you. A fair number want Britain to declare war on France for not giving you up sooner. And some just want to say they've seen the murderess of Park Lane. I imagine a few think you're a

189

kind of revolutionary who has stood up for servants everywhere.'

When we reached a small waiting room inside the courthouse, he opened his leather bag and took out two sandwiches of white bread and butter wrapped in a large napkin, and gave one to me.

'My wife always ensures I am well prepared,' he said. 'Please eat, Marguerite. It will help calm you.' He poured two small cups of coffee from a traveller's flask.

The courtroom was sweltering and packed with people. I had a crashing pain at the front of my head and could scarcely look up. Now, in the room at Newgate with Mr Godfrey I did not want to think about what happened at Bow Street, about the moment when Mademoiselle Julie came in and everyone fell silent and I heard only the pounding of my heart, her heels on the parquet floor and the swish of her black silk gown.

In the witness box, she lifted her veil, and looked straight at me, a look that said Inspector Druscovich had delivered my message – but that it did not change a thing. She hated me for what I had done.

She insisted to the judge that she would speak only in French. She wanted me to hear her words unfiltered. That was a way of hurting me, of reaching inside my heart.

In the meeting room at Newgate, Mr Godfrey said: 'You must remember, Mademoiselle Diblanc, that no matter what happens tomorrow at the Old Bailey, you must never give up hope.'

He was telling me I was doomed.

'I should warn you, however. Whatever the evidence of the other witnesses, it is Doctor Wadham's post-mortem report that... Well, you already know it is not good.'

'But I have told the truth.'

'I have no doubt about that but it is impossible to argue with what it says. Facts are facts.'

'Does the doctor say I murdered her?'

'It is not like that.'

'How can he say I murdered her? This is not true. It is an injustice.'

'The evidence will speak for itself.'

I gave up.

Everyone thinks I am guilty, so I must be.

'One further thing, Mademoiselle Diblanc. Tomorrow, in court, please keep your hands in your lap.'

'My hands?'

'If the men on the jury see them they will have thoughts about you strangling Madame Riel. Let's not let their imaginations condemn you.'

'I did not strangle her. She was alive after I... she got up from the floor.'

'Mademoiselle Diblanc, your hands are strong, and they look strong. The newspapers have already remarked on them. When the killing was first reported, they hardly believed the person who did this could be a woman, and then they insisted that a woman could only do it with a man's help. Murder, murder like this, is supposed to be a man's crime. Most of our female murderers reach for the poison bottle.'

Just after the bells tolled eight in the morning, the Governor of Newgate, an elderly prison matron and a warder were at the door of my cell. I checked my cap was straight and my hair tucked in and then we walked down the iron spiral staircases and through the gaol, the Governor in front and the others behind. At each locked door we stopped and the warder came forward with keys in hand and opened it, and then returned to his position. I knew where we were heading – the graveyard, where I was taken every day with the other female remand prisoners for an hour of exercise. Under the stones on which we performed our slow circular perambulation lay the bones of all the felons hanged within the prison. Their names were inscribed on the perimeter walls.

At the back of this dismal corner was an entrance to the Old Bailey, and here we descended a staircase and walked through a dank curving passage covered on every surface with white tiles – the only sound being the clank of the warder's keys and the echo of our boots – until we reached the underbelly of the courtroom, where we passed through more doors and more corridors to a small chamber. I was invited to sit on a metal chair at a table in the centre of the room.

Twenty minutes later a sheriff's man came to the door, we all stood and together, in our formation, now with the sheriff's man at the very front, climbed the stone stairs up to the courtroom. Finally, we reached a heavy wooden door guarded by a court officer who inspected the papers, nodded, unlocked it, and delivered me, like a newborn, into the back of the dock.

CHAPTER TWENTY-EIGHT

Every seat was occupied. People were wedged in, shoulders up. In the centre of the court amongst a pool of clerks and officials, lawyers in charcoal-grey gowns hovered over their papers, fingers running across documents, heads together, dusty wigs slipping, and on the bench before me a host of high officials conferred with each other, all dressed in scarlet, black and white, gold regalia glinting in the harsh summer light coming through the huge arched windows behind them. I caught a waft of beeswax mixed with cigars and yesterday's beef and potatoes.

The Governor directed me to sit. He was one side of me, the matron the other, with the warder directly in front on a chair in the well of the court. I kept my eyes down and my hands in my lap as Mr Godfrey had told me to. I could not stop looking at them, the thick fingers, the square nails. I had used them to pound beef steaks and twist off bottle caps, heft tubs of soapy water, stroke Iris's forehead – and to stop Madame's words.

The whispers in the court grew. Newspapers rustled. Outside the court, heels clopped on the marble floor. The double doors opened. A court officer strode in and made an announcement. The Governor nudged me and we all stood. My mouth was dry and I started to shake. The judge, in scarlet robes and ermine, processed in and, a clerk in attendance, took his seat. He was grey, old and kind-faced – I had a surge of hope, which I quickly cut down. An appearance of kindness means nothing.

This was my chance to look about me. A quick glance to the gallery – it was full of gentlemen and ladies in sombre clothes. There was Abbé Toursel in his clerical robes, there was Madame Gérard, there was Théo Riel and his wife, the other Madame Riel. Sitting below the bench, directly in front of me was Julie, flanked by Mademoiselle Guy and Madame Antoine.

The journalists leant forward, notebooks and pencils in hand. I caught the eye of a court artist. The clerk said something and then the judge, the officials made more announcements, and the lawyers stood to talk, first this one, then another one, then this one again, then that one, and at last the prosecutor, the man whose aim was to hang me, turned towards the jury and spoke. He seemed to go on for hours. I understood nothing but I heard *Madame Riel* and *Mademoiselle Riel* and *Jacques Bouillon*, and *the prisoner*, which was the English title I now went by. I wanted to ask Monsieur Albert, the translator, why I was not permitted to know what was being said about me, but he was far away on the other side of the court.

All was quiet. The judge nodded to the clerk, who bellowed out something. A door opened and Eliza came in, smaller than I remembered her. She wore a black velvet bonnet and a black raw silk dress with elaborate ruffles and a bustle. It was one of Madame's. Julie must have given it to her.

The lawyers talked and the Governor stood and left the dock by a little gate and sat next to the warder in the court, and then Monsieur Albert crossed and took his place next to me so that he could whisper his translations in my ear. The to and fro of the questions confused me. The prosecutor spoke. Eliza answered. And while Monsieur Albert translated for me, the spectators fidgeted, Eliza looked to the floor, and the advocates shuffled their papers. Each time he finished, Monsieur Albert nodded to the judge. The judge nodded at the advocate. The advocate asked another question. And round and round they went. Starting, stopping, speaking, whispering, nodding.

Eliza spoke truthfully, as far as I could tell. How I went out to get food on Saturday evening, how on Sunday morning when she came into the kitchen with the empty coal scuttle I was in the basement area and told her Madame had gone out and accidentally locked me out there, how Eliza had gone to the pub for beer and how I kept her waiting on the porch for fifteen minutes, about Madame Crosnier arriving, waiting and leaving, and how I put on my waterproof and announced that I was off to church. She knew nothing of the argument between Madame and me the night before or anything that Madame Riel said or I said on that final morning. No one knew that but me.

'After the prisoner left the house on the Sunday evening, what did you do?'

'I stayed up till midnight, because I was worried about Madame, and I was expecting Marguerite... I mean the prisoner... to come back. Then I went to bed.'

'And the next morning ~ the Monday?'

'I got up just after six and went into Madame's bedroom on my way down. She was not there, and everything in the room was just as it was the day before. At seven I went into the drawing room and from the window I saw a cab bringing Mademoiselle Riel and her friend.'

'You were expecting them?'

'Yes, sir.'

'I hate to bring back unfortunate memories to you, Miss Watts, but I must ask you what occurred next, after Mademoiselle Riel returned to the house.'

'I told her that Madame had gone out the previous morning

and not returned and that Marguerite had also gone out, in the evening, and not returned.'

'And what was Mademoiselle Riel's reaction?'

'She sent me to get...' – she hesitated – '...to get assistance from someone, and shortly afterwards the police came.'

Julie must have sent her to fetch Lord Lucan, who summoned the police.

She wrung her hands, stretching them, rubbing them, bending them back. I heard tears in her voice.

'You were in the house when Mademoiselle Riel opened the pantry?'

'No, sir. It was opened while I was out... getting help. Mademoiselle had her own key to the pantry. Afterwards, after I had returned to the house, I went to the pantry door and... saw Madame there. Doctor Wadham, who lives next door, he was fetched by Mademoiselle Riel herself. He came and I saw them, him and the policemen I mean, carry Madame into the parlour.'

Now it was the turn of my advocate, Mr Powell. He sighed as he rose from his table and passed a hand across his brow before he spoke.

'I suppose your mistress sometimes found fault with you without a cause?'

'*Always* without a cause, sir.'

The people in the court laughed. They did not know Madame Riel.

'Do you understand French, Miss Watts?'

'No, sir, not at all.'

'So you didn't understand whatever was said between Madame and the prisoner?'

'No, sir. Marg... the prisoner speaks very little English.'

'How did *you* communicate with the prisoner?'

'I had to use actions and signs and suchlike to make myself understood. And she did the same.'

'Would you say Madame Riel was of a suspicious disposition, Miss Watts?'

'Yes, I would say that. She thought things happened that never happened, and blamed people unjustly, myself included.'

'And what did she do when she was thinking such things? Did she make her feelings plain?'

'She would use her hands a lot. A good deal, actually. She would throw her head up and her hands would go out, like this.'

More laughter.

There was no mention of the fire in the yard. Yet I had told my solicitor about it.

'Madame Riel was a lady of rather quick temper, a passionate person, wouldn't you say?'

'I don't know about her being a passionate person. She would certainly speak very loudly.'

'In English?'

'In French usually.'

'But you say she was not quick-tempered.'

'French people always sound angry even if they are not.'

More laughter.

'Was Madame Riel *ever* ill-tempered to you?'

'Yes, she could be.'

'Did you complain to the prisoner about it?'

'Yes, I did.'

She never complained to *Madame Riel* about it though.

'And how did you do that if, as is clear, the prisoner did not speak English and you do not speak French?'

'As I said, we communicated more by signs and by looks on our faces.'

The advocate was wasting his breath on this. What did it matter? The jury should have been hearing about Madame Riel's behaviour to me.

'What did you have for lunch on that Sunday, the day the prisoner disappeared from the house?'

Eliza glanced over at me.

'Bread and cheese.'

'Anything else?'

'Beer, from the public house.'

'Was that a normal meal for you and the prisoner?'

'Some days, yes.'

'Were you hungry?'

'At times.'

She should have said Madame Riel was a thief. Starvation is a form of stealing.

'The day before the prisoner disappeared from the house, the Saturday, did she go to buy food for herself?'

'I believe so.'

'Did she often buy her own food?'

'Sometimes. Yes.'

'Did you work on Sundays?'

'Usually. At least part of the day.'

'That is all. No further questions.'

While Eliza got down and the lawyers put their heads together, I looked over towards Mr Powell. He avoided my eye. He had not asked Eliza about the time Madame put her hands on my neck after the lunch for Théo Riel and his wife. I had told Mr Godfrey about it. Eliza had been there. She had seen it.

Then I heard, 'Call Miss Julie Riel.'

In the witness box, she looked ahead, straight at me, poised as if she were about to begin a performance and awaited only the cue to start. She used her stage voice, the one she practised with me in the kitchen.

And again she insisted she must give her answers in French.

'On around the twentieth of March I gave the prisoner notice to leave. It was one week's notice, as we have in France, but she said she wanted to stay the month.'

It was not like that. I had been obliged to explain the English law to her. She bribed me into staying by offering me a hand-me-down frock. She was just like her mother. A liar and a cheat.

If she had just paid me what she owed me I would have left there and then, even though I had nowhere to go, but she persuaded me to stay. I think that is what happened but our words are lost in the air now, like everything in my story. It made no difference what I remembered. In court her story counted. Mine did not.

'On the thirty-first of March I left London for Paris, and I returned to Park Lane early on the eighth of April, Monday, about seven o'clock in the morning. Eliza opened the door to me. She told me that, in the morning of the day before, Maman had said she was going out to Green Park for a walk with our little dog, but she had not seen her since, and that the prisoner had gone to church the evening before, and that she thought the prisoner had stayed overnight with her friend.'

'And what did you think about Eliza Watts's statement? That your mother had gone out and not returned?'

'I sent her out at once to bring somebody to me and while she was out, we, my friend and I, looked about the house to see whether Maman had left a note. I looked everywhere, in all the rooms upstairs, and then I came down to the kitchen and the coal cellar, and at last I went to the pantry. It was always kept locked – there were two keys to it, one Maman had, and I had the other.'

'Let me just stop you there, Mademoiselle Riel, so that the jury can understand what you are saying. And I must apologise for causing you to remember so vividly the events of such an awful day. Please tell the court exactly what you saw when you opened the door of the pantry.'

'The first thing I saw was my mother's cloak on the floor.'

She paused.

'I lifted it up' – her voice cracked and she spoke softly – 'and under it I saw her.'

She took a handkerchief from her pocket.

'And did you see anything else, Mademoiselle Riel?'

'I saw that the safe on the wall was open. The safe where I kept my jewels.'

'And what did you do next, Mademoiselle Riel?'

'I ran out into the street, and then I remembered that a doctor lived next door, and I went to him.'

'Did you touch anything at all in the pantry?'

'Nothing at all.'

'You asked Doctor Wadham to attend?'

'Yes, he came in just a few minutes – and by then the police were there.'

'I believe some banknotes were missing from the safe. Is that correct, Mademoiselle Riel?'

'Yes. Before I left for Paris, I had given my mother some banknotes, about thirty pounds.'

'Do you remember which denomination they were? Five-pound notes or ten-pound notes?'

'I'm afraid I don't remember. I didn't look at them. I gave them to Maman either on the Thursday, Friday, or Saturday before I left. I don't know the exact day.'

She is lying. She remembers perfectly well. Such a huge sum of money. She's acting as if the money had nothing to do with her.

'And your mother put these banknotes in the safe in the pantry?'

'Yes, that's correct. It's where she kept money and our other valuables. Jewellery and share certificates.'

'Who gave the banknotes to you, Mademoiselle Riel?'

'I had got the banknotes from Lord Lucan, to give to my mother.'

Now there was a surge of murmuring across the floor of the court. I took a breath in. The air was already vile.

She is brazening it out, but she is telling the world that it is not she who was the mistress but her dead mother. She has made a pact with Lord Lucan to lie.

'When did he give you these banknotes?'

'Perhaps only ten minutes before I gave them to my mother.'

'Returning to the safe now, Mademoiselle Riel. After the body was removed to another room, the parlour, I believe, a police detective asked you about the safe and its contents. Is that right?'

'Yes. I went into the pantry and saw that there were no banknotes in it. I looked in the little box containing my jewellery. Everything was still there. The certificates were there.'

'Was anything *else* missing, Mademoiselle Riel?'

'A red leather coin purse the servants used for buying provisions.'

'Did the police in Paris show you any items after the prisoner was arrested?'

'Yes, the purse. And some banknotes.'

Now it was Mr Powell's turn to question Julie. He lumbered to his feet. I wanted to march over to him, grab his arm and whisper: *She is beautiful but she is clever – you must watch for her lies.*

'Mademoiselle Riel, my sincere condolences on the death of your mother. I must ask you a few questions about the events that led us to being here in this court. Please tell the court how and when you came to live in England.'

'I have been here since the war with Prussia, September 1870. We left Paris just before the Siege started. And we moved into Park Lane a few weeks after that.'

'And you work in London as an actress, I believe.'

'Yes, in London at the St James's Theatre. Until... until the death of my mother.'

'I will turn now to the pantry and the safe, in which a box of your precious jewels was kept. What can you tell us about those items?'

'I was in the habit of wearing them, for my stage appearances, and stored them in that box for safekeeping.'

'The jewels are valuable? They are real rubies and pearls, or diamonds, or suchlike?'

'They are.'

'I see. You brought them from Paris?'

'Some of them.'

'And the others?'

'I acquired them in London.'

I felt sorry for her. The banknotes and now the jewels. He was shaming her for something that was Madame Riel's fault.

'I see. And the box was not missing?'

'No.'

'And the jewels were not missing?'

'No.'

'But the banknotes that, er, Lord Lucan gave you, for your mother you say, those were missing. But you can't remember when he gave them to you? Is that right?'

'I cannot say which day it was. It was before I left for Paris.'

She smiled slightly, like a true Parisian, to tell him how much she hated him. 'You can't remember which day but you do remember that you gave them to your mother straight away?'

'Immediately.'

'Was she in the house when Lord Lucan gave them to you?'

'Yes, she was.'

'Kindly explain to me why he gave them to you, if they were intended for your mother, if she was in the house. Why did Lord

Lucan not give them to her himself? Why would he give them to you?'

'I suppose...'

'Please go on.'

'I suppose she may have been indisposed.'

'No further questions, My Lord.'

As Julie got down from the witness box, our eyes met properly for the first time. What was in her expression? Everything: pity, fury, hurt, sadness, grief.

CHAPTER TWENTY-NINE

The court broke for forty-five minutes during which I was taken into a side room and given sugared tea, chicken broth and a hunk of coarse bread. Then we filed back, with the warder in front and the matron behind, and took our places.

The clerk called William Peat. I had never noticed this fresh-faced, nervous constable who said he normally stood at the junction where our branch of Park Lane split off from the main part of Park Lane. Usually, when I left No. 13, it was to walk in the opposite direction, towards Piccadilly.

'At a quarter to eight in the morning I was called to No. 13,' he said, 'and there I saw a lady standing at the door, the friend of Mademoiselle Riel I believe, and in consequence of what they said I went into the house to a room at the end of the passage leading from the front door, and saw the dead body of a woman with her face to the floor...'

He was speaking too quickly, without stopping, his voice trembling, and Monsieur Albert could not keep up with him.

Was it his first time in the witness box or was it his first dead woman?

The judge spoke to him. Perhaps it was to tell him to slow down and to address the judge himself and not the jury.

'Madame Riel's feet were at the door end of the room, as you went in, you say,' said the prosecutor.

'Yes.'

'And what action did you take when you were in the pantry?'

'I moved the body about eighteen inches, as near as I can say, from the safe out towards the middle of the room. A rope was wound once round the neck, with a slip noose under the left cheek, and–'

The judge spoke again to the constable. He stood up straight and started speaking almost comically slowly.

'...the other end was twisted twice round the handle of the door of the safe. The rope was tight round the neck.'

Had I done things I didn't remember or were they making this up? I could not believe I put the rope around her neck in that manner.

My stomach turned over. I should not have had the soup.

'Thank you, Constable. Were you still in the pantry when Doctor Wadham arrived?'

'Yes, I was.'

'Was that when the body was moved to the sofa in the parlour?'

I saw Madame Riel in my mind, with her little crow feet hanging over the armrest.

'Yes it was. We moved the body at Doctor Wadham's request, so that he could make a preliminary examination.'

It was difficult to follow, but he said he found Madame's bonnet with some false hair in it in the pantry.

Everyone in the court looked over towards the exhibits table as a clerk held up the bonnet and the hairpiece. I kept my head down and stared at my hands. And then it was back again to talk of the safe, and how I took the banknotes but left the jewellery.

My advocate, Mr Powell, was asking the policeman about Madame Riel's rings.

'She was wearing only one gold ring, sir, with a diamond in it, and no wedding ring,' said the constable.

'I am sorry. Just for clarity – there was a ring with a diamond set in it but no wedding ring. Am I correct?'

He was trying to suggest to the jury that there was a possibility Madame was not really married, or that she thought so little of her dead husband that she would not wear his ring. He was telling them that she was worthless because she received banknotes from Lord Lucan that were really for her daughter.

One of the detectives came into the witness box and said that he found cinders and chips of wood, and a small fish bone, in Madame's false hair. Disgust rippled across the courtroom.

'I surmised that those items had attached themselves to the hair while the body was in the coal cellar. On the mat in the coal cellar I found a hairpin, and another on the stairs leading to the kitchen,' he said.

'Did you search the prisoner's room at 13 Park Lane?'

'I did. I found the prisoner's box there. The lock was broken. There were some pieces of cloth, for patching dresses, I imagine, and some old boots and two *cartes de visite*. A pawn ticket issued in Paris.'

'The photographs were of the prisoner?'

'They were. And of an unknown woman and child.'

'Was the box packed, as if ready for the prisoner to leave the house?'

'No, sir. Her things were lying in different parts of the room, underclothes and such, and a brown dress was hanging on the back of the door.'

We broke for half an hour. In the side chamber, the matron brought me a glass of water. We returned to the court.

Jacques was next.

He will sink me. The money will be the death of me. They will say I did it to steal, so that I could pay my debt to him and Victoire.

Monsieur Albert left the dock and stood near the witness box to translate Jacques' account for the court.

I began to sweat.

'When the prisoner came to your door on the evening of the eighth of April was she alone?'

'Yes.'

'Did she have luggage?'

'Only an umbrella. She said she had come from her employer, who was staying in the Rue des Malesherbes.'

'Were you aware that the prisoner's clothes, a green dress, a bonnet and a waterproof cloak, and the banknotes were in your premises?'

'I had no idea. She must have left them in the room where she was sleeping.'

'You were arrested, I believe, on the Friday.'

'Yes, and my wife the Sunday following.'

'And you were detained at a prison in Paris?'

'Yes, in Saint-Lazare, for several weeks, and our son was born there.'

I was the cause of this. I had betrayed Victoire and worse – her baby. The child would never be able to wipe away the shame of a prison birth.

'Did she pay you for her bed and board, when she lived with you in Paris, during the Siege and afterwards?' said the prosecutor.

'She was unable to pay me anything due to lack of work. She owed me a lot of money. She gave me some English sovereigns in payment of that debt, which I accepted.'

He did nothing to try and save me, but I had known that he wouldn't.

The next morning, our dismal caravan took the iron spiral staircase again, through the graveyard, through the doors and the corridors and the echoing tunnel and into the waiting room in the bowels of the Old Bailey. Mr Powell came to see me there for the first time.

'Please say she was late paying me and that we went hungry, Eliza and me. How she set a fire. How she was constantly insulting me. How she pinched the back of my neck. Tell them about Lord Lucan and what he was doing and how Madame made Julie–'

He sighed. He was bored.

'Miss Diblanc, I can say nothing about that.' His French was slow but better than Mr Godfrey's. 'It is not relevant to your case. Lord Lucan is not on trial here. Whatever His Lordship does with a young lady who is of age has no bearing on you killing the young lady's mother. Even you must be intelligent enough to see that. Remember, we are in London, not Paris, and we follow our own laws.'

The air in the courtroom was as rancid as it had been the day before. My mouth was parched. I couldn't stop biting on my lips. I must have looked ghastly, like the ghost I feared I would become.

I flinched at every little sound: the closing of a distant door, a laugh between the advocates, the thump of a cane on the floor. In my lap, I wrung my hands.

The prison governor sat himself next to me in the dock while Monsieur Albert went to the side of the witness stand.

Monsieur Gérard's blue work suit was freshly pressed. His chemise was bright and crisp. He removed his cap and set about declaring that he hardly knew me, but when he said it, he had pain in his face as if he was shooting a favourite horse, but none of what he said was untrue.

At his coal yard, he said, I confessed to him that I fought with Madame.

'She told me that in the customs house at Calais she saw Mademoiselle Riel.'

Julie let out a sound and Mademoiselle Guy and Madame Antoine both bent towards her. But what was that moment at Calais? Nothing. If Julie had seen me then, I would have made up a story about why I was there. It would have made no difference. Her mother would still be dead. We would all still be here at the Old Bailey – and I would still be days from my death.

The clerk called Lord Lucan. There was a ripple of whispers.

The judge asked for quiet.

The door opened.

Lord Lucan, in an immaculate black gabardine topcoat, came in, steadying himself with his cane as he walked, no longer the bellicose old gentleman interrogating me outside Monsieur Dumas's shop.

Is he stooping on purpose? Is he pretending to be more frail than he really is?

His booming voice was modulated for his performance. Yes, he did go to his bank and afterwards, yes, he did hand six five-pound notes to Mademoiselle Riel to pass on to her mother.

He tried to step down from the witness box. The judge reminded him that the defence would ask him questions.

'How well did you know Madame Riel?'

He looked on Mr Powell as if on a worm.

'I saw her from time to time.'

'Please tell the court what Madame Riel was like.'

Ah, he said, she was just like a good many French ladies. He used a word – she was a little *vive*, as if she were skittish, like a racehorse.

'Did you ever see her lose her temper?'

'No, nothing like that.'

'And did you have an opportunity to observe her demeanour towards her servants?'

'No, not really. Not at all.'

Again, he moved to get down but the judge signalled for him to stay.

'I am intrigued by this word *vive*, Lord Lucan,' said Mr Powell. 'We were told yesterday that all French people were passionate.' Was it only me who saw his eyes lingering on Julie? 'Do you mean to say Madame Riel couldn't control her temper?'

'I had no opportunity of judging. She was animated. I do not even mean that she was a person who used more gesticulation than English people are in the habit of using. If she had been an Englishwoman I should describe her as hasty and *vive*, as I just said. I would not go beyond that. French people, who are used to such, would not remark on her manner at all.'

Mademoiselle Julie had made her face a blank.

'The banknotes – what was the reason for the transaction with, er, Madame Riel?'

'I was in the habit of helping... advising' – he coughed – 'Madame Riel on her finances. The money was return on investments I had made on her behalf.'

'No further questions, My Lord.'

I looked at the prison matron and signed for a drink of water, but she shook her head slowly.

Then Eliza was back, being questioned about my green dress and my brown dress, and when it was Mr Powell's turn he said, 'The prisoner desires me to ask you, while she was living at 13 Park Lane, whether you knew her to buy any clothes or spend anything on herself, to your own knowledge' – and of course she said no, she never saw me do so, because I had not.

Mademoiselle Julie was called again. This time she admitted

that her mother had a quick temper, but when the prosecutor asked if she ever used abusive language she said, 'Never, never!'

The judge announced that the court would adjourn for lunch.

This time, in the waiting chamber, I took only a little tea.

When we were called back, the end of my story started.

Doctor Wadham was fifty-ish, portly, with thick fingers and a mass of yellow hair. Although he lived at No. 12, next door to us, in the months I was at No. 13 I had never seen him, and when he was questioned he said he had never met Madame Riel nor Mademoiselle Riel, until that Monday. He did not have to explain why.

Monsieur Albert whispered his translations to me as the doctor talked of Madame's face, her knees, the buttons on her dress, the rope burn under her jaw, the blood from her mouth, her broken nail. When he examined her she was cold and stiff and had been dead some twenty hours.

She was taken to the mortuary, he said, where he found a bruise on her cheek, scratches on her nose, loose front teeth. He opened her and removed her brain, lungs, heart, liver and kidneys. It was if he were telling a friend he had unlatched a grandfather clock to wind it. Mademoiselle Julie bowed her head when he was talking.

Her organs – they were all perfect.

He must be wrong. I heard her wheezing. Her skin was like tissue paper. She looked like a victim of the Siege.

He spoke of her throat and her windpipe and a broken bone in her neck.

It must have been done with very great violence, he said.

Very great.

He spoke of powerful hands, of boxers punching each other in the face, of German surgeons strangling living people almost to death to record the effects, of experiments he himself had done on the dead to prove you cannot break that exact same bone unless a person is alive. The lawyers fiddled with their wigs, and cleared their throats and rearranged their documents, and the judge passed his hand across his forehead and Julie looked at her black lace gloves. I glanced over at the jury – one was nodding and jerking, fighting sleep, another, arms folded, snored, but ten men were alert and listening.

And finally, the doctor hanged me.

'I hardly think one hand could grasp all the parts at once, so that the various injuries could be the result of a single sudden act. In my opinion it is utterly impossible for one single blow to have produced all those injuries.'

CHAPTER THIRTY

On the third and final day, Monsieur Dumas came into the court and announced that I had been a good and honest employee. He had allowed me to look after his young daughter and he had never seen any violence from me. It was not enough.

The opposing advocates gave speeches, but I had no idea what was in them because Monsieur Albert was not permitted to translate. I don't know why. While they spoke I played with my fingers as I used to in church with Iris. Counting them up and counting them down.

Then it was the turn of the judge. No whispers, no rustlings. No one moved. After five minutes, from the street, the rollicking whining notes of a hurdy-gurdy ground out, mocking. The judge stopped, exasperated, and sent a clerk out to silence it.

Eventually, the jury stood and filed out.

After half an hour they came back. I felt nothing, not even fear.

They took my chair away so I stood as each juryman's name was called out and answered to.

The foreman read slowly from a paper.

I knew what it was before Monsieur Albert started whispering his translation.

Guilty.

But Monsieur Albert was still whispering.

The jury, he said, recommended mercy because I had not planned to kill Madame Riel.

The judge nodded.

I thought the judge would say I was to go to prison but a clerk was arranging a black cap on top of his wig.

'Do you have anything to say why sentence of death should not be passed?'

I had no intention to kill, I said to Monsieur Albert, who lifted his chin and spoke the words for me. The judge nodded at him.

'You will be taken back to Newgate, and hanged there, and you will be buried inside the prison walls. May the Lord have mercy upon your soul.'

Then an official asked me: 'Are you pregnant?'

I glared at him.

'No,' said Monsieur Albert.

The matron touched my elbow and we went through the doors and back down into the depths.

Behind me was the sound of laughter and conversation as the crowd pressed to get out into the fresh air.

CHAPTER THIRTY-ONE

Sleep was my refuge. Eighteen, nineteen, twenty hours a day, drifting in and out, floating, drowning. I dreamt no dreams.

A rota of matrons sat with me to stop me doing the hangman's job for him. All day, people came. The chaplain of Newgate asking if I wanted a Catholic priest; matrons delivering meals, collecting my tin plate and removing my utensils; the Prison Governor to inform me of the date of my hanging.

On the third day, it was Mr Godfrey the solicitor.

The matron made me stand to receive him.

'How are you keeping, Mademoiselle Diblanc?' he said in his terrible French.

When I did not answer, he said, 'You will no doubt find some peace in your religion, Mademoiselle.'

Nothing could help me. I would be taken into the yard, escorted up the scaffold, hooded and hanged. After that, I would be cut down and cast away under the pavings in the yard where people would walk around in circles a metre above my bones.

I came from nothing. I would go back to nothing. Forgotten. Trampled on.

God had deserted me. He should have stood by me.

My mother and sister – where were they?

'Do not worry yourself, Mademoiselle Diblanc,' said the solicitor.

I laughed. 'How can you say that? That is ridiculous. If you were me, you would *worry*. I am not worrying for no reason. What a thing to say. I'm not stupid. I know what's coming.'

'*Diblanc*,' said the matron warningly.

She did not understand what I had said but she heard how I said it.

'There is nothing left for me. Everything has gone.'

'You may be wrong there, Mademoiselle Diblanc,' said Mr Godfrey. 'This matter is not over, by any means. I am hopeful...'

'And I am not. Please, do not encourage false expectations. Do not play with me.'

'We are working as hard as we can.'

'What good will that do?'

'It may make all the difference. Between your life and death.'

'My family has abandoned me.'

'There may be a reason for it. They could be unwell, Marguerite.'

'No, I have shamed them.'

'Time is short,' he said, as if I did not know this. 'I must go – there's much to do.'

The following morning, the matron came into the cell, a dress of spring yellow cambric draped over her arm.

She handed me a note that had been pinned to the collar:

The Condemned Prisoner Marguerite Diblanc, Newgate. From Mlle. JR.

It was her reward for me staying in the house to look after her mother, the dress that was in Julie's luggage when I saw her at Calais. Now it was the dress I would wear to the gallows.

The fabric at the cuffs was worn through, the threads of a seam had come loose at the shoulder. The matron insisted I mend it. She allowed me a needle and cotton and watched me closely to make sure I did not stab myself.

CHAPTER THIRTY-TWO

There was a rap on the cell door.

It was two weeks before my execution day, the first of July, but still I panicked.

Against the gloom of the corridor I saw one of the lady superintendents and behind her, the dark robes of the Abbé.

He is here to prepare me for death.

The Abbé asked me to sit on the bed while he took the stool. He faced me.

I looked at my hands in my lap.

'They should do it now, as soon as possible. I can't go on.'

'You must, Marguerite.'

'I am in despair.'

'It is a sin to despair. You have friends.'

I was grateful that he did not mention God. God, who had deserted me.

'Your solicitor has asked me to speak with you. He needs more information about you, for the plea to the Queen for mercy. He thinks I will be better at getting this than he will.'

He asked about my life in the village and my mother and father, and my brothers and sisters in the graveyard, and why I had gone to Verdun. I did not tell him about the Widow Larue, but I did say I had spent seven years with Madame Soulier and Iris. He wanted to know who I had worked for in Paris and what I had done there through the Siege and the Commune.

'You told me, when I first met you, that you left Paris because you couldn't make an honest living there. Was that true?'

'Yes, Father.'

Of course, I said nothing of Chantiers. After all, I had done nothing to deserve that punishment. Nor of Lieutenant Marçeron – Henriette would have to answer for that.

He asked me whether I had set fire to Paris in the fighting after the Commune fell.

'No! I'm not a criminal. I would not do that. Why do you ask me?'

'I have no doubt you did not, but I needed to hear it from you. When the newspapers first reported that Madame Riel had been found dead, they said you had been a *pétroleuse*, running about the city setting fire to the Tuileries and other buildings. I must be able to firmly refute these rumours.'

'I would never do that. I kept myself to myself at that time.'

I told him I did not understand why Madame died.

'I sinned, Father, I know this, but what I did... it shouldn't have killed her. Her heart must have been weak.'

'Leave that aside. You said it yourself – that you committed a mortal sin. You have confessed and repented.'

'I was deceived into going to that house. That man, Lord Lucan, he was there. At night.'

'I know this, Marguerite.'

'Madame Riel shouldn't have spoken to me in that way.'

'No, she should not. But evil language does not merit a killing.'

'It was more. There was more. She said nothing I did was good.'

'Again, it's not enough.'

'I only stayed because…'

And here I stopped. I wanted to say, because Mademoiselle Julie begged me to, because she promised me a dress, because she practised her plays with me, because I sewed on her buttons, she treated me as a person, she touched my arm with her soft hands, she was everything I was not, and because the trip to Highbury showed me something I did not like but loved at the same time, and did not want to let go of.

Instead, I said, 'Because I had nowhere else to go.'

'I need to be able to say that you are contrite, Marguerite, truly remorseful. That after you take your punishment you can one day be returned to live in the world. That you would be grateful for mercy and spend your time in a worthy way.'

'I am sorry, Father. I am.'

Yet I was not. I was not sorry for Madame Riel – only for what had happened, for myself and for Julie.

———

A week before my death day, I heard footsteps outside the door. It was the Governor and, behind him, Abbé Toursel and Mr Godfrey.

'Stand up, Marguerite,' said the Abbé, coming forward. 'The Governor has news. Do not be alarmed.'

The Governor started reading from a document, and at the end of each sentence the Abbé translated:

Her Majesty the Queen has granted you mercy.

Your sentence has been commuted to hard labour for life.

CHAPTER THIRTY-THREE

They moved me from Newgate to Millbank Prison, a stinking bastille by the river. Grit lined every crevice of its four storeys, and the whole place, inside and out, reeked of marshland and blocked drains. The rats were kings.

When I arrived, with five or six other women, I was herded into a room where the matrons cut off our hair, gave us rough uniforms and led us through a warren of corridors and staircases to a crooked gallery of cells. Our labour was to shred ship's ropes, which they called oakum, by hand. We were forbidden to speak to each other. This was supposed to make us truly remorseful.

Another prisoner showed me how to wind a length of rope onto an iron hook gripped between my knees and how to pare off the old tar with my nails and unroll the corkscrew strands, which fell in a heap to the floor and were collected at the end of the day in sacks. Day after day, except for fifteen minutes of prayers, our meal breaks and an hour of exercise when we paced slowly in twos around the yard at the centre of the gaol, I sat in my cell pulling apart the fibres, which cut my fingers and made black callouses on my palms. I didn't care. I relished the challenge I set myself to be the fastest and the best.

The women in Millbank were mostly mad or broken. They had sores, burns, scars and open wounds. They talked to themselves. They ranted and raved. They lacked teeth, eyes, fingers and peace of mind. They cried for their children. When they scratched faces, shoved and slapped, and threatened death – their own and others' – they were hauled away by male officers to the punishment cells.

The distant roars from the men's wings, the constant clash of doors, and the outbursts of weeping and screaming kept me awake at night, but it was the feelings of dread – the certainty that only by staying awake could I escape dying – that frightened me more. The lack of sleep pushed me into a kind of insanity. To stay in the world, at night, I mumbled the prayers I was taught as a child:

May Almighty God have mercy on us, and having forgiven us our sins, lead us to eternal life. Let it be so.

Over and over, until the words became mere sounds.

I comforted my soul by conjuring up my life with Madame Soulier. I was in her warm kitchen and Iris was playing with my fingers, but sometimes I wandered to the market in Verdun. From there I would be dragged to Berwick Street and the French greengrocer selling radishes and chicory and before I could stop myself, I would be back inside 13 Park Lane, with Eliza upstairs and Madame Riel lying dead on the flagstones like a bird brought down with a slingshot.

I resolved to keep myself to myself, to live within my head, without comradeship, not difficult in our regime of silence and with no ability to speak English. In that silence, the seeds of bitterness germinated. Icicles pierced my heart. I saw that my biggest mistake had been to allow myself to think that Julie and I had had a friendship. From now on, I would permit myself nothing of that kind. To take that path meant crossing quicksand.

After two months at Millbank, I was put to making linen shirts for male prisoners. A month later I moved to a quieter corridor and was allowed to sit in the doorway of my cell to sew. From time to time the matrons gave me the other women's botched work to fix. Most of them had never been taught to use a needle. They had not led that kind of life. I could not escape the idea that important men outside the prison were thinking up impossible tasks for prisoners, so that all they would ever do was fail at them.

Millbank was the fourth prison I had been in, if you count Paris, and it was not the worst. Even though it was a labyrinth whose twists and turns confused the warders – who chalked their routes on the walls so they could find their way back, like children dropping crumbs of bread in the woods – its routines could be relied on. The knowledge that every day would be the same, that at a quarter to six the bell would sound and I would be up and dressed, with my mattress and blanket rolled up at the foot of the iron bed, and waiting by the door of my cell for the matrons to unbolt it – that's what helped me survive. In the meals served at the same time every day, the tins from which we ate a pint of gruel, the prayers mumbled by a matron who could hardly read, and working under the light of the gas jets – in those endless unchanging timetables I found solace.

After I was trusted enough not to fight with the other women or tear my clothes in protest at life, I was sent to work in the laundry. Here the air was laced with carbolic and soap, fresh, almost, compared to our cells. Wearing wooden clogs because the floor was slick with water and with our skirts hitched up we starched the matrons' white caps and kerchiefs, rotated, rinsed and mangled the uniforms, theirs as well as ours, drowned the fleas and the bedbugs, soaked and boiled the coarse sheets, blankets and towels, and carted them to the drying horses and from there to the ironing tables. Every Friday afternoon we collected sacks of rags used by the women for their monthlies, left them in tubs of cold salted water and scrubbed them by hand.

Laundry can never be done alone – you always need someone to help wring or haul, to hang the sheets and fold the blankets – so we were allowed to speak in low murmurs if it was necessary for our work. It was hard labour indeed, requiring sweat and muscle, harder than sewing shirts or picking ropes apart, so our dinner tins included an extra hunk of bread and butter at breakfast, and a second ladle of soup and a cube of cheese with our supper.

My hands became red and sore, just as they had when I worked with Henriette at Madame Wilhelm's laundry. I tried not to think of my friend and how she had given me up to the police without a second thought.

If anything out of the ordinary happened to me during the day – a reprimand from the matrons, for instance – it was Madame Riel who entered my mind and refused to leave. At those times she was always Madame Riel alive, telling me I was fat and ugly and a whore from the streets, pinching the nape of my neck, standing by the pantry door and implying that I was a thief. Each time she squeezed through my defences, I would be flooded with anger, and then I would think of Mademoiselle Julie dancing in the kitchen and how she had looked at me at my trial, and then I would see her hand on the pantry door and my heart would be seized with a juddering sorrow.

One January morning, a matron came to my cell with an elderly male prison guard, who told me in cockney French that I would be leaving Millbank for a place called Woking Female Convict Prison. I must have smiled because he said quickly, 'Used to work the steamboats to Calais.'

The next morning, twenty of us were brought down to a forecourt between high walls of the wings of the prison where an omnibus stood, the horses' breath blowing white clouds in the chilly air. Despite the matrons' firm instruction not to speak during the journey, my companions' wonder at the sights proved too much and they exclaimed at the size of the roads and the crowds on the streets and the enormous width of the river. Confinement had miniaturised their memories.

At Waterloo Station, people stared as we huddled on the concourse. I would have done the same. A herd of shabby unfortunates shrouded in brown woollen capes, in the charge of two severe-faced female warders and a prison guard. It was an opportunity to pity poor wretches and feel satisfied that you didn't share their fate. I kept my head down. Only a few months earlier I had been in all the illustrated newspapers. At Millbank one of the matrons had gleefully pointed to a picture showing that Madame Tussaud had made me into a waxwork and put me in the Chamber of Horrors.

We boarded a third-class carriage and left London, chugging past frosty winter fields and damp spindly woods. Even at that desolate time of year, the sight of their decay, imbued with the promise of new life, brought me a sliver of hope. This new prison in the English countryside could not be worse than Millbank.

At Woking Station, two black vans drove us for five kilometres or so through farmland, orchards and gardens. We slowly climbed a long hill and when we got to the top, we stopped while our escorts waited for entry. A great iron gate swung wide and when we were in the courtyard we were decanted in front of the vast frontage of the prison halls, each four storeys high with serried rows of small windows.

Those who were not admitted directly to the infirmary were led into a building where we were issued with Woking uniforms. By then, I had completed my probationary period and reached the second class, so I was given a green serge dress and cape, which I wore with a white straw bonnet and a pair of black boots.

In the central hall, wire netting had been stretched over the lowest tier to catch those that jumped. We climbed an iron staircase up to a landing and each of us was directed through the narrow door of a cell.

High up, a barred window gave onto the outside. I stood on the bed and looked through. In the distance, on the other side of the far wall, I saw the tops of trees.

CHAPTER THIRTY-FOUR

Woking Female Convict Prison
24 December 1891
Twenty years after the trial of Marguerite Diblanc

The sky was a thick grey mattress and the rain came down in daggers. You wouldn't have known it was daytime. As Miss Legge escorted me across the central courtyard, behind us my fellow kitchen women were carting the empty milk pails and bread baskets back from the wards – thirty wooden clogs splashing through the puddles and 'Hurry on! Hurry on!' from the matron.

Miss Legge pushed open the door of the Governor's lodge and held it for me. I stamped my feet on the mat and at her nod unbuttoned my cloak, turned around and shook it off in the porch. I knew which hook to hang it on – I had done this many times before.

The women who cleaned the lodge had decorated it with fronds of evergreen. Apart from the chapel, where we were allowed a few sprays of holly, there was no other sign that it was Christmas.

'Hang up your bonnet too, I think, today,' she said. 'Or you'll catch your death.'

Normally we kept them on indoors but the straw was soaked through.

She directed me to sit on the bench next to her.

Somewhere above, rain drummed on a skylight. I tapped my feet on the mosaic floor until Miss Legge said: 'Stop that, Diblanc.' Later, she said, 'If your release was granted where would you go?' She was young and new to her job, with cheeks like freshly steamed buns. It was not for me to tell her that it was against the rules to converse with me like this.

'Home.'

'France?'

'Belgium, ma'am.'

'They won't permit that. If they let you out, you'll be on licence for life. You'll have to go somewhere they can keep an eye on you. In case you go wrong... and if you do, you'll have to come back in. Got any family?'

'My sister.'

'In Belgium?'

'Yes, ma'am.'

'She married?'

'Yes, ma'am.'

My eyes were hot; my forehead was burning. I was not ill but fiery with anticipation. I wanted to slide to the floor and cool my skin. I knew what the Governor would say, and yet there might still be a chance for me.

Miss Legge pulled a tract from her pocket and opened it on her lap.

She whispered to herself as she read and followed the lines with her finger.

After a few minutes she said, 'Do you believe in God and Jesus Christ Our Saviour?'

'Yes, ma'am.' I was not going to argue with her.

'You could do no better than to contemplate Christ. I mean really contemplate. He's the saviour of us all. Open your heart to Him. He loves and forgives everyone, even you.'

I didn't answer.

From the landing, the Governor's clerk called down: 'Miss Legge, please bring the prisoner up. The Governor is ready to see her now.'

The Governor himself opened the door to us.

I stood behind the line on the floor in front of his desk. Miss Legge was to my side.

'Marguerite Diblanc. Prisoner number Y120?' he said.

'Yes, sir.'

He glanced down at the papers in front of him.

'Your petition for release – I have had a reply from the Home Secretary.'

I worked in the kitchen. Week in, week out we made dinners of mutton or beef stew with onions and potatoes, soup on Saturday and cold pressed beef on Sundays. The quality was not high, but I knew how to trim it, and tenderise the meat and flavour it to the English taste. Breakfast was a hunk of bread and milky chocolate. Supper was gruel with molasses and more bread. The women who had spent time in workhouses told me they had never eaten as well as they had at Woking.

I was in charge of the cooking. Even the matrons deferred to me. It was me who decided when to peel the potatoes, how much salt should go in the stewpots, how many loaves to order from the bakehouse. When a new woman joined us, if I thought she showed potential, I taught her to weigh the onions, the flour and the beans and vegetables – slowly, patiently, side by side, in the same way that Madame Soulier had once taught me.

We were a team of nine in the kitchen. Everyone worked hard. We washed out the milk churns, swabbed the long table, blacked the ranges, cleaned four hundred dinner tins, wiped and sharpened the knives, rinsed sacks of potatoes, served the dinners and scrubbed the floor. The heat blasted out by the coppers, the stove and the steamers was overpowering, especially on hot summer days, but I would rather have been there than anywhere else in the prison.

If we kept our voices low, we were allowed to speak to each other. There was snappiness, of course, but if feelings boiled over the matrons stepped in and sent the transgressors off for a week or two of cleaning the blocks or sewing shirts for the men's hospital prison, a huge infirmary adjacent to our premises, where they kept the criminals who were terminally ill and feeble-minded.

Our day started at six and continued until half past five, with breaks of thirty minutes after breakfast and in the afternoon, and an hour after lunch was sent out. The prisoners took their meals in their cells, so the prison courtyard was criss-crossed with almost constant traffic – lines of women going between their work and their cell blocks. Meals punctuated our days.

Of all the enterprises in the prison – the orchard, the sewing room, the laundry, the fire service – the kitchen was the showpiece, of greatest interest to prison visitors. Everyone has an opinion on food and how to prepare it – *a good way to save money is this, a better way to make a gravy is that, that is disgusting, that is delicious, that is not worth the money.* We never knew the names of the fine gentlemen and ladies who watched us ladle soup or baste the meat or scrape out the enormous baking trays. We did not deserve an introduction.

I overheard them ask the Lady Superintendent out of the side of their mouths:

'I heard the Road Hill House murderess has been moved out. Is that true?'

'Which one is Mrs Maybrick?'

'Please point out to me the Park Lane Murderess.'

And I heard the Governor say: 'The story of Diblanc demonstrates that even the worst can lead useful lives.'

I was the worst. Why did he not say that about Mrs Maybrick? Why was she not the worst? She poisoned her husband. She planned his death. And why am I merely Diblanc and she Mrs?

I knew the answer to that: The world on the inside works much like the world on the outside.

These fancy people, who never so much as boiled an egg, peered at our ovens and opened our meat store. One whiskery old gentleman with the smell of cigars and brandy on him, who put me in mind of Lord Lucan, said, pointing to the griddle, 'And what is that?'

'A mutton chop,' said the matron.

'A mutton chop!'

The Governor looked toward the matron in alarm.

'For a very sick prisoner in our infirmary,' she said.

'We do not feed such vittles to the, erm, ordinary prisoners,' said the Governor, chin up.

'Even so, these are extraordinary delicacies for criminals,' said the gentleman. 'No wonder our courts are clogged, if convicts have the prospect of such luxury. It is not for me to tell you how to do your job, Governor, but the women have only themselves to blame for their situation. Whatever condition they now find themselves in is their own doing. I cannot accept that a convict deserves to live off the fat of our land. If she is ill, it is most likely to be because she has done something to make herself ill.'

At association time, Mrs Maybrick and I walked in circles together around the yard.

'Well, he was certainly a nasty man,' she said. *Nay-asty may-an*. She was from America and spoke through her nose, adding to her words, dragging them out so far that sometimes I could barely understand her. I had learned English from the cockneys, who sliced and stopped their words, and used their own argot for the most commonplace things.

Mrs Maybrick and I were starred prisoners, first-time offenders who had committed one, but only one, serious crime. A few of the starred were thieves of vast treasure who had led lives of crime but had been, in the end, nabbed, but most were infanticides who had committed their desperate act because they could see no other way. Mrs Maybrick and I, and poor sad Curtis, were the only true murderers.

The prison authorities regarded us, the starred, as the backbone of the prison. They could not run it without us. We were to be incarcerated for decades and for that reason were more likely to *knuckle down and make the best of it*, in the words of the Governor. He was not wrong. We were, in the main, well behaved – we did not spend our time in perpetual conflict with ourselves, each other and the prison authorities. The matrons trusted us, even me, not to explode if we were looked at the wrong way. We would just sigh and think, *I'm too tired for that, and I've seen it all before*. We were not hauled off to the punishment cells for destroying our bed clothes or smashing windows. When a starred prisoner was released, the matrons did not fold their arms, nod to each other and say *I give her three months before she's back* as they did with the others.

Mrs Maybrick was a complainer. The uniforms were itchy, the boots did not fit, the matrons were rude, she should not be made to walk around the courtyard alongside the *contaminated poor*, the ugly women, the defective women, the women who had never been able to escape the terrible lives they were born into. '*We* should be kept separate from them,' she said, as if I had once been like her and danced in frothy gowns at balls and married a rich old man and poisoned him a little bit every day when I got bored of his ways. '*They* are drinkers and sinners, Diblanc. And Lord Almighty, do they never cross their legs? There's no hope for them.'

I had heard that she had taken a lover, who had deserted her the minute there was suspicion about her husband's death. The story she told me – of dissipated Mr Maybrick, whom she was pushed into marrying when she was not even twenty – brought me hideous visions of Mademoiselle Julie and Lord Lucan, so I had a grain of sympathy for her, although I could never regard her as a friend. I did not believe in friendship. In prison, with nowhere to escape its consequences when it soured, friendship was a risk. Whenever she was sounding off about the other women I deliberately contradicted her, although she hardly noticed and ploughed on with her grievances. After a while, I grew tired of her and dropped hints to the matrons, who also despised her as a constant complainer, that she should be assigned to the scullery in the officers' mess. It worked.

On my first day of respite from her, she sought me out in the association yard.

'The work is so harsh over there, Diblanc, so harsh. Twenty-five covers, five meals a day. You have no idea. I will be writing to the Home Secretary.'

She begged me to put in a good word for her with the matrons and to request she be sent back to the main kitchen and, of course, I said I would and, of course, I did not.

Just as I had avoided friendships, I also evaded small talk, the gossip that wove in and out of prison life and bound us and divided us: who has the better boots, who has a thicker blanket, who had played a trick on the matrons, who had been sent to the punishment cells, who would be leaving next Friday. I had seen that in Chantiers – it was meaningless noise, a waste of energy.

Instead, I concentrated on my work in the kitchen, and in the evening, until the gas jets were turned off at eight o'clock, I sat in the doorway of my cell and knitted socks. I had read everything in the prison library from cover to cover many times: from *The Penny London Reader* to *Chambers' Miscellany, Stories for Summer Days and Winter Evenings, The Home Friend,* and the three French books.

It was not as if I lived completely without affection. I found it in the corners of life. In the trust of the matrons, in a kindly glance from the Governor, in the letters from my sister, Marie, who started writing to me five years after the trial. And in the greetings of the rougher women, who ribbed me when I did the breakfast rounds.

'Dye-Blank's here at last. What kept ya, Frenchie?' they would say, ignoring the efforts of the matron to impose silence. 'Oh, I shouldn't upset ya, should I – you might bang me with the saucepan.'

Their teases, so close to insults, were not darts of love but of tenderness tipped with vitriol. They made me smile.

What more could I want? I had my job, a visit to the prison library once a week and the guarded respect of the matrons. The years passed. Every six months I wrote my petition for an early release, pleading, until she died, that my mother needed me, that I would lead a good and upstanding life at home in Belgium – and every time I was refused.

This time, I thought the news might be different. I was coming up to twenty years. What good would it do anyone to keep me?

In the Governor's office, I held my wrist behind my back and stood as straight as I could. I looked down to check that my feet were still behind the line.

'Diblanc, your petition has been turned down,' said the Governor.

A white noise in my head.

'You need to reconsider how you write them. Your petitions, and I have read them all, will not succeed if you insist that you were not to blame for the murder of which you were found guilty.'

To make his point, he proceeded to read aloud my latest petition because he wanted me to hear it with the ears of the grand lawyers in London.

Your petitioner humbly begs for mercy.

She has done nineteen years out of a life sentence. She begs your Lordships to forgive her and grant her liberty. Please give her justice like you have done for others. She has seen other women being discharged after doing much worse crimes. But because she had no money to defend herself when she was tried, she has been kept in prison for a lifetime for a crime she committed in a moment of passion without premeditation and because she was provoked with taunts and false accusations.

'The judges will not have liked this, Diblanc. You are saying you did not get a fair trial.'

I had written that petition in the depths of winter. In over three months I had received no letters from my sister – I had not known that her husband was ill. I was bitter and some days I was in a pit of despair.

'You need to give them more,' said the Governor. 'Tell them about the day of your crime. What you did specifically and how you regret each and every wrong turn you took. Be honest. You have nothing to lose by it and everything to gain. Will you consider this for next time?'

I promised that I would. I could do nothing else.

'Put yourself in her shoes, the victim, and put yourself in the Home Secretary's shoes too, if you can. He has the final say-so.'

Miss Legge and I crossed the courtyard back to the kitchen. All the women knew where I had been and from my face knew the verdict. I took my place in front of the sink and set to work.

A few days later, Hart arrived.

CHAPTER THIRTY-FIVE

Every morning just before eight, we shuffled into the two chapels, Roman Catholic or Protestant, which had been built back-to-back in the centre of the prison. I always attended the Protestant service because the minister spoke in English, and because belting out even the most dreary of hymns took me beyond the prison walls. There was always release in singing, even if it was tuneless.

Sometimes the prisoners became overwhelmed and broke into weeping, which spread across the congregation like an infection. On occasion, before we reached the end of the refrain, the whole chapel, including a handful of the matrons, had tears streaming down their faces.

In those fragments of time, the fifteen minutes in chapel, when I was surrounded by coughing or snorting or whispering women, I could think privately. Alone in my cell, I was constantly observed or interrupted. Here, I was just one woman in a sea of many, unnoticed, and this gave me freedom, not to plan my spiritual improvement, as the minister suggested, but to contemplate my situation and what I could do about it.

Usually, in the days before I was eligible to write a new petition, I would compose the sentences in my head, so that they were ready to set down on the special blue form provided, and the matter could be completed as quickly as possible. However, I had promised the Governor I would consider a new way to write the petition. On the day I first saw Hart, as we all got to our feet for the Lord's Prayer, so deep was my mind occupied in puzzling out what I might write five months hence, I was not paying attention to my surroundings.

At the end of the service, I looked up and saw the back of her as she stood in the pew in front of me. She wore the lilac uniform of a prisoner of the first class, which meant she was a new arrival. At the nape of her neck a short curl of chestnut hair, the same shade as Mademoiselle Julie's, had escaped her linen cap. There was the familiar curve of her neck, the same way of holding her back straight with her head tilting a little to the side.

A hand closed over my heart.

She must have been about Julie's age the last time I saw her – twenty-five or twenty-six – and when she turned to look about her, glancing up to the rafters and over at the matron bashing at the organ, I saw her big brown eyes. She had all of Julie's full-cheeked prettiness.

The next morning she arrived in the kitchen in the custody of one of the junior matrons. A white star embroidered on the shoulder of her dress told me she was a first-time offender, like me, and that she was not a murderess. Mrs Maybrick, Curtis and I, and the infanticides, had red stars, the colour of blood, with an L for Life underneath. It spelled out that we had escaped the gallows.

Hart stood next to me as I taught her to clean the knives.

She said: 'Are you a cook on the outside?'

Are.

She means were.

'Yes. You?'

I was trying to be polite.

'Actress.' That was no surprise – the way she held herself: shoulders down, head up, as if she expected to be listened to. 'Smaller places, you know, music halls, public houses. Not plays. Entertainment, if you know what I mean, for the men.'

I didn't want to hear her story. Knowledge is a burden. But I also wanted her to confide in me.

I resolved to pick my steps carefully lest I trod on glass.

'Rub a small amount of emery powder along the blade like this,' I said.

'I shouldn't be here. In prison, I mean.'

'None of us should. We're all innocent.' I laughed, hoping to keep things light. 'A little less powder. That's right. Hold the sharp side away from you. We don't want to injure ourselves.'

I prayed she would not ask about what had brought me to this place. Even my reprieve from an ignominious death felt grubby.

'I was the one they all blamed for what happened,' she said. 'I stood there, you know, looking round that courtroom. They were all men, every single last one of them. How would they know how hard it is to be a woman in London and keep your head above water, eh? How would they know what it was to live on the edge, not knowing where your next meal was coming from? And I clocked a couple of them, lawyers and the like, you know, from my line of work. No one even mentioned his name, not once.'

'Who? Your husband?'

'No, no, that rat scarpered long ago. No, the gentleman who gave me a tenner for them, for the girls. *Him*. I didn't think it was a big deal. I did the same at their age. It's natural. You know what I'm saying, don't you? It didn't harm them.'

'You sold them, these girls?'

239

'No, no. They was willing and it's not like they didn't take the money when I gave it to them. I got a slice, that's all. They went to the police, or the police got a-hold of them, more likely. But it was only me what got done and ended up in here. Five years they gave me. He was never in the court at all. They never even used his name, just called him *the old gentleman* and acted like he was just doing what came naturally. Me, who did what he wanted and what them girls wanted – because they liked the money, believe me – it was me who was the villain.'

———————

The next morning, Hart was ahead of me in the line of women waiting for Mrs Hood to unlock the kitchen. She was whey-faced.

'They cut a woman down in my block last night,' she said as we sawed shins of beef at the long table. It was Curtis, who had the cell next to hers. She was a child-killer who'd strangled her son when her man abandoned her. Hart said she had sewn a noose from strips of bedsheet and threaded it through the grille in her window. 'She's in the infirmary. The matrons said she'd live. She'll have a very sore throat, though.' She laughed sourly.

'I heard them say it was all a pretence to get attention and go to the infirmary. Is that true? Looked serious to me. She was nearly dead when they carried her out.'

I have seen women tie ha'pennys to turn the wounds they made with stolen scissors into a septic mess. I have seen madness faked and real.

A few days before, Curtis had stood next to me in chapel, weeping.

'She's given me over,' she hiccuped out, as the rest of us sang 'O God Our Help in Ages Past'. She pushed a scrap of paper torn from a library book into my hand. I knew who it was intended for. She had pricked out the message with a pin. We are not allowed pencil and paper.

I will kill her who has taken you from me, I no longer care what happens.

I passed it to the next woman and so it went from hand to hand down the pew until it reached Burford.

When she first arrived at Woking, Curtis had been almost mute and spent every association time pacing alone or sitting on a bench staring at the floor. She had tried several times to end her life and with each one the goodwill of the matrons faded further. Then Burford, who was barely seventeen and gleaming with life, arrived and Curtis emerged from her casket of grief. Curtis had a job cleaning the staff quarters and she begged the matrons to let Burford work with her. Burford, in return, shone a light of adoration on her – until she swivelled to Seymour and after she was transferred to work with her new love in the infirmary, where fires roared in the grates and the women had the pickings of the invalids' leftovers, Curtis descended into despair.

'It's so awful here,' said Hart to me. 'It will finish me off. Five years. I'm just about ready to give up, like whatshername last night. Do you... did you ever think about it? A quick exit, I mean.'

'No.'

I did not want to revisit those times in the dungeon at Paris.

I felt obliged to ask. 'Do you, Hart?'

'It comes on me at night. Ever since I was arrested.' She turned towards me, her eyes bright. 'I wish I had your strength, Diblanc. I'm so feeble. Look at me. I'm full of bravado, me – not like you. You just get on with it. I crumple at the first... You have so much courage. You don't let things tear you down.'

I wondered what she wanted of me.

'You remind me of my friend Florence, on the outside. She's like you. Nothing bothers her. And always so loyal to me. I couldn't have a more loyal companion. She'd have fought lions for me if I'd asked her to.'

Protection. Was that what she wanted?

Mrs Hood looked over at us with an expression that said, *Stop chatting and get on with your work.*

At association time, as we circulated the yard, Hart slid her arm around my waist under my cloak and I felt the weight of her head on my shoulder. I wanted to give in to it.

'Hart, you mustn't do that. It is not allowed. Stand up straight. The matrons, they will mark your record.'

'I need looking after. I need you to care for me, Diblanc. I never had a mother and I'm lonely in here.'

'They will mark me down too. If there are marks on my record, it will delay my release.'

She straightened herself.

'Oh, I would not want to do that, Lord help me.'

There was ice in her voice.

'You must work hard, Hart, otherwise you'll sink. It'll keep your mind busy. That is how I survived.'

It was nearly time to start the afternoon shift.

'Are you sorry? For what you did.'

Her question was so abrupt that at first I thought she was berating me for hurting her feelings.

'It wasn't murder. She only had herself to blame, my Madame. She was a wicked woman.'

'I expect you were betrayed by people you thought you could trust. Diblanc, you must have suffered.'

'No one at my trial told the truth about her and how she abused me.'

'No respect,' she said.

'No one asked me about what I had been through, how every day was worse than the last.'

I had an urge to tell her about Verdun and Madame Soulier, and the Siege and the prison at Chantiers, and even about Marçeron and Henriette, but I did not.

'You are a good person, Diblanc. It's obvious.'

She laid a hand on my arm.

Why did I feel she was insincere?

I said: 'I just think I was not treated in a fair way.'

'I know what you mean! It's the same for me,' she said. 'That man, the rich one I told you about, the old gentleman who gave me money for the girls – he's swanning around as free as you like. Gets my goat. I wish I'd got him like you got your Madame.'

'It wasn't like that. You mustn't think it was like that.'

She tilted her head to one side.

'You don't seem like the kind of person who should be in here,' she said. 'I know some of the girls are well brought up and from good families and all' – she meant the infanticides – 'but you – so intelligent... and being foreign... and well-mannered... I was half expecting you to say you never done what you done and was innocent.'

'No, I did it, and I confessed. But that house...'

'Was it a brothel?'

'No – not really, but... something happened to me before I ever went there...' I stopped.

'But you don't have the words for it? You can tell me. I look young but I've seen everything.'

'I can't speak of it.'

'Marguerite, I have so many stories like that, so many that you would never be able to shut me up.'

'It wasn't like that.'

'That husband of mine, he was the one who put me out to work after he forced me to... you know. Anyway, I would say every woman in here, including the matrons, has a story. We all have to fend them off, all the time.'

Miss Legge was ringing the bell.

'Hurry up, ladies! Form your lines. Times up.'

CHAPTER THIRTY-SIX

Every day we were searched for implements that we might use to harm ourselves or others. Outside our cells, we were made to stand in front of the matron and turn out our pockets. Because they trusted me, the matrons would rarely take more than a quick glance around my cell and a flutter through my library book.

'Right you are, Diblanc,' the matron would say, not wanting to test her knees by peering under the bed frame. None of them ever discovered my trove of treasures: a butter knife slid between the bricks where the mortar had dropped out, a matron's cuff button in the window recess, a contraband scrap of paper on which Hart had pricked out with a pin *Thank you for your friendship.*

Three months after she arrived at Woking I was seconded to the kitchen of the officers' mess, which was in a corner of the prison precinct, reached across a lawn. I was to cover for the sickness of a matron who normally oversaw the four prisoners working there. 'There's none of us staff who know how to cook like you, Diblanc,' said Mrs Hood, as she walked me over the grass to the squat red-brick building. 'And we don't want to disappoint the Governor, do we?'

The mess kitchen was a cramped galley; its shelves overflowing with the bits and pieces most people had at home – mixing bowls, chopping boards, tea sets, copper saucepans, lemon graters and dish-covers – quite unlike the crude equipment we had in the main kitchen. There was barely enough space for two women to work at the same time, let alone three. The fourth, Mrs Maybrick, was stationed in the scullery, washing and drying the sets under a cold-water tap, and complaining.

For six days, I turned out perfect omelettes, trays of steaming chicken pie, herb-filled broths and roast joints of pork and beef, cherry pies and apple puddings.

'We'll have to get you back for special occasions, Diblanc,' said the Governor, who had come into the kitchen especially to praise me.

On the Sunday morning, with the officers' luncheon in the oven, the potatoes parboiled, the pickled vegetables in jars on the counter ready to heat up, we were escorted to the chapel. When we were halfway across the lawn, Mrs Maybrick whispered, 'Have you heard?'

I turned my head.

'About Hart.'

'No.'

A pulse in my kidneys.

'Transferred to Fulham. Gone.'

We were soon shuffling into the pews. My insides trembled. I was once more marooned. I looked about for her. Perhaps Mrs Maybrick was lying or mistaken.

We sang 'How Firm a Foundation' and the minister started speaking. 'The commission of sin has led you here... lost sight of virtue... deceived your own hearts... rushed into sin... brought you suffering... fears of Hell... you must humble yourselves... that he may pardon you...'

I was hot and sweating and feared I would vomit.

'Diblanc, keep still,' the matron at the end of the pew whispered to me.

Absurde! Stupide! I heard myself muttering out loud.

She cannot leave me!

I stood up.

Mrs Maybrick said, 'Shhh, or they'll come for you.'

I squeezed past the women.

I had to be outside.

Move, move, move!

Hands grabbed me and tried to shove me back to the pew.

Diblanc, calm down.

Diblanc, this will not do.

Fetch Mrs Hood. Fetch Mrs Price.

I didn't hear them. I didn't see them.

I scratched at my neck. I tore off my bonnet.

I slapped, I struggled, I hit.

I was hauled out by my clothes.

'Punishment cell!' I heard behind me. 'I never would have thought Diblanc would do this.'

I woke surrounded by high black walls. Daylight bled in through the perforated steel fixed to the window. My bed was a plank.

'Did you sleep?'

It was the Governor.

'No, sir. Not much. There's something wrong with my heart. It keeps rushing and stopping. I feel like I might die.'

I sat up and staggered to stand, as we must in his presence.

'Diblanc, I have this morning received a letter,' he said. 'I think you should sit down.'

He waited.

'A letter from Paris, from a certain Madame de Saint-Germain.'

I knew that name.

'Yes, sir.'

Julie.

'She has asked for permission to visit you.'

CHAPTER THIRTY-SEVEN

'Everyone is allowed one breakdown, Diblanc, even the starred prisoners,' said the Governor. 'In a way, it's strange that you have never had one before.'

He could have put me on cleaning duty but he sent me back to the kitchen as if nothing had happened. The women did not speak of it and I suspected that Mrs Hood had ordered them not to.

About two weeks later, Mrs Hood walked me across the courtyard and into the lobby of the visitors' block. I had never been inside it before. The last visit I had was over eighteen years before, from Abbé Toursel, who had made the journey because the newspapers falsely reported that I had died by my own hand. We had been allowed to sit together in the Catholic chapel, with a matron nearby. He had spoken of forgiveness and told me that he was retiring to France and this was the last time we would meet.

Mrs Hood and I entered one of the narrow suites of the block.

'Sit there, Diblanc,' she said, pointing to a chair facing a large wire grille set in the wall.

I peered through the grille and saw, a yard or two beyond, a second wall in which was set another grille. Mrs Hood took her seat in the chamber between the two walls. Anything that was said by me or by the visitor through the grille on the other side would pass by her.

Julie has come to forgive me.

No, she has not.

She will tell the Governor I deserve to go back to Belgium to live with my sister.

No, she will not.

She will accuse me.

Why has she come?

What does she want from me?

I heard a door open on the other side. The matron accompanying Julie was instructing her on where to sit.

From my seat, I made out a maroon cape, a bonnet, a pale face, still beautiful.

Mrs Hood in her in-between space nodded at me and then at Mademoiselle Julie.

'Diblanc, you must not speak of prison matters, nor of your treatment within the prison, nor anything that happens in here. And you must speak at all times in English.' She turned to Mademoiselle Julie. 'You may proceed.'

'Marguerite Diblanc,' said Mademoiselle Julie.

'Mademoiselle Julie.'

'You must address me as Madame de Saint-Germain,' she said, raising her voice so that I would be sure to hear her. She was on her guard.

Her English flowed, unhurried but not halting. She did not have to search for words as I sometimes did. I learned English haphazardly from the other women, whose thoughts, fears and furies piled up in their heads and gushed out like waterfalls.

'You're probably wondering why I'm here. There are some things that I need to say to you and some things I need to ask you. Matters I can't express in a letter... I have thought often about you, Marguerite. I have come from Paris to see you.'

'Yes, Mademoi– Madame de Saint-Germain. I am the same, about you. I think about you.'

'I have come here to speak to you about that day.'

I closed my eyes. This is what I feared.

She wants to punish me.

She must hate me still.

'I am not looking for reconciliation. I am not intending to forgive you. I know that is my Christian duty, but I am not willing to do so. First, I want to start by telling you how the loss of my mother has affected me. I will tell you this because you cannot know it and you *should* know it.'

She waited for my acknowledgement.

'Yes, Madame.'

'I'll say straight away that what you did destroyed my life and my career. Utterly.'

She hates me, but I knew she would.

'I was on the point of a good future, a very good future, on the stage. Monsieur Le Directeur was about to promote me to better parts. You took everything from me. I have done almost nothing on the stage since. At first no one would employ me because they said ghouls would come to the theatre to stare at me and not to watch the plays, and I was shunned, as if I were tainted. I don't say this to make you feel guilty, because I don't care about what you feel, but as the perpetrator of the act you should know the consequences of what you did.'

She is lying. She wants only to add new layers to my guilt. She is her mother's daughter.

'Yes, Madame de Saint-Germain. I understand.'

'I have a different life now. I am married and have a son.'

'I am very happy to hear, Mademoi– Madame de Saint-Germain, about your family. I... I did not mean to hurt you or ruin your–'

'I know this and I am not interested in your excuses,' she said. I thought I could hear her sighing. 'I need to tell you something else. After your trial, I fell into a dark place, an indescribable misery. The worst was not when I came home and...'

Her hand on the pantry door.

'And it was not when the police were tracking you down in Paris and we were all waiting for your extradition, nor even having to go to your trial and stand up in public and speak of personal matters.'

I closed my eyes.

Lucan. The banknotes. The jewels.

'And it wasn't even having our circumstances exposed to the public, or people we did not know talking about us, printing lies. All of that was not the worst. It was afterwards, when everything was over and I had to live my life, when I had to go about my business in Paris and all the time, inside I was saying to myself, "I am not like other people. My mother was murdered and her body was mistreated, and I found her... I found her body myself," and at the same time I was asking for a leg of mutton or a string of onions. Have you ever thought about what that would be like?'

'No, Madame. I'm sorry, Madame.'

Was that true? Did those things make her different to everyone else? The National Guards' bodies stacked up like fish at the market, the man shot in front of us by soldiers on the march to Chantiers, and baby Edith in her winding strips made of my petticoat – those deaths ruined our lives too. Each of us had our own loss and grief – it is what made us all the same.

I was being foolish, though. If it had not been for me, she would not have suffered in the way she did.

'But I also need to hear from you, Marguerite. I need you to tell me why, otherwise I will feel this pain until I die. I don't want the answers you gave the magistrate in Paris or the excuses you gave your lawyers. I want to hear the truth from you.'

'It was not a robbery.'

'No.'

'I could have robbed you and your mother at any time. I could have stolen the jewels on a night when your mother stayed late at the theatre and then taken the morning train to Paris. But I didn't.'

'I know that. You don't need to tell me. I don't have time to go over old ground. And I know she, Maman, could be... difficult. I think I said so at the time. I know all this but the story you gave cannot be the whole truth – so tell me what it was.'

I could think of nothing to say.

'There was something wrong with you when you were with us. From the time I first met you, I saw it. You were jumpy, nervy, touchy. You reacted to everything. As if you were looking over your shoulder, as if you were already a criminal.'

That was not how it was. When she arrived at No. 13, I was clear in my mind that I was ready to go to Madame Evans. It was she who was on tenterhooks, she who argued constantly with her mother, she who came down to the kitchen for respite from the whirlwinds upstairs.

'When you were away in Paris, Mademoiselle... I mean, Madame de Saint-Germain... she, your maman, was acting like a madwoman. She had set a fire in the back yard and she had broken into my box. So when she said I was a...'

But I couldn't repeat Madame's words. Mrs Hood would have objected and the visit would have been terminated.

'No, Marguerite. This is not what I am here for.'

I had angered her.

She had come all this way for something I could not give her.

'I know all this, but I also know you, or thought I did. What made you so full of fury that you would do such a thing? Put your hands around her throat? Strike her dead?'

Should I tell Madame de Saint-Germain about the stone I carried in my heart after she told me, told me so coldly, that I was sacked? And the feeling I had when I heard the cab draw up and Lucan's cane on the stairs? These were not matters for my next petition, but they must be what Julie was seeking.

'Madame Riel...'

'No, it was not my mother, Marguerite. She did not make you do what you did. I need to know what it was.'

'Do you really want to know what my life was like?' I was speaking loudly, on the verge of shouting. 'Is that it? You want me to tell you about scratching a living in Paris, about my fear of being cast onto the streets, of having to line up in... what was it called... Mount Street, for the workhouse? Do you want to know about the bombs falling in Paris, about babies starving? What does that do to a person, Madame? It destroys them. Is this what you have come for? You, in your beautiful gowns, you have no idea what it was like to be me.'

Mrs Hood turned her head and said, 'Diblanc, moderate your language, or I will call an end to the interview.'

My heart was pounding in my chest. A surge of hatred for the old Julie, the Julie in the yellow wrapper who had pretended to be my friend, and for the Julie in court who cut and trimmed so carefully around the truth, and for this new Julie, who had come to demand I speak of matters that I had buried.

'Marguerite, I can see that I have confronted you with no warning, and I am sorry for that. I have asked too much of you. Perhaps you could consider my question away from here and the answer will be easier to find. You can write to me through the Governor. But Maman... I know she could be awful. Not just to you but to Eliza too, and the servants we had before you. I know this.'

'And she was horrible to you too.'

It felt brave to say it.

'But not always. She could be kind and generous and sweet when life was good. She fought like a tiger for me, she fought the Riels, who hated her, she fought for my education at the Conservatory but... well, things, certain things, matters to do with money, made her anxious and if they did not go the way she wanted she saw only catastrophe ahead. It caused her to make poor decisions and say things that she shouldn't say. I do think she was not well in her mind. She panicked easily and that made her sharp with people.'

She asks me to scratch at my scabs but bandages up her own.

Then, abruptly, she said: 'Why did you move her?'

We were back inside No. 13.

'So Eliza would not find her. I thought she might open the cellar door to get coal for your mother's room. And also that I should not have put her in such a dirty place. I did not mean to hurt her body.'

'But you put a rope around her neck.'

'It was to pull her up the stairs.'

'It was around her neck, Marguerite.'

I bit my lip and looked down at my hands.

To stage this tableau was, of course, the true reason I moved Madame Riel to the pantry. No one kills themselves folded over in a coal cellar, but a person might crawl away miserably like a dying cat to die in the confines of a cupboard under the stairs.

'They were right... when they said I wanted it to look like suicide.' I could not look over at her. 'I thought it would not be so sinful to do that because she was already gone and would never know. I didn't remember doing it but I must have done so. Nobody else could have done that. I am truly repentant, Madame.'

'And then you took the money.'

'Because I needed to get away and go to Paris.'

'She didn't deserve it.'

'No. Nobody deserves it.'

'I spent a long time being angry with her, after she died, for pushing you so hard, but you must understand that she was not a monster.'

She wiped away tears.

'She had no childhood. She had nothing, Marguerite. She was abandoned by her mother and brought up by the Sisters, who taught her millinery. She wanted me to have everything that she did not have and she thought the important parts of life could be bought. In Paris, in her atelier, she was not like she was in London. I want you to know this. You should have seen her. She tried hard to make herself into a new person in London but it was as if she was only fragments of herself. In London she had no purpose. She put everything into me, and sometimes forgot that we were separate people, and because she was so harsh on herself, she was harsh on me.'

I thought of Hart and her callousness towards those young girls. They were goods for sale, like Julie had been. She forgot to see them as people.

'The Governor has told me that you are one of his best prisoners.'

'I try. That is all.'

He has not told her about my breakdown in the chapel.

'What work do you do?'

I hesitated.

'I am a cook. In the kitchen. The chef.'

She laughed.

'I have learned a lot here,' I said. 'That people are the same everywhere and want the same things: respect and safety. They don't always know the best way to get them.'

'What do you mean?'

'They want to know they're doing a good job and they want other people to see it too.'

'They want appreciation, you mean.'

'Yes, exactly, Madame.'

'Have you found it, in this place?'

'Yes, Madame, I think I have.'

'Three more minutes,' said Mrs Hood. 'Please begin to say your farewells.'

'Inside me, I know what I did. I did a terrible thing to your mother. I did a terrible thing to you. I am truly sorry, but there is nothing I can do to change what I did. I can only try to live a better life, even in here. I am helping people. In a small way. I blamed your mother for everything that was wrong. If I myself had been more well, in my head, it wouldn't have happened.'

She waited for me to continue.

'I was frightened. During the Siege, during the Commune and after... I tried not to be...'

'Please now say your farewells,' said Mrs Hood.

Julie whispered something I did not hear. I cupped my ear.

'I think she saw some of herself in you,' said Julie quietly. 'I think that is why she bullied you. Worse than your predecessors.'

I am nothing like her. This cannot be so.

'She...'

Mrs Hood rose from her chair.

'She was always an outsider.'

We were out of time.

'Please conclude now,' said Mrs Hood. 'Diblanc, stand up.' She turned to Julie. 'Thank you, Madame, your visit has ended.'

'Marguerite, consider what I say. There is more to this.'

That night I didn't sleep.

Her words bashed at the sides of my head: *She saw herself in you.*

CHAPTER THIRTY-EIGHT

'Here it is, Diblanc, let's hope it's the very last one,' said the Lady Superintendent. She held up the special blue printed form we write our petitions on. 'Sit at the matron's table. It'll help you concentrate.' She had laid out the blotter and the pen and ink. 'If you can't spell a word… well, I'm sure Miss Legge will be happy to help, but I can't guarantee she'll know the answer.'

The Superintendent handed me a scrap of paper on which she had written out the two sentences that should always begin a plea:

Your petitioner humbly begs you for mercy. She has completed so-and-so many years and such-and-such many months out of a life sentence and begs Their Lordships to forgive her.

'The rest must be your own words,' she said unnecessarily.

At first, my hand was shaky but as I wrote my handwriting improved. No blotches, no smears. If my schoolteacher, Mademoiselle Lambert, had seen my looping Ys and my fine capital Ts she would have squeezed my shoulders.

She is very sorry for the crime she committed which was done in a moment of passion without premeditation.

I must write of myself as if I am not myself.

She did this, she did that. She is not the woman you once judged her to be.

One of the kitchen women told me that a new law permitted prisoners to stand in the witness box and tell their side of the story to the jury. If the jury had heard what happened from my own lips, they would not have found me guilty of murder but of manslaughter. Here was my chance to set it down. So even if Their Lordships kept me in prison for ever it would be in a record somewhere. Someone would read it and know.

I told them of Julie going to Paris and leaving me with her mother, and how I could have robbed the house and fled at any time if I had wanted to but didn't. After murder, robbery was the worst crime so it was important to make this clear.

It was the injustice of Madame's insults, I said, that made me lose my control and strike the fatal blow. Then there was the dreadful journey around the house, hiding Madame Riel's body. Every word I set down caused me to bite my lip and look away. I said nothing about placing the rope around her neck.

I included something I had never before mentioned, that Madame Antoine tricked me into working in the house, how it was only to help Miss Riel that I stayed after being sacked and she had promised me a dress in recognition of this.

I had a good character, I wrote, and Madame Soulier had had no complaints about me.

I covered two whole pages, four times as much as all my previous petitions.

Was I truthful?

Yes.

Did I tell the whole truth?

No.

CHAPTER THIRTY-NINE

'Now, the formal bit, Diblanc. Are you ready?'

The Governor picked up a paper, stood and read it out: 'The prisoner, Y120, Marguerite Diblanc, is to be informed that the Secretary of State has decided to grant her discharge from prison when she has completed twenty years and eight months of her sentence, conditional upon her conduct.'

'When do I leave, sir?'

'On Friday the third of February. For now, you must carry on as if nothing has happened.'

'Where will I go, sir?'

'Mrs Meredith's Discharged Female Convict Aid Society, who run a laundry, say they will take you for their kitchen. You will lodge nearby and a police officer will check on you every week. I have every confidence that you will do well.'

'Will I be allowed to return to Belgium?'

'That is not my decision, Diblanc. My advice is to wait a year or so before you make an application.'

On the last day in the kitchen, at the end of the shift, the women gathered round to say goodbye and several of the matrons came to wish me well.

I woke at half past five. A matron brought me a cardboard box containing my belongings. In it, tied with string, was the hair that had been cut from me at Millbank, as well as the primrose yellow dress that Mademoiselle Julie had sent for my hanging. I donated it to the prison stores. I folded up my prison uniform and put on the navy winter suit, white blouse and bonnet that my sister had sent from Belgium.

CHAPTER FORTY

For two years, I lived with Mrs Brown, a widow, and her numerous unmarried sons and daughters, plus nieces, nephews and grandchildren, and sometimes also a nurse child, all of us crammed into a small terraced cottage in a side street off the Clapham Road. Every morning at half past six except for Sundays, I walked the three hundred metres to the steam laundry, where I worked in the kitchen serving boiled beef, mutton pies and brisket for a hundred laundrywomen. I knew some of them from Woking, and recognised a couple more, the older ones, from my Millbank days. There were plenty of infanticides but as far as I knew I was the only murderess on the premises.

Every Saturday afternoon, a constable from the local police office called on me at my lodgings to check that I was abiding by the terms of my release. At first, I was embarrassed but Mrs Brown told me that she remembered my crime from reading about it in the newspapers and was not troubled by the weekly visits from the police.

'You've paid your dues, Margaret,' she said, 'and I can see

you're no bother. Any that gives you argy-bargy about it, send them my way. I'll set them straight.'

No one ever did. By then, I had started to call myself Margaret Blake and had concocted a story about how I was the French widow of a British sailor who had died at sea decades earlier, but I never had to use it. No one was particularly interested in me. I was merely a poor old foreign woman working to keep body and soul together.

The work in the laundry kitchen was not hard, certainly nothing I couldn't manage after the years at Woking. Mrs Meredith, a kind woman who ran the Society, would come in to see me from time to time, and occasionally I sat in on the daily prayers led by her volunteer ladies but usually I had a perfect excuse not to – I was too busy getting the lunch ready.

Was I happy? The question never occurred to me. I was lonely but that was to be expected. At times I yearned for the camaraderie of Woking, for although I did not make friends in all the years I was incarcerated there – except for Hart, that is – there were times, such as when we all wept in the chapel, that we were bonded into one.

With the constant comings and goings of Mrs Brown's brood, the house was as busy as a railway station. It was not chaotic – Mrs Brown insisted on keeping what she called a decent house. On Sundays the entire family went to St Stephen's for the morning service while I took my walk.

I walked anywhere and everywhere, in all weathers, to Norwood, Richmond, the Tower of London, along the embankments, up to Highgate. Occasionally, if I had enough in my purse, I took an underground train or an omnibus. Every week was the same. Work, home, work, home, and Sundays, walking. My sister wrote to say that she and her husband would be happy to come to see me, but I made sure never to pin down a date. I turned down their offers to write to the Belgian Embassy on my behalf.

What drew me back to Soho? It was not choice but an opportunity. Mrs Meredith had suggested that I was ready to move on from the laundry and join what she called *real life*. I tried to ignore her advice, because it felt so much like rejection, but a month later she appeared in the kitchen and told me that one of the laundry's sponsors, a reverend gentleman, knew of a place for a cook in an industrial school for girls and that he had arranged an interview at nine o'clock the next morning.

The matron in charge showed me around and questioned me about my understanding of nutrition and my attitude to girls who might be tempted by an easy life. I did not correct her and say that from what I had observed there was nothing easy about that kind of life. Mercifully, she did not ask about my own past or about my opinions on religion and at the end of the visit she said, 'So we can expect you on the first of the month. Naturally, I will write to Mrs Meredith,' as if I had no voice in the matter.

I walked back down Charing Cross Road and stopped at Cranbourn Street, where Henriette had lived with Monsieur Miray. To my surprise, I started to weep. Great tides of sobs welled up in me, as if I was standing at a grave.

I was not ready to return to the laundry to continue my shift – it would harm nobody if I took an extra hour for myself – so I walked through Leicester Square to the French Church. It had not changed. The confession boxes, the pews, the portraits of past abbés on the walls were all the same. Abbé Toursel had been added – he had died about ten years earlier.

The grief that had overwhelmed me in Cranbourn Street had not subsided but settled around my heart. It was not a heaviness, more a new clarity. I knew what I must do.

CHAPTER FORTY-ONE

Sunday 26 May 1895
St John the Baptist Industrial School,
Manette Street,
London W

Dear Madame de Saint-Germain,

You will be surprised to hear from me and probably a little alarmed. Please do not be. A clerk at the Embassy of Belgium in London sent this letter on my behalf via your husband's manager. I have no knowledge of your address and have no wish to. I will not write to you again unless invited.

It is more than two years since your visit to me at Woking. A few weeks afterwards, I was released on licence, and I am now living and working in London.

I want to start by saying I am sorry that I was not able to give you the explanation you were seeking when you came to see me. It was only later that I properly understood what you were asking of me. For years, I could not shake off the feeling that a great wrong had been done to me by your mother, and this clouded my thinking. I lived my sentence blaming her.

You were right when you guessed that there were other reasons for what happened.

Those reasons were long-hidden, even from myself. They concerned events that I swore I would never speak of. The time to break that vow has come. It is painful to think of them – I am sure you will understand when I say I must overcome feelings of dread and fear when I set them down in ink and paper.

Although I did not tell you much about it when I was at No. 13, you will remember from what was said at my trial that I was in Paris during the Siege and that I remained there during the Commune. When you came to Woking, with the matron listening, I could not say more about what happened to me after the end of the Commune. I did not then, nor even so many years later, fully appreciate the effect it had on me.

You will have read newspaper reports about those weeks in Paris, and I have no doubt that you knew others in the city who have told their stories. I can only speak of my own experience when I say that the Commune, whatever its faults, gave me the first glimmer of hope and happiness since I arrived in Paris. We who lived towards the bottom of the pile felt that at last there was some justice in our lives and that our welfare was something to be considered.

We basked, knowing full well that a storm would come. On the day it ended, which was a warm Sunday in May, my friend Victoire and I were sitting under the cherry trees in the Tuileries Gardens at a free outdoor concert. Madame de Saint-Germain, if you had been there, with the afternoon sun glinting off the windows of the palace and the gentle breeze brushing you... For humble people like us to sit next to ladies and gentlemen in their fine clothes as if we were of equal worth was like heaven.

And the entertainment! You would probably think nothing of it but I had never seen anything like it: real opera singers and a proper orchestra – it was a dream. Like all dreams, it had to end. When the concert was over, just as we were getting up to leave, the ground beneath us started to shake and people were shouting. Shells were landing metres away in the Place de la Concorde. At that moment we knew the dream was over. The crowd scattered and Victoire and I ran towards her place in the Rue Saint-Denis and then we heard that the government troops were moving through the city from the west and that we'd best stay off the streets. Victoire's husband, Jacques, refused to allow me into their apartment so I decided to head north and take shelter with an old widow woman I knew.

I heard soldiers behind me and hid in an alcove. They were going from house to house pulling men out into the street and shooting them. Later, near the Boulevard Haussmann, I walked past a huge pile of corpses. As night fell, I even tried to talk to a dead woman who was sitting on the bottom stair of a house. And when it was dark, the bodies lay in black mounds in the middle of the road. A cart went over one, and I heard the driver say, 'Bah! Oh well, it won't do him any harm now.'

That night, the widow and I climbed to the attic of her building and went out onto the roof. The whole city was alight. The air was full of smoke and fiery embers. Every so often, there was a crack of guns, and below in the streets the sound of soldiers' boots on the cobbles. The buildings trembled as bombs landed and in the distance cannon pounded. It was just as terrifying as the bombardments of the Prussians, but this time it was the government trying to kill its own people.

At dawn, I was itching to leave. I had a strong desire to return to my family in Belgium. Paris had been a disaster from the beginning and now it was the end. I knew if I stayed I would be poor, homeless and hungry for ever. I would have to take a path I had seen other women take, just to be able to eat. I'm sure that I don't have to spell out what I mean.

The streets were full of upside-down furniture and carts and the corpses of horses, and where there had once been barricades, cobblestones were scattered across the thoroughfare like dice. In amongst this terrible bric-à-brac were the bodies of National Guards, their faces bloodied, arms and legs at strange angles, their mouths open, and of women, their skirts up, and the children... Madame, I am glad for your sake you were not there to see it.

Eventually, by hiding in nooks and darting down alleys, I got as far as Clignancourt. I heard rifle fire and dipped into the doorway of a café. Government troops in the upper floors of buildings either side of the barricades were picking off the defenders. There were more government soldiers coming up behind me so I tried the handle of the café. The door opened and I took shelter inside. The staff had fled. For hours, I cowered in the basement, while trying to block out the screams and cries from above, until about five o'clock in the afternoon when I crept back up to the pavement. When I emerged, I saw the barricade was rubble and all the defenders dead or disappeared.

I had gone only a few metres up the street when I was seized from both sides and thrown to the ground. My head smacked the kerb. My attackers, who were soldiers, beat me when I tried to tell them I was just an ordinary woman who was trying to get home. One said: 'We should do her.' The other said he couldn't be bothered and wanted a drink. They shoved me along the street until we got to a small square almost entirely filled with captured National Guards, and I was pushed into a corner with a crowd of women and street boys.

I tell you this, Madame de Saint-Germain, not so that you will pity me, for many went through much worse than I did, but only so that you understand what led to some of the things that happened later.

When the captives numbered a few hundred, the soldiers lined us up in rows of eight and ordered us to walk through the city, the women and boys first and the men behind. At some point, I can't remember where exactly, a young man was hauled out of the line and accused of being a certain Communard politician, I forget who, which he loudly denied. They shot him and left his body in the road. Plenty of others died on the way.

We walked and walked, on and on. By now it was raining hard. Our feet grew heavy, our clothes dragged us. As we passed stacks of blue-coated bodies, we whispered encouragement to each other. We were marched past the quays of Paris and on through Porte de Saint-Cloud, which was full of charred and burning buildings, and through Sèvres, where onlookers pelted us with mud and pebbles and screamed Whores! and Monsters! at us.

Eventually we arrived at Versailles and were taken to Chantiers Prison, which is only a few hundred metres from the royal palace. The men went on somewhere else. I heard it was even worse. We were completely bedraggled by then; our faces, hair and feet filthy. The Sisters of Mercy, who were lined up to receive us in the prison courtyard, told us we had made ourselves outcasts and warned us that a terrible fate awaited us.

As we shuffled in, I felt a tap on my shoulder from behind. It was Henriette Pompille. You may know, Madame de Saint-Germain, that after my crime she was the girl who informed the English police that I would have gone to Victoire in Paris. I hadn't seen Henriette since before the Siege when we both worked at a laundry in the Rue du Faubourg Saint-Honoré. She told me that during the war with the Prussians she had been a first-aider and that her husband was a Communard who had been killed the day before and that soldiers had raped her and taken her young stepsons away, God knows where.

You may have read of Chantiers Prison. The newspapers might have described it as a clean and orderly place, where the authorities were fair but firm with wayward women. That was not the truth. It was atrocious. I doubt you would be able to imagine the squalor. The main building was an old granary, where the women slept on the first floor on bundles of rotting straw, two hundred of us crammed together in one open room, with four slop buckets between us, and we were watched at all times by the guards, even while dressing.

There was no peace, night or day. We would not have got through it but for the boys, the naughty, brave, daring street boys who had been incarcerated with us. When we first arrived, they ran about the courtyard like flies trapped in a lamp, bouncing up the walls, climbing the buttresses and rattling the doors of the wash house. I suppose the authorities thought we would look after them, and of course we did. We washed their clothes and fed them bacon and potatoes and loved them as much as they allowed. We heard them in the night on the floor above us, calling out for their mothers or fighting dream-time battles. Some sleep-walked down to us and curled up next to our litters.

The boys were in charge of the fires of wood and stones on which we cooked our rations, and they cleverly cut us spoons from pieces of tin. There were a few I became especially fond of, including Ranvier, who was thin and small for his age and used to help me and Henriette wring out the laundry. We were among the few women who had no one on the outside to send in cash to buy provisions, so we earned a few sous washing the other women's clothes at the pump behind the granary.

The man in charge of the prison was Lieutenant Marçeron, who was tall and thin with a luxuriant dark moustache. He was always excessively polite to us. On his weekly tours, he bowed at the waist before he addressed us and used vous, even to servants like Henriette and me. It was he who ordered canvas awnings to be put up around the high walls of the courtyard so that our skin would not burn in the summer sun, and it was he who permitted the shopkeepers of Versailles to set up stalls to sell us wine, sausage and soap. We even had a doctor who dispensed laudanum, which we all took eagerly. From his impeccable manners and occasional acts of kindness, you'd never know what a demon Marçeron was.

For the three months we were there, we all made fast alliances and just as quickly broke them. The smallest matters took on the greatest meaning: who had borrowed and not returned, who had been favoured with the best potatoes. I tried not to get involved. The political women befriended us and then lectured us. I tried to ignore them too, but an ember of anger about what had happened to Paris and to our destroyed hopes of a better life burned deeply. That is not to say that I was a socialist, or whatever such people are called. As you know, Madame de Saint-Germain, I was always aware of matters of fairness and I did not see why I, just like anyone else, should not be treated with respect.

The guards mocked the politicals and said they would all be sent to the tribunals and guillotined for setting fire to the buildings of Paris. Communard firemen had put petrol in their pumps, they said, but it was the women, ugly crones, young as well as old, who had done the worst damage. We had toured Paris secretly sprinkling gasoline from milk cans, and it was our fault all the beautiful and important places of Paris – the Tuileries Palace, the Palais Royale, the Palais de Justice, the Sainte Chapelle and the Theatre of the Châtelet – had gone up in flames. They had a name for us: pétroleuses.

Those guards were lads from the countryside and to them we were all traitors, and not only traitors but filthy city whores. When they weren't boasting of slaughtering savages on faraway islands, they spoke in disgusting terms about us. I hesitate to put their words into a letter that you might read in your drawing room. I will just say that they preferred to punish the young pretty women because their humiliation had the greatest value in the eyes of their friends, but we were all in their sights.

And then came the day of Ranvier. This part is very hard for me to describe, Madame, so please be patient if I falter. In all these years, I have tried not to remember it but I know that to put it down means that it will no longer churn about inside me.

The actual date I no longer recall. I know only that the courtyard had been baking in the sun and by the end of the afternoon was radiating out a pulsing heat. Most of the women were sleeping on their straw beds in the granary or dozing in the courtyard under the awnings. Henriette and I were taking down washing when the bell was rung and the call went out. We were ordered to gather around in the yard. All the boys, except for Ranvier, were lined up by the wall.

Ranvier had been tied to a bench, face down, and Marçeron was pacing in front of him, a cane in his hand. His spoke clearly and slowly and, as ever, his tone was courteous.

'Ladies and young gentlemen, here we have Ranvier. He has not answered my questions which, I might say, are perfectly reasonable, about his criminal father. How very brave of Ranvier! Well, we'll see just how brave he actually is. You all condemn him, I'm sure, and for that reason he will be punished not by me but by his peers. And, dear ladies, you also will benefit by watching. As part of your moral education.'

He handed the cane to the first boy in the line, who struck Ranvier on the back and returned it; and then the next and the next. Auclair came forward – I knew him; he was one of the roughest of the street boys, burly and full of bravado – struck Ranvier and handed the cane back.

Marçeron nodded, took a step towards the line and put his hand out, fingers wide, to halt the next boy. I thought it was the end of the scene, but he said, 'What are you, a coward, Auclair? This is a beating, not a kiss. Do it again.' The boy came back, took the cane and delivered another stroke, much harder.

Children should not be thrashed. Perhaps I was thinking of my own mother and the beatings she gave me.

The sun was hot on my face. My clothes were sandpaper on my skin. I began to push my way through the other women. Henriette tried to hold on to my arm but I shook her off.

'Good God! Stop! Stop this!' I shouted.

I was in front of Marçeron, face to face. It was one of those slow-moving fragments of time, when the world around you distils into soundless chaos. Hands were on me, Marçeron was pinching my neck, he was ordering guards to remove me to his office. Behind me, I heard him calling the next boy forward and Ranvier, who had not emitted even a whimper up to this point, begging for mercy.

When I say Marçeron punished me you will know what I mean and while he was punishing me, he spoke of authority and challenge and lessons to be learnt but by the end he was spitting out the same words that your mother used that day in the kitchen.

I never spoke of Marçeron's punishment, to anyone. Nor could I think of it, nor yet forget it. I tried to squash down the memory but it festered. At No. 13 it was as if it was not just Madame insulting me but Lieutenant Marçeron too. I could say, and I have done so, that it was her words that tipped me over, that they were a match to a keg of gunpowder, and she should not have used them on me – it was unjust of her, and made the tension between us worse. Of course, Madame de Saint-Germain, she was not to know they had a special meaning for me.

After I was brought back to the sleeping room at Chantiers, as I lay on my straw bed, Henriette sat beside me and held my hand. She told me that Ranvier was in a terrible state but was expected to live. I wasn't listening and drifted into a place that was not in the world, trying to convince myself that what had happened had not happened.

A few weeks later, some time at the end of July, a nine o'clock roll call was called and the names of a hundred or so women were shouted out, mine and Henriette's among them. We were instructed to step forward and form a line by the wall while the others were sent back. Then we were called forward, one at a time, to answer questions put to us by a man in a dark suit and gold-rimmed glasses. How old are you? What is your work? Who is your husband? Who is your father? Have you ever been in the lock hospital? It was Magistrate Macé asking the questions, the same man that later questioned me in Paris after I was arrested. In Chantiers, Henriette and I were of so little importance that he didn't even bother with us – he just told us to stand to one side with the others. Then he climbed on a chair and announced that we had all been imprisoned for not behaving as obedient wives and mothers of the glorious republic of France should. He told us that our degeneracy was written in our faces and bodies and that we should be grateful for his kindness and mercy, as if he were God himself. He was letting us go. The French women were to return to their families and the foreigners, if we knew what was good for us, should leave the country.

It was twilight by the time the Sisters lined us up at the prison gate to receive a loaf of bread and a few coins to see us on our way. Henriette said we should not risk staying in Versailles – we might be arrested as vagrants – so we retraced the route of our forced march and arrived back at the gates of the city at dawn.

It is midnight now, Madame de Saint-Germain. I must rise early tomorrow to be on duty, so I am forced to stop writing and will resume as soon as I can.

CHAPTER FORTY-TWO

A week has passed since I wrote the first part of this letter. Nothing of importance has happened between that time and this except that I have prepared myself to tell you about the events that followed my release from Chantiers.

I am not trying to squirm out of responsibility for it. Although it is true that Henriette alone took the decision to do what she did, I am guilty of ignoring the clues and signals she gave me, and of keeping her secret.

We left Chantiers and headed for Victoire and Jacques' place in the Rue Saint-Denis because we had nowhere else to go. I felt sure Jacques would relent and offer us shelter because our only other option was the streets and I knew Victoire would never forgive him if he pushed me in that direction. She was brought up strictly in exactly the same way I was, to be an honest girl.

I was right and Jacques reluctantly let us have a room in an unoccupied apartment upstairs. Victoire was newly pregnant and in bed, suffering once more from uncontrollable nausea.

Although Magistrate Macé had told us to quit France

there was no law that compelled us to do so. However, we were keen to leave and take our chances in London. It was the hopelessness of our situation in France rather than the opportunities there that led to our decision. By then Henriette had discovered that her stepsons' grandfather had put them in an orphanage and, as she had no rights over them, having never married their father, she had nothing to stay for.

We washed our clothes and hung them to dry in the yard. Victoire gave me an old brown cotton dress. Henriette did some cleaning for the woman who had the glove shop in return for two good sets of underclothes and a bonnet. Jacques lent us the train fare, more to ensure that we would be out of his hair than from the goodness of his heart.

I could not say Henriette was acting out of character at this time. When we had worked in the laundry she had been a chatty girl who burbled on about her admirers and this song she'd heard and that fair she'd been to – but that Henriette no longer existed. The Henriette I knew in Chantiers was serious and sad. A few times in the week before we left for London, I woke to find she had left the apartment. She would return two or three hours later, saying that she'd been at the Père Lachaise cemetery contemplating the wall where the government troops had shot hundreds of National Guard. The mortar was still stained with their blood. Her husband's was probably amongst it.

On the morning we were due to leave for London, Henriette insisted we set off from the Rue Saint-Denis at six o'clock. I was puzzled but I did not question it. Our train was not until nine and we had already purchased our tickets with the money Jacques gave us. It was only a thirty-minute walk to the Gare du Nord and we did not have much to carry. Our paltry possessions were packed in a carpet bag that we carried between us. 'Wrap the tickets and your book of testimonials into your shawl, Marguerite,' Henriette said. For some reason, I also tucked my cartes of Madame Soulier and of myself in there.

I thought nothing of Henriette's strange behaviour and looking back, I was a fool to believe her when she said we needed to get to the station early to exchange our currency and claim our seats, and too distracted to notice that she was steering us in the wrong direction through the Second Arrondissement and up towards the Rue du Quatre-Septembre.

As we came to the back of the Church of Saint Augustine, she confessed that she had told me what she called a tiny white lie. She had an important errand to run, a surprise for me, which was the work of but a moment. She refused to tell me what it was and insisted that I stand on the back steps of the church facing the Rue de la Bienfaisance. When I saw her, she said, I was absolutely not to call out to her or the surprise would fall apart. I think you'll be pleased, she said, but be ready to run. This did not alarm me as it should have done. She seemed as elated as a child awaiting her saint's day gift, so I did not challenge her. I should have looked into her eyes. I suppose I expected some kind of practical joke. I was also anxious that she might be jeopardising our plans – the fare would be lost if we missed the train – and wanted her to get whatever it was over and out of the way.

Madame de Saint-Germain, I could scarcely believe it. With the carpet bag at my feet, I stood on the steps as Henriette had instructed and waited, looking left and right for her. There were only a few people about – I recall a postman with his sack who disappeared into the apartment buildings and a cleaner washing down the pavement. Then I saw a tall gentleman in a dark blue military roquelaure and cap striding along the pavement opposite, too far away for me to see him clearly. At that moment, Henriette came running up the street behind him and in my worry about getting to the station as it was now half past seven, I almost forgot her instructions and called out, but at that same moment she shouted something I could not hear. The man turned around and she threw a liquid at him – that it was water was my first thought but I soon knew that it was not. It was terrible. He was screaming and clutching at his face.

Over twenty years later I can hardly bear to think of it. Henriette raced over to me and shouted Hurry, hurry, hurry, we must go now, don't just stand there, came up the steps to grab my hand and in my stupefied state I tried to put the carpet bag over my arm but for some reason I couldn't co-ordinate and Henriette was screaming Leave it, leave it, we must go. Run, Marguerite. So I left it.

We bolted towards the Rue Saint-Lazare, and after a while Henriette said Slow down, we must not attract attention. We caught our breath as we walked at a normal pace and by the time we turned up towards the station, I was in a state of shock. The tickets and my book of testimonials were safe and I understood now why Henriette had been so insistent earlier that I take charge of them. If she had been arrested, I would still be able to get away to London. We had thirty minutes before the train was ready, which we spent skulking behind the pillars on the concourse, hiding from the sunlight.

When we took our seats, she uttered only one word: Marçeron. She never spoke his name again, at least not to me. In fact, we never spoke directly of the surprise. I never told her that I was horrified by what she had done. I can only suppose that she convinced herself that her revenge was for my benefit, but I knew it had been more for hers.

I would be lying if I did not confess to you that it was the possibility that I would be held to account for Henriette's crimes that kept me awake rather than the harm to Marçeron. The carpet bag I left on the steps of the church contained nothing of real value. I was wearing my brown dress, and I had already pawned The Splendour of Paris Under Napoléon III, but I left behind my white leather prayer book, which my mother had given me and in which I had written my name and the place and date of my First Communion. My guess is that the bag was stolen soon after we ran or that nobody ever connected it with the attack on Marçeron.

I was sure I would be arrested for Henriette's crime. I had the perfect motive. But, Madame de Saint-Germain, I would never have done that. I am not vengeful. You may doubt me but every outburst I have had has been on the spur of the moment. I never planned my furies. Henriette, however, had calculated when to pounce. She had imagined the pain she would cause and that had excited her.

I was never right after that. I was twitchy and touchy, as you noticed. I thought I would go mad. Madame Dumas sometimes complained that I was absent-minded. I always blamed lack of sleep. Henriette, on the other hand, was serene.

In London I was so convinced that I would be arrested and taken back to Paris that I became reluctant to leave Monsieur Dumas's shop, and whenever I did so I was constantly looking about to see if I was being observed. I overheard the shop boys saying that the French government had sent spies to watch all the Commune refugees in London. I was stuck. This was the state I was in when

Madame Antoine came into the shop and persuaded me that I should go and work for your mother. Away from Soho, I thought I could lie low.

I no longer go to church, Madame de Saint-Germain, but I did at that time and on each occasion, I prayed for Marçeron's recovery. I also prayed that Paris would forget Henriette's surprise. At Monsieur Dumas's I skimmed through their French newspapers for reports about him and I did the same at No. 13 whenever I could, but never found anything, so I have no idea whether he survived or whether the police ever identified a suspect.

At No. 13, before you came, with no one to talk to, even about the weather, I was afraid and alone. I hope you won't take offence when I say I saw in you a fellow survivor. You seemed as relieved to find me as I did you. I thought we were of one kind.

When you said that Madame and I were alike, it distressed me in a way I can't describe, and it has taken me two years to recognise the truth of it. Perhaps in me, poor and fearful, she saw herself as a young person. We were both unrecognised for what we could bring to the world. Your mother's achievements in Paris were eclipsed, never to return – and in retrospect I can see that she must have felt herself to be redundant.

Madame Riel, you, me, Henriette, we are all sisters. We are all the same. Show me a woman who has not been sidelined, talked over, pushed aside, disregarded, reduced, ignored, underpaid, undervalued – you cannot. Our treatment is so routine, we don't notice it. I was always ready to speak up for myself and I was constantly urged to keep quiet, to submit, to nod and agree. I confess, I came to No. 13 in the expectation that I could rebuild myself. I thought it would be a place I could at last be seen as a person. I soon understood that was a false hope, but when you arrived my hope surged again. It is ironic, or fitting, that the place I found most appreciation, for my work and for myself, was at Woking, where I had been sent for punishment.

Finally, I must address something that I hoped never to think of again. It would be surprising if, in this spirit of candour and honesty, I did not bring it up. It is a delicate subject, and I regret for your sake that I must write of it. Madame Riel accused me of listening at doors, which I strongly denied. However, she was not wrong. In doing so, I became aware of certain events in the house. This will not be news to you. What I must explain to you is that after this, my understanding of those events became entangled with the way I had been brought up to think. So however much I admired you, I also condemned you and I condemned your mother. At the time, I thought as the world thought and blamed the women. And this fed my fury and a mix of outrage, disappointment and jealousy – yes, I admit to a strong jealousy, even though I know I had no right to feel it.

I have laid my heart on the table, Madame de Saint-Germain. My dearest hope is that you believe me when I say that I accept that your mother was herself, in all of this, a victim of a whirlwind of fate and chance, and a victim of me. I take responsibility for my actions on that day. What I cannot do is take responsibility for all the wrongs done to me.

You will need time to absorb what I have told you – after all, it has taken me half a lifetime to bring it up from the depths. Do not feel that you need to reply to me. You owe me nothing.

And be assured that from now, I will be gone. I will be leaving England. The clerk at the Embassy who forwarded these letters to you helped me draft a request to the

Ambassador to apply to the British Home Secretary for permission to return to Belgium. Any day now, my papers will come through.

I write knowing that the contents of this letter will cause you pain, and naturally I regret that, but from the information in it I hope you will find some of the peace you seek.

I remain, Madame, your most grateful and humble servant.

Marguerite Diblanc

CHAPTER FORTY-THREE

Saturday 13 July 1895

I am sitting on a bench watching the passengers as they promenade or look out across the sea. The day is fine and clear and the boat dips gently. Despite the grind of the engine, it is a peaceful scene.

My bag is by my feet. I have little in it: two dresses, underclothes, indoor shoes and a couple of books. Tucked inside the pocket of my coat are my papers and Julie's reply to me.

A young girl of perhaps eight or nine, Belgian, bids me good day and we converse in French. She tells me about the games she will play on the beach at Zeebrugge with her brothers and the excursions her parents have planned. Her mother calls to her and she jumps up, announces that she's pleased to have made my acquaintance, and runs off. I wish she would stay longer; she reminds me of Monsieur Dumas's daughter.

Now that I am alone, I face the memory of that awful night-time crossing to Calais when I sheltered under Madame Riel's umbrella by the stack, with my stomach tightening and my heart pounding, wanting both to die and to live. I am not a fugitive this time, of course. No, I have a destination and someone who loves me waiting on the quayside.

Marie and I are to live together in Virton, a few miles from our village. She is a widow now. In our kitchen we will make touffaye to our mother's recipe and warming soups, and I will bake madeleines and profiteroles. Our neighbours will know who I am and what I have done, but they will not want me to speak of it. For them, those events took place far away, a long time ago.

This will never be true for me. Madame Riel still visits me occasionally in my dreams, calling for Ulysses or pleading to be let out of the pantry. I always wake in a sweat, but by the time I start my chores the horror dissolves to nothing. I know it is not her spirit that haunts me but my own sense of guilt.

I think often of Julie. She and I are forever bound to each other – by my terrible act but also by our strange friendship. My letter to her is now ashes. After she read it, she threw it into the fire, so only she and I know of Henriette's crime. She will keep my secret. I no longer fear arrest, and I doubt Henriette, wherever she is, does either. The attack on Marçeron will exist only as a paragraph in a discarded newspaper. It was wrong of Henriette to do as she did, but I don't waste sympathy on the man himself, for he expended none on me.

I told you at Woking that I would not forgive you for what you did, Julie wrote to me, *but I don't need to. Rather, we need to forgive ourselves. You have been honest with me and I can tell that it cost you a great deal to set your words down on paper and make them real. Now it is my turn.*

She wrote about how her mother transacted her to a man called De Corneville when she was fifteen, and that for years she had tried to fend off her uncle, as well as the tutors at the Conservatory. Her mother pushed her to become the mistress of

Lord Lucan – she had no real choice. *She had done the same, my mother, when she was young. It was all she knew. It was expected.*

I stand by the railings on the deck, pull her letter from my inside pocket and tear off little pieces. One by one I cast them into the sea.

THE END

HISTORICAL NOTE

Deep in the stacks of the archives at the Bibliothèque Nationale de France (BNF) is a small, fat photograph album, barely a handspan in height. It has been designed to hold *cartes de visite*, photographic 'calling cards' that were popular in the latter part of the nineteenth century. 'Commune de Paris 1871' has been tooled in gold leaf on the red leather spine and inside, held in place by linen tape, are sixty of these *cartes* measuring 85mm by 55mm, all of them created by Eugène Appert, a society photographer and enthusiastic early pioneer of the techniques of photomontage. The collection illustrates the brief and doomed left-wing insurrection in Paris against the French government in the spring of 1871.

The portraits depict both prominent defeated Communards and the so-called heroes of the conquering French Army. There are also copies of Appert's now-famous staged tableaux purporting to show atrocities committed by the Leftists, as well as scenes of the ruined boulevards and burnt-out buildings of Paris.

Women hardly feature in the album. Apart from Appert's famous photomontage of dozens of Communard women in

Chantiers Prison, the collection includes only one other *carte de visite* of a woman, a smudgy vignette labelled 'Marguerite Disblanc'. The image is strangely flat and the pose is unnatural. The subject's forehead is unusually shallow and her hair is plastered to her scalp, making a plateau of the top of her head. Over her dark evening dress she wears a tawdry gauze blouse with cut-aways revealing the flesh on her shoulders, a style not typically worn by domestic servants. There are copies of this *carte* in other archives in France and elsewhere that have had *pétroleuse* scrawled on them – this was the contemporary term used to refer to one of the band of terrifying insurrectionist women alleged to have set Paris alight during the violent fall of the Commune. Although Communards did indeed set fire to buildings as part of their strategic retreat, the *pétroleuse* was a figment of government propaganda.

So who was Marguerite Diblanc? I should start by saying that Diblanc is the correct spelling of her name, which appears in some sources as Dixblancs or similar. She was born on 31 July 1843 in Meix-devant-Virton in the Gaume area of Luxembourg, the third of eleven children of Thomas Diblanc and Catherine Gillet. Alain Diblain's French-language non-fiction book *L'histoire hors du commun d'une personne ordinaire*, which details the facts of Marguerite's early life, her parents' origins, the births and early deaths of most of her many siblings, is available as a print-on-demand publication. I am grateful to Diblain, who claims distant cousinship with Marguerite, for his meticulous research.

Marguerite was known to have been a good school student. As a teenager she worked at the local sugar beet factory in Berchiwé, just outside her village. After she was arrested in Paris for killing Madame Riel, the Belgian press published details of an earlier crime against the Widow Larue for which Marguerite was sentenced to eight days' incarceration and stated that afterwards she fled to Verdun. I have discovered no other details or official document to corroborate these stories. In Verdun, she was employed for a number of years by an unknown family. In 1868 she went to Paris, and in the summer of 1871, after living through the Siege and the Commune, arrived destitute in London. She joined the Riel household in January 1872.

The murder victim, Madame Riel, born Marie Caroline Besson, remains an enigma about whom even her daughter was evasive. I have found little information on her origins before her name started to appear in fashion magazines as the designer of hats, with a shop in the Rue Laffitte. Many of the birth, death and marriage records for the inhabitants of Paris were lost during the fires at the end of the Commune. However, among the few documents I found was a record of the marriage in 1849 between Marie Caroline Besson, aged twenty-three, to forty-one-year-old Jules Riel, a divorced merchant dealing in trinkets and souvenirs, at which point her two-year-old daughter Julie's surname was changed from Roberts to Riel.

As for the nature of Madame Riel's relationship with her husband, I have found no evidence apart from a comment from one of the French detectives who arrested Marguerite Diblanc in Paris who told her that he had heard that Jules Riel had died as a result of Madame Riel's scandalous behaviour.

As a designer, Madame Riel was best known for her styling of the *chapeau Lamballe*, a flat straw picture hat with a small saucer-shaped bonnet and long ribbon ties, named after Marie Antoinette's friend the Princesse de Lamballe (who had the misfortune to be torn to pieces in Paris in 1792 by a Revolutionary mob). I found some waspish and intriguing criticism of the style in a book by *flaneur* Adolf von Ebeling who noted that Madame Riel's design had been heavily criticised in the press. Von Ebeling insinuated that Riel was not French but Prussian and, like her hat, not entirely ladylike. Similar criticism appeared in newspapers and in response Madame Riel asserted that her critics had no appreciation of fashion and beauty, and so must themselves be old and ugly.

Apart from Alain Diblain's work, Madame Riel's killing has not been studied in detail. It most often appears as a chapter in a compendium of murders or as a passing mention, of interest primarily because Madame Riel is often supposed to have been the mistress of the 3rd Earl of Lucan, a figure best known for the ambiguous, and catastrophic, command he gave before the Charge of the Light Brigade in 1854.

This is an understandable error given that the age gap between Lucan and Madame Riel was twenty-six years compared to the forty-seven between Lucan and Julie Riel, and because both Lord Lucan and Julie Riel deliberately tried to give that impression. Evidence of Lucan's interest in much younger women is provided by his maintenance of another mistress, Elizabeth Powell (no relation to Marguerite's barrister John J. Powell), at the same time that he was pursuing Julie. Powell was a milliner forty years Lucan's junior who lived in a villa in Maida Vale, less than three miles from Park Lane, and who bore him four children between 1868 and 1881, each of whom was granted the right to use the Lucan family name of Bingham. At his death in 1888, Lucan left £6,000 in trust to Elizabeth and their offspring.

When Julie returned to the house after her week in Paris and was told her mother had been missing since the previous day, she sent the maid, Eliza Watts, to fetch Lucan from his home a ten-minute walk away in South Street, off Park Lane. Some of the initial newspaper reporting described how Lucan with an unidentified man came to the house, saw the body in the pantry, and then walked to the traffic junction, approximately where the London Hilton Hotel stands now, to alert the traffic constable on duty. Lucan led the way back to the house, which he opened with his own latchkey. After this, the press avoided comment on Lucan's involvement. Although there is no proof, the most obvious explanation for this would be that his lawyers pressurised both the police and the press to say as little about him as possible. Nevertheless, he was forced to appear as a witness both at Marguerite's Bow Street arraignment and at the subsequent Old Bailey trial in order to prove the provenance of the banknotes that Marguerite stole, and to give evidence on Madame Riel's character. A transcript of the interchanges while he was in the witness box, available on the Old Bailey website, documents his discomfort at the questions put to him.

Confirmation that Lucan's relationship was with Julie Riel rather than with her mother is sparse but compelling. In a section titled English Gossip in *Harper's Bazaar* published in June 1872 in New York, where editors were not intimidated by English libel laws, 'R. Kemble, of London' wrote:

The catastrophe [the killing of Madame Riel] has made a great sensation, not only because Mademoiselle Riel was a beautiful and popular actress, but because of her delicate relations with Lord Lucan, an ancient veteran better known (from his inactivity when in command of the heavy cavalry in the Crimea) as Lord "Look-on." He is a brother-in-law of that "gallant gay Lothario" the late Lord Cardigan, who commanded the Light Brigade; and it is said that they were on such bad terms throughout the campaign that they never spoke to one another. They seem, however, to have had some tastes in common.

This snippet from the Paris newspaper *Le Figaro* appeared a year later:

> Miss Riel, the victim's daughter, is leaving the theatre. Fortunately, a certain English general, who had had to appear as a witness before the court, is generously taking charge of the future of the poor orphan.

———

If her mother had not been killed in the basement kitchen of 13 Park Lane, Julie Riel would probably have had a good stage career in Paris and London. After leaving the Paris Conservatory, she was engaged first at the Gymnase and then joined the company at the Vaudeville. She and her mother fled Paris in September 1870, just before the Siege. At some point before the taking of the census in April 1871, mother and daughter moved into 13 Park Lane, a house gifted to them by Lucan. After her mother's death Julie returned to Paris almost immediately. All of her theatrical engagements in London had been cancelled. In 1881 she married the comedy actor François Victor Arthur de Saint-Germain Gilles, otherwise known as Gilles de Saint-Germain, with whom she had appeared on stage. She died in Paris in 1921.

Many of the other characters in the story were real people, notably Monsieur Dumas, who kept a delicatessen in Soho and employed Marguerite before she was persuaded to join the Riel household; Victoire Bouillon, Marguerite's childhood friend, and her husband Jacques; Thomas Gérard, at whose coal yard Marguerite was arrested; the veteran French actor Irma Crosnier, who visited on the afternoon of Madame Riel's death; and Marguerite's friend Henriette Pompille (although her back story is entirely fictional). Lieutenant Marçeron was a real and notorious figure and his beating of Little Ranvier, the son of a Communard commander, a documented event. Madame Antoine is a fiction although an unnamed French dressmaker in London recommended Marguerite to the Riels, tempting her with a ten-shilling bonus. Abbé Toursel assisted Marguerite when she first came to London and interviewed her in Newgate after her sentencing. His notes on their conversation, in which Marguerite related the vicious insults Madame Riel had thrown at her and the night-time presence in the house of a 'rogue', are in the National Archives.

Jules Riel, Madame Riel's deceased husband, had a brother, Félix, who lived in London for at least ten years. I have changed his name to Théo. As I have given him fictional criminal proclivities it seemed only fair to do so.

Nathaniel Druscovich, the son of a Moldovan boatbuilder and an English woman, whose meticulous handwritten reports on the pursuit and capture of Marguerite are in the Home Office files in the National Archives, and whose intelligence and talent for languages led to his appointment as one of the youngest detective chief inspectors in the Metropolitan Police, was the golden boy of the Division. Alas, he came to a sad end a few years after Marguerite was convicted. Loyalty to a wayward younger brother dragged him into a major betting fraud and he was convicted in 1877 of corruption at the famous Trial of the Detectives and sentenced to two years' imprisonment. He died at the age of thirty-nine, of tuberculosis contracted in Coldbath Fields Prison. The story of his meteoric rise and catastrophic fall is yet to be properly told. I am crossing my fingers that someone will pick it up.

A real woman called Louisa Hart was incarcerated in Woking after her trial at the Old Bailey for 'feloniously aiding and assisting a man unknown in carnally knowing Rose Shires, a girl under the age of 13'. Florence Maybrick, the Mississippi-born socialite convicted of killing her dissipated husband, was in Woking at the same time as Marguerite and released from prison in 1904. She died in obscurity in the United States thirty-seven years later.

As this story features a host of French women, there were far too many Maries to cope with. While Marguerite's surviving sister remained Marie, Marie Caroline Besson Riel (Madame Riel) I renamed Caroline. Julie Riel's friend Marie Guy became Isabelle.

To simplify the story I have trimmed the Diblanc family tree considerably, although her numerous short-lived siblings are not fictions. I have no evidence that her mother suffered poor mental health. Her father died in 1891.

Jacques Bouillon, who was married to Marguerite's childhood friend Victoire, provided the police in Paris and London with information about Marguerite's movements during the Siege and the Commune. There is no direct evidence that Marguerite was ever in Chantiers Prison, and she does not appear in Appert's photomontage of the women incarcerated there. I found a single mention of the arrest by government troops of a Marguerite Diblanc at the barricade at Clignancourt in the final days of the Commune in a document in the Bibliothèque Marguerite Durand in Paris. There is no certainty that this is 'our' Marguerite but I have not come across any other woman of that name in Paris at the time. The magistrate Gustave Macé questioned the women at Chantiers Prison and also heard the charges against Marguerite in Paris.

The house where the killing occurred, 13 Park Lane, was destroyed during the Blitz. Millbank Prison was closed in 1890 and later demolished, replaced by housing and the art gallery that is now Tate Britain. Woking Convict Prison was closed in 1895 and later used as an army base. A few houses originally built for staff is all that remains.

Marguerite Diblanc was released on special licence on 3 February 1893 after serving twenty years and eight months. According to the published Register of Habitual Criminals (which, contrary to its name, published the release details of all convicts, habitual or not) she was discharged into the care of the London branch of the Royal Association for the Assistance of Discharged Prisoners, an organisation licensed by the Home Office to receive ex-convicts. I have no specific information linking her to Mrs Meredith's operation in Stockwell, South London, which offered employment in a steam laundry to convict women on licence. However, in one of Marguerite's petitions for release she mentions Mrs Meredith and her willingness to work there.

Despite the harshness of institutions like Millbank it would, in my view, be a mistake to assume that all operations within the prison system in the Victorian era were run by cruel taskmasters focused only on punishment. Woking Prison and Mrs Meredith's laundry, and doubtless dozens of other organisations, could be viewed in part as compassionate enterprises, in which one of the aims was rehabilitation. Before Marguerite's time, Woking trained women as mosaicists, a programme abolished when it was clear that there was no demand for such workers post release. Women also asphalted the paths around the prison, worked for farmers in the surrounding orchards, and ran the steam laundry and the kitchen. The less able and less privileged prisoners sewed mailbags and uniforms for the Greenwich boy sailors. It is interesting that Woking eventually closed because the system was not convicting enough women to fill it.

The terms of Marguerite's release stipulated that she was to remain under police supervision for life. The Home Office files include a letter to the Home Secretary from Baron Soloyns, the Belgian ambassador, which notes that he had asked for information on her in November 1893, eight months after her release. I have not found anything further about her whereabouts after this date and have no evidence that she made it back to Belgium.

Around the time of Marguerite's Old Bailey trial, the London Stereoscopic Company (LSC) published a *carte de visite* of Marguerite and registered it at the Copyright Office in London. It is a copy, not the LSC's original work, and shows a young Marguerite in a skirt and blouse, wearing a maid's cap. My feeling is that it dates from the period before Marguerite came to Paris and my guess is that it was found in her box or provided to the police by Henriette Pompille. The image formed the basis of line drawings of Marguerite published in magazines such as *The London Illustrated News*.

Appert's *carte de visite* of Marguerite the *pétroleuse* is a fake. Using his photomontage expertise, he cut out the head of the LSC *carte de visite*, slicing off Marguerite's maid's cap, and imposed this on an image of the shoulders and bust of another woman. The effect was to render Marguerite frowzy, lumpen and lazy-looking.

At the time he made this confection, Appert was facing bankruptcy. Coupled with ill-judged copyright lawsuits, his money-making scheme to photograph hundreds of imprisoned Communards had been financially ruinous. He sold *cartes* of the Communards to the public as collectible souvenirs and used them in a series of photomontages in which he superimposed their faces on the figures of actors engaged in staged scenes of alleged atrocities. Copies of this series, known as Crimes of the Commune, are included in the album in the BNF's archives.

Unfortunately for Appert, after the trials of the most prominent Communards, the French government was keen to persuade the public to forget that the Commune had ever existed and banned both its visual representation and the trade in such *cartes*. The counterfeit portrait of Marguerite may have been an attempt on Appert's part to cash in on her notoriety as a murderess rather than a Communard. Individual collectors may have mistakenly labelled her *pétroleuse*, based on erroneous press allegations about her behaviour during the Commune published soon after the killing.

The main primary sources for this story were the transcript from the trial of Marguerite Diblanc at the Old Bailey, the Home Office files on the case at the National Archives and press reports published in Britain, France and Belgium.

Any historical errors are entirely mine.

ACKNOWLEDGEMENTS

Without the writing group that grew out of Sarah Leipciger's novel workshop at London's City Lit this book simply would not exist. Ranjabali Chaudhuri, Janine Fortune, Brigid Green, Oli Griffiths, Marian O'Connor, Meital Sharon, Carolyn Tobin and Helena Wright have offered unfailingly helpful criticism and suggestions, and top-class support. The professional guidance and feedback of Caroline Green (aka the writer Cass Green and C.S. Green), whose online course on crime writing at London's City University pushed me towards a new way to look at my work, has been equally invaluable.

Special mentions must go to my first draft readers Michele Colyer, Mandy Glass and the aforementioned Janine Fortune, and to Sara Cox, the brains behind the Cheshire Novel Prize. In 2023 I submitted the first chapters of this book to this annual competition and while I did not make the longlist, the detailed advice from the readers was amazing. Likewise, I am grateful for the crime novel expertise of my friend Karen Robinson, creator and former editor of The Times' Crime Club.

Without the work of history scholars, historical novelists would be catastrophically adrift. The full list of sources I used to research this story is too long to give here but contact with historians working in the relevant subject areas brought me detailed insights. Heartfelt thanks go to Summer Brennan, who rooted around on my behalf in the Paris police registers of *insoumis* (a type of freelance courtesan) for Madame Riel (she was not listed); Pamela Joan Stewart of Arizona State University, who shared her perspectives on blame attaching to women after the fall of the Paris Commune; Paul Frecker, for his specialist knowledge of *cartes de visite*; and Dr Joanne S. Turner of Staffordshire University, whose research, with Helen Johnston, into nineteenth-century women's crime and punishment helped me with the Woking Prison passages and the role of Discharged Prisoners' Aid Societies in particular; and lastly, but not leastly, my friend Erika Hobbs, who organised a translation of a passage set in German gothic type, one of few published references to Madame Riel.

The details of Marguerite Diblanc's story would not have been retrievable from history but for the work of the National Archives at Kew and the British Library (and by extension the online British Newspaper Archive). Images of Madame Riel and Julie Riel are preserved, and freely accessible, in the Bibliothèque historique in Paris and the Musée Carnavalet, Paris. Google and archive.org have made a plethora of useful primary sources available. During the Covid-19 lockdowns these were lifesavers. I traced family trees using Ancestry and tracked down criminal registers on FindMyPast.

Now I turn to the help and encouragement of close friends. Notable amongst them are Hedda Archbold, Diana Gregory, Caroline Jefford, Nick Jones, Georgio Konstandi, Louise Lyon, Alison McIndoe, Adam Roberts, Barbara Segall and Sharon Wright. Jane Cook enthusiastically helped me wrangle aspects of the characters during a long train journey. Special thanks go to my friend and fellow podcaster Lena Augustinson.

Finally, or almost, family. First among these is the eagle-eyed sub-editor and typo-killer Tim Clifford who is, conveniently, also my partner in life, closely followed by our progeny Lily and Izzy, whose good humour and patience were always able to divert me when the writing was not flowing. Through her work in the prison service my sister Madeleine Klein helped me imagine the ordeals Marguerite may have encountered inside; my brother Paul Klein gladly dived down research rabbit holes and always came up with treasure.

To finish, a huge round of applause to you, the readers of the published book. My hope is that you enjoyed it. All reviews help a writer so please consider leaving one.

Naomi Clifford, August 2024
naomiclifford.com

ABOUT THE AUTHOR

Naomi Clifford grew up in London. After reading history at Bristol University, she lived in Nashville, Tennessee, and following her return to London worked for many years for a variety of magazines and websites. Her non-fiction books focus on women and crime.

A NOTE FROM THE PUBLISHER

Thank you for reading this book. If you enjoyed it please do consider leaving a review on Amazon to help others find it too.

We hate typos. All of our books have been rigorously edited and proofread, but sometimes mistakes do slip through. If you have spotted a typo, please do let us know and we can get it amended within hours.

info@bloodhoundbooks.com

Printed in Great Britain
by Amazon

49628264R00179